THE SNOWBALL EFFECT

THE
SNOWBALL
EFFECT

Holly Nicole Hoxter

HARPER TEEN
An Imprint of HarperCollins*Publishers*

HarperTeen is an imprint of HarperCollins Publishers.

The Snowball Effect

Library of Congress Cataloging-in-Publication Data
Hoxter, Holly Nicole.
    The snowball effect / Holly Nicole Hoxter. — 1st ed.
        p.   cm.
    "HarperTeen."
    Summary: Having lost her stepfather, grandmother, and mother in the span of
a year, seventeen-year-old Lainey unexpectedly reconnects with long-lost relatives,
copes with her five-year-old brother's behavioral problems, and endangers her
long-term romance when drawn to a young man with an unexpected connection to
her mother.
    ISBN 978-0-06-175571-2 (trade bdg.)
    [1. Death—Fiction.   2. Brothers and sisters—Fiction.   3. Family life—
Maryland—Fiction.   4. Emotional problems—Fiction.   5. Baltimore County
(Md.)—Fiction.]   I. Title.
PZ7.H8513Sn 2010   2008055722
[Fic]—dc22   CIP
                                                                          AC

Typography by Amy Toth
10   11   12   13   14   15   CG/RRDB   10 9 8 7 6 5 4 3 2 1
                                    ❖
                              First Edition

For my mother and father.
You gave me life, confidence, a sense of humor,
and everything else I ever needed or asked for.
I have been incredibly lucky.

THE SNOWBALL EFFECT

1

THE FIRST DAY OF
THE REST OF MY LIFE

I wouldn't say I'd been worried about Mom, but I'd known for a while that things were bad. She still cried every day about Carl, my stepfather who'd been dead since January when he drove his stupid Kawasaki off the side of the highway.

When our neighbor, Mabel, called me at work three days after my high school graduation, my first thought was: *Oh no*. She'd called my cell phone first, and I'd let it go straight to voice mail. When she called back two minutes later on the kiosk phone, I knew something was wrong. I'd never given Mabel the number for Perfume World.

"Sweetheart," Mabel said, "do you think you could meet me at my church after you get off work?"

I should have said, *Sure, why?* And maybe she would have told me that she wanted help sticking address labels to the newsletters, or her car had a flat and she needed a ride home. But I didn't ask. She'd looked up Perfume World in the phone book. Something had to be wrong.

"Uh," I said to Mabel. "Sure."

"Just come straight here, all right? I need to talk to you about some things."

When someone wants to talk to you in person instead of over the phone, your mind immediately goes to the worst possible scenario. I guess it's some sort of coping mechanism—if you're expecting the worst possible thing, then whatever it really is won't seem that bad. My mind went straight to Mom.

I told Mabel what time I got off work. She reminded me again to go straight to her church. She hadn't said anything reassuring like "nothing's wrong" or "don't worry," and Mabel loved to say stuff like that, even when the situation didn't call for it.

Mom's hurt, I thought.

No, Mabel could have told me that over the phone. She was dead. Definitely dead.

Or maybe it was Collin?

No, Mom would have called if something happened to Collin.

Maybe it was Mom *and* Collin. There could have been a car accident or a carbon monoxide leak.

Then I thought about the mothers who made the news for drowning all their children in the bathtub before they killed themselves. Mom had three kids, but

2

of course she would have killed only Collin. My older sister was long gone, and there's no way Mom could hold me underwater.

When had I seen Mom last? It hadn't been that morning. She'd still been in bed when I got up for work, even with Collin in his room, right next to hers, shrieking and playing the drums. They weren't actual drums, just a bunch of boxes and crates that he'd set up in a circle and banged on with sticks. It must have been the night before. I tried to think if anything unusual had happened, but I couldn't remember. She'd probably just sat in the recliner after dinner and cried while she pretended to watch TV.

When Katie got to the kiosk to work the afternoon shift, I grabbed my purse and ran to my car.

There's a church every few blocks in Corben, and Mabel's church wasn't far from our house. Their congregation was so small that I'd probably met everyone even though I'd only been to two Basket Bingo nights and one spaghetti dinner. I recognized the pastor, who was standing outside with Mabel, even though he was dressed in shorts and a T-shirt. He was a little younger than Mabel, kind of handsome, but not so handsome that you had guilty thoughts about him. As I sat there in the car, I wondered how I could ponder the pastor's good looks when I knew that as soon as I got out and walked over to him, he would tell me that my mother was dead.

I got out of the Grand Am and walked up to the church.

"Hi, sweetheart," Mabel said. She took my hand. "Let's go inside."

We walked down the stairs to the basement and sat at one of the long folding tables. It felt strange to be there without the entire congregation, with no crepe-paper streamers hanging up everywhere. I'd always thought the streamers looked cheesy, but without them the basement just looked old and sad.

Mabel sat beside me, and her pastor sat across from us. Mabel took my hand, but before she could say anything she started crying.

"Is it Mom?" I asked. And I waited for her to tell me no, it wasn't Mom. It wasn't Collin. It was . . . I don't even know, but it wasn't Mom or Collin.

Mabel nodded. She squeezed her eyes shut and tears pooled at the corners.

Yes. Yes, it's Mom.

I looked at the pastor. "She's dead?"

He reached across the table. I gave him my free hand.

"Your mother took Collin to Mabel's house this morning and asked her to watch him for a few hours," the pastor said. He held my hand tightly. I stared at his hairy knuckles.

"She gave me money for ice cream," Mabel added. "And we went to Cold Stone. You know how excited he gets."

I nodded.

"After she left Collin with Mabel, your mother called Officer Callahan."

I had to think about it before I could place the name. Mabel had nicknamed him Officer Sexpot. He was a big burly guy, nice enough but not real attractive, and she'd thought he wanted to put the moves on Mom. He came over a lot after the accident, mostly because Mom called him and asked him to.

"When Officer Callahan arrived at the house, he let himself in, as your mother requested. And he found her . . . her body."

"What happened?" I asked. *Do not tell me she did this on purpose.* I said a silent prayer to God for an unfortunate accident. Carbon monoxide leak. Grease fire. Fall down the stairs.

Mabel wiped her eyes. "I'm sorry, Lainey. She hung herself. Down there in the basement. Officer Callahan found her in front of the washer and dryer."

Mabel let go of my hand and blew her nose. "It's just terrible. I can hardly believe it." I couldn't look at her face, so I looked down at her dress. Yellow with lots of big pink flowers. Mabel owned about ten million different flowery dresses. She squeezed my hand. I could feel the pastor's hand on my shoulder.

"We'll get through this," he said. "I know it may seem impossible right now, but we will." I glanced up at him. He frowned and looked all distraught, like he could actually be seriously devastated over my mother's death after meeting her three times in his whole life.

"It's not like this is a big surprise," I finally said.

Mabel nodded. "She never got over losing Carl, did she?"

I'd never understood how Mabel could be sympathetic to Mom's pathetic reaction to Carl's death. Mabel had lost her husband too. She had been with him for over thirty years before he got cancer and died. They didn't have any children or even a goldfish, so she lived all alone in the house where they'd lived together. I couldn't imagine how tough that had to be. But she didn't give up and hang herself in the basement.

"Mabel and I thought you might like to stay with your father," the pastor suggested. "At least for a few days until the investigation is over."

"Investigation?" I looked at Mabel.

Mabel shook her head. "It probably won't be anything for you to worry about. Officer Callahan said he'll try to take care of it quickly. He knew your mother, and he took my statement, and they certainly don't suspect foul play, so there doesn't seem to be much to investigate. It may even already be over for all I know. We just thought it might be easier if you go stay with your father for a bit. We've already called and talked to him. He said you can just come on over."

I shook my head. "I can't stay with my dad."

She and the pastor just stared at each other. I waited and held my breath, knowing there was a chance that they could make me go. I was almost eighteen, but "almost" might not matter. "I'll go stay with Kara," I said.

The pastor glanced at Mabel and then back to me. "She's a friend of yours?" he asked.

"My best friend. She has a . . . real stable family, you know? Like, her parents—they're great."

Mabel nodded. "Do you want me to call Kara's parents and explain . . . what happened?"

I nodded. The pastor pulled a pen out of his shirt pocket and I wrote down Kara's number on the back of one of the church's newsletters.

"And what about Riley?" Mabel asked. I wrote down his number too and then passed the newsletter to Mabel.

"I'd be happy to give you a ride," she said.

I shook my head. "That's okay."

"You'll be all right getting to Kara's?"

I nodded. I was so ready to get out of the church basement. I hugged Mabel, shook the pastor's hand, and ran out to my car.

I got in and turned the key in the ignition. Nothing. I sighed and climbed back out. I opened the hood and jiggled the wires to the battery. I tried it again. Nothing. Jiggled the wires. Tried it again. The car started. Thank God. One more try and they would have come running out of the church to rescue me.

As I pulled out of the church parking lot, I realized I hadn't even asked about Collin. I thought about turning back, but I couldn't stand to face them again. He'd probably been playing somewhere else in the church with one of Mabel's church friends. Maybe I should have wanted to be with him, but I knew Mabel would take care of him better than I could.

I'd spent most of my life as an only child. Mom and Carl didn't adopt Collin until I was sixteen, and my older sister from Mom's first marriage moved to Colorado with her dad when I was practically a baby. Maybe that wasn't much of an excuse, but it's why I didn't go back inside and find Collin, or ask if Mabel had figured out how to get in touch with my sister. It just didn't seem like the thing to do. So I drove the Grand Am through the streets of Corben, alone. Sure, it felt selfish, but it also felt right.

<hr>

We'd had pamphlets and books on death and bereavement sitting around the house all year, so I knew that the first stage of grief was denial. It wasn't necessarily actual *denial*, like when you lied and said you didn't do something. It was more a feeling like *How can this be happening?* You couldn't wrap your mind around it. It shouldn't surprise me, though. Mom had all but announced she would kill herself. But it still felt surreal. I felt numb. And terribly unlucky. Everyone was leaving me.

Carl had been first, in January, which I wouldn't have considered a huge loss to humanity in general, but it had certainly been a crushing blow in Mom's world. She checked herself into the psych ward at Bayview for two weeks while Collin stayed with Mabel and I stayed with Kara. When she came home, things weren't much better, so Grandma Elaine came up from Florida. Grandma Elaine was Dad's mom, but she'd always thought of Mom like a daughter.

I loved when Grandma Elaine visited, because she was the one person in our family who didn't fill me with disgust. I was her only granddaughter, and she liked me the best, too. I was even named after her, sort of. My dad wanted to call me Elaine, but my mom was dead set on Tiffany. Mom and Grandma Elaine both liked to watch this stupid soap opera, *Heartstrings*, so one day Grandma Elaine said, "Why don't we name her after that beautiful Lainey St. James?" And that's what they did.

We lived with Grandma Elaine until I was a few months old, and then Mom and Dad got their own apartment. They didn't stay together very long after that. Dad moved away, and Mom and I moved back in with Grandma Elaine. We lived there until I was about seven. When we lived with Grandma Elaine, we shared a bedroom and we ate real meals, and during the summer we watched *Heartstrings* every day at one P.M. Then my aunt Liz in Florida got pregnant and wanted Grandma Elaine to move down there. Grandma Elaine tried to convince Mom to come with her, but Mom said no even though we didn't have anything keeping us in Corben. Sometimes when Mom was in one of her moods, she'd say that we were going to move and be with Grandma and I'd get excited, but then she'd find a new boyfriend or a new job or a new hobby, and we'd stay.

Grandma Elaine was already sick when she came back to take care of Mom. She'd gotten over lung cancer the year before, plus had a heart attack, but she came anyway and treated Mom like she was a little kid with the flu, making her favorite foods and letting her do nothing but watch TV all day. But Grandma Elaine kept getting sicker and sicker, and Mom wasn't getting any better. Grandma Elaine finally gave up and went back to Florida so Aunt Liz could take care of her.

On the day before she left, Grandma Elaine and I made a big dinner together and Mom cried all through it saying she didn't know what she was going to do. I didn't know what I was going to do either, but I didn't cry about it.

I drove Grandma Elaine to the airport the next morning. The Grand Am always took forever to heat up, so even after we were halfway to the airport, it was still freezing cold. We both wore our hats and gloves and scarves. I could see my breath.

"I bet you're happy to be going back to Florida," I said with my teeth practically chattering.

She reached over and patted my leg. "I won't miss the cold, that's for sure."

"I wish you could stay," I said. "I would take care of you."

"I know you would, sweetheart. But you have plenty here to take care of already."

And then she started coughing. She leaned forward, and I knew the routine. I pounded on her back until the coughing stopped.

"You all right?" I asked. I rubbed her back.

She nodded. "That's good. Thanks, honey."

I drove along and kept one eye on Grandma Elaine.

"Lainey, you have to promise you'll look after your mother for me," she said.

I nodded, but I must have looked really unsure, because Grandma Elaine added, "She needs you."

"I know."

"She won't get through this without a lot of help."

"I didn't even like Carl," I blurted out. "And I don't know what to do when she cries. I don't know what to say to her. I just sit there and look stupid."

Grandma Elaine nodded. "You just need to be there. Hold her hand. Tell her it'll be okay."

I shrugged. "I'll try."

"I know you will. And I know you'll look after poor little Collin, too. That boy needs a lot of love."

A few days after she got back to Florida, she had a stroke and died. Obviously I was glad I'd gotten to spend so much time with her before it happened, but who knows how much longer she would have lived if she'd stayed home in Orlando resting and taking care of *herself* instead of flying to freezing cold Baltimore and taking care of my crazy mother.

Mom got worse after we found out about Grandma

Elaine, but it's hard to say if that had anything to do with it. She'd mostly stopped talking to us, so I assumed that she was just still upset over Carl.

I know he was her husband and all, but Mom acted like she didn't have a kid to take care of. Two if you counted me, which I didn't. Her behavior would have been typical of Old Mom, the mom who raised me, who was paranoid and scared and mopey. New Mom, Collin's Mom, just didn't act like that. New Mom had it together. But after Carl and Grandma Elaine died, she'd just sit in Carl's old recliner and cry. I tried telling her it would be okay, but anything I said just made her cry harder.

Fortunately Mabel started coming over all the time to cook for us and talk to Mom. With Carl dead, she and Mom finally had something in common. Before, she'd invite Mom to her Tupperware parties or Basket Bingo night at her church, but Mom always had an excuse not to go (she didn't want to leave Collin with Carl). But a few months after he died, Mom gave up on excuses and let Mabel drag her anywhere.

Mabel thought she would save her. I could have told her that was a waste of time.

⋯⋯⋯

I didn't want to drive straight to Kara's house. That would have taken about two minutes, and I wanted Mabel to have plenty of time to call and talk to Kara's mom. Instead I went driving around Corben.

I'd lived in Corben my whole life, and it wasn't awful

but it wasn't the greatest place to live, either. In Corben, the coolest place to go on the weekend was the flea market. You could buy anything there—porn, NASCAR memorabilia, bunny rabbits, groceries, furniture. Kids could bring in their report cards and get free BBs for their BB gun for every A they got. I think that says everything you need to know about Corben.

I'd lived in three different houses and three different apartment buildings, and as I drove around Corben, I inadvertently went back to those familiar places. First the apartment where I'd lived briefly with my parents when they were still in love (or at least still together). Then to the house we lived in with Grandma Elaine. The apartment building I lived in with Mom (and, at various times, a Daddy Whoever). The other apartment building we lived in. The house we rented before we moved into the house that we bought.

I made sure that my drive didn't take me anywhere near the house I currently lived in, the house where my mother had just offed herself, the house where police officers might still be hanging around.

The *Corben Courier* did a big story once about how seventy-five percent of Baltimore County's registered sex offenders lived in Corben, like that was shocking news. Where else did they think they would live? Did they think an ex-con pedophile was going to get a high-paying job and afford a half-million-dollar house in the ritzy part of the county? Of course not. He would get a job at a gas station working for minimum wage, and he'd rent a cheap-ass apartment in Corben.

After Mom starting making more money, transformed from Old Mopey Mom into New Peppy Mom, we did have a choice, but she wanted to be near the people who supported her. For the last few years, Mom had worked as a life coach. She taught workshops out of our house, and she wanted to be near the women in her groups. I knew the women would have followed her anywhere, though.

I drove past the big shopping center on Corben Avenue, close to the beltway, where Riley worked in the auto repair shop. I drove past the mall and then turned into Kara's neighborhood.

When Kara opened the door to let me in, her face was almost as red as her hair. I felt guilty that she'd been crying, even though it wasn't *my* fault that my mom decided to hang herself. Kara had been my best friend since middle school, so she'd known my mom for a while. She was closer to her parents than anyone I'd ever known. After Mabel called, she probably started thinking about what she'd do if she lost both her parents and her grandmother all in the same year.

"I don't want to talk about it," I said to Kara. I could feel my cell phone vibrating inside my pocket. I checked the caller ID. Riley.

She nodded real quick like she didn't want to talk about it either. She rubbed my arm as I walked inside. I let Riley go to voice mail.

"Hi, Lainey!" Kara's mom said in a fake-happy voice. It rubbed me the wrong way, but I knew that she didn't know how to act. I didn't know how I wanted her to act.

I sat on the couch between Kara and her mom, leaning up against the quilt that Kara's grandmother had made. We didn't say much. We watched TV until her dad got home from work. Then we sat in the kitchen while her dad made chicken parmesan for dinner. I pushed my mom—my entire family—out of my mind and listened to Kara's dad talk about his day.

"So this woman comes in, asking about some rugs that she ordered. The girl at the counter tells her we have no record of it. She gets pissed—pardon my French, Lainey—and she wants to talk to a manager. So I come out and look it up, and I can't find any record of it either. That really sets her off. She tells me I'm incompetent. Tells me she's never shopping here again. On and on and on. Finally, I tell her we'll go in the back and look for them. I can still hear her screaming and hollering as I'm walking into the back room. Of course the rugs aren't back there, and when I come back out, the woman's gone."

Kara's dad stopped and opened a can of green beans. He took his time emptying them into a pot. He never told a whole story straight through. He always stopped and waited for one of them to ask how it ended.

"Then what happened?" Kara's mom asked.

He tossed the empty can into the trash and smiled at us. "About five minutes later, she *calls*. She asks if I'm the manager she was just talking to and I say yes. So she tells me that she actually ordered the rugs at Masterson's down the road. But she wasn't calling to apologize for screaming at us." He shook his head. "No, of course not. She tells me that she actually ordered the rugs at a different store, and then says to me, 'I can't believe you all didn't know that!'"

"Like you could possibly know that!" Kara exclaimed. She and her mother laughed.

"Exactly!" her dad said. "Exactly!"

I couldn't make myself laugh, but I forced a smile.

After a while, dinner was ready and we all sat down and held hands and Kara's dad said grace. If someone took a picture of that moment, we could have passed for a family, sitting around the table in the happy orange and yellow kitchen. Kara's dad had dark hair and brown eyes like me, and except for the flaming red hair, Kara looked just like her mom. She could be the sweet but slightly rebellious younger daughter. I could be the lovably sarcastic older daughter. It certainly made for a nicer family portrait than the picture Mabel had taken of my real family on the day of Collin's graduation. Maybe I'd just stay here with Kara forever. Or at least until she moved out.

". . . and God bless Lainey and her family. Please hold them near to you and help them through this troubling time. Amen."

Kara's dad squeezed my hand and gave me half a grin. "We love you, kiddo," he said. And that was that. That was the closest anyone came to mentioning my dead mother.

After dinner Kara went to her room to take a nap before work. I sat on the couch with her parents and we watched the news. I hated the news. It was just a daily count of murders and scandals and four-alarm fires. But once I'd sat on the couch between Kara's parents, I couldn't find any way to extricate myself, so I tried to think about other things. My mind wandered to Riley. But then I remembered that I hadn't called him. I still didn't really feel like talking to him. Or anyone else.

"I'm going to do the dishes," I announced during the first commercial break.

"Oh no, sweetie," Kara's mom said. "I'll take care of that later."

"It's the least I can do," I said. "To thank you for dinner."

"You don't have to thank us," Kara's dad said.

I motioned toward the TV. "I just can't . . . it depresses me. Everyone . . . dying."

Kara's mom frowned and looked at her husband. That, right there, was the Poor Lainey face. They both looked so sad for me. Like their hearts were just breaking in half for Poor Lainey Pike.

"Please don't feel sorry for me," I mumbled. "I just want to do the dishes. I like to wash dishes. Ask—" I trailed off. I'd almost said, "Ask my mom." When I was aggravated or annoyed, I went straight to the kitchen sink, because for some reason, washing the dishes relaxed me.

Kara's parents were still staring up at me. "Ask Kara,"

I said, although that didn't make sense, because Kara didn't know I loved to wash dishes.

I went into the kitchen and turned on the faucet. A few minutes later, Kara's dad came into the kitchen and grabbed a towel. "I'll dry," he said. He picked up a plate out of the rack.

"I really do like washing dishes," I said after a minute.

He nodded. "I've always been fond of mowing the lawn when I need some time to think about things."

I shook my head. "I don't really want to think about things."

He nodded again. "Understandable."

As much as I didn't want to think about anything, I couldn't shut my brain off. I thought about Riley again, just to have something occupying my mind. I wondered what I'd do if Riley died. Would I feel like I'd never be able to love anyone again? Would I feel like he'd been my last chance to be happy? How long would it take before I felt normal again, like I could live without him?

No, I told myself. *Stop. You're not going to pretend it makes sense. You're not going to make excuses for her.*

And then I guess I started crying. Kara's dad dried a few more plates before he noticed. Then he muttered, "Oh, kiddo. Hold on." He dropped the towel on the counter and then disappeared into the living room. I stared down at the soapy water in the sink. I closed my eyes and remembered the way Kara's parents had looked at me. I remembered the same look on the faces of Mabel and her pastor. *Poor Lainey*.

Kara's mom walked into the kitchen. "Honey," she said. She touched my shoulder. I let go of the dishrag and she pulled me into a hug. We stood there together in front of the kitchen sink, and I cried into Kara's mom's shoulder. My hands were soapy, and I knew I'd gotten the back of her shirt wet, but she didn't say anything. She just held me.

When it started to feel awkward, I pulled away and asked if I could take a shower. She went into Kara's room and found me some clothes to change into—a T-shirt and a pair of sweatpants that I knew were going to be too tight, but I took them and thanked her.

I checked my cell phone on my way to the bathroom. I had nine missed calls—a combination of Riley, Mabel, my dad, and a Florida number that I first thought was Grandma Elaine and then realized had to be my aunt Liz. I listened to the messages, and they were all generic "I'm worried, please call," messages. I'd call Mabel and Riley back later. Maybe even Aunt Liz. But not Dad. No friggin' way.

I couldn't believe he thought he could step in and play hero now. Every time I'd ever needed him when I was a kid, he'd let me down. Every time I'd asked for something, he couldn't give it to me.

Honestly, I'd never gotten over our visit to Chuck E. Cheese's when I was seven. I hardly knew my father then, because his visits were as sporadic as the child support checks. But even though I barely knew him, I asked him if I could move in with him.

"Honey, you know you have to live with your mommy," he said.

"I don't want to!" I started crying. "I don't want to live with Mommy and Daddy Steve anymore. I want to live with you."

"Does she make you call him that?" Dad asked.

I nodded. She always made me call all her boyfriends Daddy whoever.

"Don't call him that anymore. From now on, call him Asshole."

I cried harder and shook my head. "That's a bad word."

"I'm your father, okay?" He pointed his thumb at his chest. "This is the only Daddy you're ever going to have."

"Then please let me live with you. Or take me to Grandma Elaine's house in Florida. Please, please, please?"

Surrounded by pizza and games and a ball pit—a little kid's paradise—and I was miserable. You'd think that would have told Dad something about my home life.

"Baby, it's not up to me," he said. "Come on, finish your pizza."

So, no, I wasn't going to call him back. I wasn't going to ask for his help. I didn't need him anymore. Didn't want him. And hopefully no one would force me to live with him. I'd be an official adult in less than a month anyway.

When I stepped into the shower, I waited for the tears to come back, but they didn't. Alone, without people staring and feeling sorry for me, I felt fine. I dried my hair and then went back to the living room. Kara's parents had gone to bed. Kara came out of her room wearing her work apron. "Go to work with me?" she asked. I nodded.

        —◦◦◦—

Kara worked at the diner right off the interstate, not in Corben but in Baltimore City, with the super-big parking lot where truckers could park their tractor-trailers. No one we knew really hung out at the diner until after Kara started working there.

Kara'd gotten some scholarships, but she still needed money for college and she actually made decent tips working at the diner. Unlike most of our graduating class, Kara would be at a real college in the fall—UMBC, on the other side of the beltway. She wanted to be a nurse.

When Christine had found that out, she'd rolled her eyes and said, "You could take nursing classes at CCC," which is Corben Community College, where about half of us were headed. After Christine's boyfriend, Wallace, decided to go there, Christine started talking about CCC like it was Harvard or Yale, even though anyone could get in; you just had to decide you wanted to go, and then you went. Christine wasn't going to college at all. All she wanted to be was a homemaker, and you didn't need even an AA degree for that.

I'd be at CCC in the fall. Riley, too. He'd taken a year off after high school so we could start together. I would major in business and he would get certified in auto repair, and then we were going to open our own repair shop. I'd be the receptionist and run the business side of it, and Riley would fix the cars.

I sat in one of Kara's booths and ordered an omelet and sausages. She found an old Sunday paper in the back and brought it out for me to read so I wouldn't look pathetic sitting all alone. She kept my coffee cup filled. When she wasn't busy, she came and sat down with me and told me stories about dumb customers she'd had. Some of the stories I'd heard before, but I let her tell them again. I knew she was just trying to get me to laugh.

When she got off, we went back to her house and her mom was up already for work. She stood in the kitchen in her robe and started the coffeepot.

"Mabel talked to your boss," Kara's mom said to me. "She told him you'd be out for at least a week, but if you want to take more time, just let us know."

I nodded.

Kara's mom kissed me on the forehead. "Sleep tight, girls."

Kara and I slept awkwardly together in her twin bed. I woke up about a million times. I finally got out of bed in the early afternoon, just in time for *Heartstrings*. I went out to the living room and turned the television on.

I must have woken Kara up, because she came out a few minutes later. "Are you kidding me?" she asked as she sat next to me on the couch. "We haven't watched this in forever."

On soap operas, everything is so drawn out and overstated that even if you haven't watched in a long time, it isn't hard to figure out who's had an affair or who's gotten killed or come back to life. The only thing that threw me was Lainey St. James's baby, who'd been born the summer I was eleven. They'd rapidly aged her. She was a grown woman now—engaged, even.

It boggled my mind to look at that beautiful girl and remember the day she was born. I knew it wasn't real, that twenty years hadn't actually passed, that it certainly wasn't the same baby actress I remembered. But still, I felt old. I felt ancient.

<hr>

After *Heartstrings* we spent the afternoon watching movies. I kept my phone turned off. I hadn't felt like calling anyone back yet. I went to work with Kara again that night. When I woke up the next afternoon, I saw that Kara's mom had washed my clothes and left donuts for us.

"I guess I should probably talk to Riley," I said to Kara as I dunked a chocolate donut in my milk. I didn't feel *too* guilty about it, though. Mabel would have told him I was at Kara's, so he could have found me if he'd really wanted to.

I knew he had to be devastated about my mom. He'd try to get me to talk about my feelings, and he'd make it into such a big deal. But I wanted to ignore it for as long as possible. Denial was my favorite stage of grief, by far. I didn't mind being numb. When you go to the dentist, who wants to feel all of that scraping and drilling? If you don't take the novocaine, you're crazy. There's nothing wrong with being numb.

Riley would understand why I'd been ignoring him. He knew me. I wasn't some fake perfect girlfriend, and he loved me anyway. Even when I let his calls go straight to voice mail.

Kara raised her eyebrows and took another donut. "You haven't talked to him? He's probably worried."

I glared at her.

"Just saying."

After we ate, I changed back into my own clothes and left Kara's house. I didn't drive straight to Riley's. I got on the beltway and drove around for a while. I drove past the spot where Carl crashed his bike. I'd done it before and it didn't really bother me. Mom, though, never went back on the beltway after Carl's accident.

I practiced how I'd apologize to Riley for ignoring him.

I'm sorry I've been distant. Or, you know, completely absent.

I just wanted to be alone. Sort through my thoughts.

I know I should have wanted to be with you.

Hey, my mom is dead. *I don't have anything to apologize for.*

Ugh, yes I do.

I was selfish. I am sorry.

Finally I pulled up in front of Riley's house. I didn't even have to knock. He saw me coming up the sidewalk, and he opened the door and stood back and let me in. Like he'd been waiting for me. Maybe he had. Maybe Kara had called him, or he'd called Kara.

"Anybody home?" I asked.

He shook his head.

Riley's family was always busy, and they were hardly ever home. His mom owned a craft store and spent all her time there. That's what got Riley motivated to open his own business. His dad was a car salesman. His brother spent all his time with his girlfriend or playing soccer.

He took my hand and led me upstairs to his room and then shut the door and gave me the longest hug of my life. He probably thought I would start bawling, because that's what he remembered me doing after Grandma Elaine died. And like I'd done when Mom said we couldn't afford to fly to Orlando for the funeral. She never went back to work after Carl's accident, but I knew she was lying about not having the money.

Riley had really wanted to take me to the funeral. He had money saved up because we'd been planning on getting an apartment together after I graduated. But Riley's mom didn't want him to miss work, and I didn't want to go by myself. I told him we should just keep the money for the apartment. I knew Grandma Elaine would have wanted us to get out on our own as soon as possible. So in the end I didn't get to go, but he'd tried.

"Are you all right?" he whispered in my ear.

"Fine," I said. "Let's watch TV."

He let go of me and pulled his sheets back so I could climb into bed. I snuggled up under the blue plaid comforter that I'd helped him pick out a few years earlier.

"Are you hungry?" he asked. "I was getting ready to make a snack before work."

My eating schedule had gotten so out of whack after spending two days with Kara that I didn't even know if I should be hungry or not. "Um, yeah," I said. "I guess."

Riley tucked me into bed and turned on the TV. He handed me the remote and then headed to the kitchen. He didn't ask me what I wanted and I hadn't told him, but I knew whatever he came back with would be perfect.

"I can't believe it," Riley said after we'd finished eating our sandwiches. He sat beside me on the bed holding my hand, like I was sick, or an invalid or something.

"I don't know why you're surprised. I mean, she practically couldn't do anything for herself the last few months."

"But she seemed happy at Collin's graduation."

Ugh, Collin's graduation. Collin didn't go to either of the elementary schools I'd gone to. Since he needed special services, he went to a school outside our zone. He was in a regular kindergarten class, but they pulled him out for one-on-one help since he didn't always do well in big groups.

The graduation thing had been outside. All the kindergartners lined up in the grass wearing their graduation gowns and sang a few little-kid songs. And then Collin almost ruined the whole thing in the middle.

While they were supposed to be singing "My Country, 'Tis of Thee," Collin turned around and bolted across the field toward the baseball diamond. His teacher looked back at him, lost her place in the song, and then looked around the audience for Mom. Mom just sat there staring off into space like she didn't know what was going on. Mabel nudged her, but by the time she figured out Collin had run away, Riley had already crossed the field and caught him. He threw Collin over his shoulder and tickled him as he carried him back to his class. Collin wouldn't stay with his kindergarten class by himself, so Riley stood with all the little kids. And he sang, too.

Mabel took a ton of pictures with Mom's camera. Mom couldn't stop crying long enough to hold the camera up to her face. Later Mabel had them printed and got a big blown-up version of the only decent picture she'd gotten of all four of us. We were a sad excuse for a family. Collin scowled and looked away from the camera as he tried to pull away from Riley. Riley looked down at Collin with his mouth open like he was telling him to hold still. Riley had his other arm around my waist. I squinted because the sun was in my eyes. Only Mom, with her face red from crying, had smiled. Trying to pretend like she wouldn't be dead in a week.

I snorted. "Were you there?" I asked Riley. "She cried through the whole thing."

"Other mothers cried too. You get emotional when your kid graduates from kindergarten."

I rolled my eyes. "She was just crying about Carl. She probably didn't even know where we were."

"Lainey, you're—"

"Let's talk about something else."

"Fine. How's Collin holding up?"

That wasn't really changing the subject, but whatever. "He's fine."

Mabel probably thought I was a terrible sister. I still hadn't actually called to see how Collin was doing.

"Jeez, I can't even imagine how he feels right now. He must be so confused."

I nodded.

"Who's watching him?"

"Mabel. Don't you have to go to work soon?"

He checked his watch. "Yeah, I should be leaving now. If I go. I'll call in sick and stay with you if you want."

I shook my head. "You should save your sick days for when we can actually have a nice day together."

He rubbed my knee through the blanket. "You can come with me."

If I'd wanted to, I *could* have gone to work with him

28

and sat in the waiting room reading car magazines and drinking gross coffee out of a Styrofoam cup. But it didn't really sound all that appealing.

"I think I'll just go back to Kara's," I said.

Riley nodded. "Maybe I can come over after work?"

"I might go to work with Kara."

"I could meet you at the diner."

"All right. That'd be nice."

"I'll call you."

I forced a smile. "I'll answer."

2

LAINEY
ST. SOMEBODY

After I left Riley's, I drove to my house. I decided if I saw police tape, I would keep driving. But when I got to my house, it looked completely normal, just like it had the last time I'd been there. I parked in the driveway and then walked up to the front door. Then I changed my mind and walked next door to Mabel's.

"Hi, sweetheart." Mabel greeted me with a big smile. Then I noticed her looking me up and down, and I knew she was thinking, *The poor girl's had on the same clothes for forty-eight hours.* "Come on in!"

As I followed Mabel into the house, I noticed the silence first. And then I noticed that all her animal knickknacks were still carefully arranged on her shelves. Those goofy animals had provided hours of conversation after Carl died and Mabel started coming over a lot. It was good to have something to talk to her about besides church and Basket Bingo and dead people. I'd buy her a grizzly bear figurine or whatever, and when I gave it to her, she'd tell me how much she loved it; then she'd tell me about her other grizzly bears and where she'd found them, and that would eventually lead into a story, and the stupid grizzly bear would provide an hour's worth of conversation between me and Mabel, while Mom sat in the recliner looking comatose.

The knickknacks were intact and the house was perfectly silent. My brother was definitely not here.

"Where's Collin?" I asked Mabel.

"Oh, honey, sit down," Mabel said. She took my hand and pulled me into the living room. I wondered if I'd been wrong. I'd just assumed Collin was okay, but maybe he wasn't.

I sat on Mabel's couch. Mabel stood beside me.

"I called Carl's mother, and she came and picked Collin up. The day it happened."

"Oh. Is he going to live with her now or something?"

"I don't know, sweetheart. Would you like some cookies?"

"Okay," I said, even though I wasn't hungry. Mabel smiled at me and went to the kitchen.

Mabel's house always smelled like tea, and not instant iced tea from a canister like my mom always made, but the kind that you made on the stove with boiling water and tea bags. I hated that kind of tea, but whenever Mabel gave me a cup, I drank it. She came back with two glasses of nasty tea and a plate of cookies (store-bought; Mabel never baked) on a tray.

"Did you talk to your father?" Mabel asked.

I nodded, but of course I hadn't.

"Good. He sounded so worried about you. Are you going to visit?"

I shook my head and then took a big gulp. The trick was to drink the tea as quickly as possible. "I think I'll go back to Kara's tonight." If my dad had been all that worried about me, he would've come to Corben already.

Mabel nodded. "Her mother sounded very nice on the phone."

I nodded. "They're all really nice."

I sat on Mabel's couch and stared at her coffee table. It was so quiet that I could hear myself chew, and it sounded like the loudest noise I'd ever heard. I finished my cookies and took two more big gulps of the tea and then put my empty glass down on the tray.

"Did you want me to walk next door with you and help you pack an overnight bag?" Mabel asked.

I shrugged. "If you want." There was no way I'd admit to Mabel that I might actually be afraid to walk into my own house.

We got up and walked outside. When I saw the red Mustang convertible with Texas plates parked in front of my house, I stopped. Mabel bumped into my arm.

"What is that?" I asked. "Whose car is that?"

Mabel stared and shook her head. "I don't know,

dear. It's probably just someone visiting one of the neighbors."

As we walked toward my house, I saw that the gate was already open. We never left the gate open, and I knew I'd shut it fifteen minutes earlier.

We walked up to the porch. Mabel turned the doorknob. It was already unlocked. She gave me a look.

"Hello?" Mabel called. "Is anyone home?" I followed her into the living room, but I left the door open in case we had to make a quick escape.

A blond girl flew into the doorway between the kitchen and living room. "Hey!" she exclaimed. She wore white shorts and a pink T-shirt with a rainbow on the front. She was tan. Really tan.

And she looked just like Mom.

Okay, she looked like what Mom would have looked like twenty years ago.

Mabel looked at me, like she wanted me to explain. But I just stared. She took a few steps toward the blond girl.

"Hello," she said. "I'm Mabel White. From next door." She held out her hand and the blond girl shook it.

"Vallery Lancaster," she said. "From Texas. I'm Lisa's daughter. I just got here. I left as soon as Lisa's lawyer called, but it's a pretty long drive." Vallery looked me over. "Hi!" she said. She held out her hand.

I knew I shouldn't be offended that she didn't recognize me. I hadn't even bothered to find her number and call her. But I just stared at her hand. "It's me, Lainey," I said. "Remember?"

"Oh!" Vallery threw her arms around me. "My God, Lainey, it's been *years*."

I let her hug me for a few seconds and then I pulled away. We stood there awkwardly in the doorway between the kitchen and the living room.

"Uh. So. Do you dye your hair now? It looks lighter."

Vallery rubbed her hair. "The sun lightened it up a lot."

I nodded.

"Do you have any food or anything?" Vallery asked. "I haven't eaten since Tennessee."

I waved my arm toward the kitchen, and Vallery turned and went in. Mabel and I sat down at the kitchen table while Vallery opened the refrigerator.

"So you're Lisa's oldest daughter," Mabel said.

Vallery looked at Mabel over the refrigerator door. "Yep."

Mabel nodded. "I'm so sorry for your loss. I'd gotten very close to Lisa, so I can only imagine how you must feel right now."

"Yeah," Vallery said. She walked away from the refrigerator with a block of cheese. "It's really . . . sad. Just sad. I don't know any other way to describe it." Vallery turned to me and made a jabbing motion with her hand, like she wanted to stab me.

"You need a knife?" She nodded. I went to the silverware drawer and found a sharp one.

"Thanks," she said. She sat at the table and cut off a wedge of cheese. "I know this is probably rude, but I'm so hungry I think I might pass out."

"Are you diabetic?" Mabel asked.

"No. Just hungry." Vallery smiled at me. "I wish you could see your face right now. You'd think I'd come back from the dead or something."

"I just wasn't expecting to see you. I didn't know Mom had a lawyer. I don't even have your phone number."

"We didn't have any idea how to get in touch with you," Mabel said. "I'd started planning the funeral with my pastor."

"Oh crap, funeral. Yeah, we'll have to talk about that."

Mabel nodded. "I bet you girls would like to catch up, so I'll go on home. When you get all settled in, you can come on over and talk to me."

"It was nice to meet you," Vallery said.

"Thank you, Mabel."

Vallery and I sat at the table and waited for the front door to shut behind her.

"How did you get in?" I asked.

"You keep a spare key hidden under a flowerpot, like every other person in the world."

She put down the knife. "Where the hell did Collin come from? Why didn't anyone bother to tell me that Mom had another kid?"

I shrugged. Vallery sighed and threw her long, tan

legs up on the chair beside her.

"I about shit myself when Mom's lawyer called. First, I was surprised that Mom had been smart enough to even talk to a lawyer. And then it was surprise after surprise after surprise." She picked the knife back up and pointed it at me. "You know, I'm not the one who didn't stay in touch."

I nodded. "Yeah. I know Mom."

"I mean, when I got a little older, I really tried to be a good daughter. I called Mom sometimes to let her know how I was doing. It didn't seem like she cared all that much, but I did it anyway. Every time I moved or changed my number, I let her know, just in case. And this, Lainey, is the very definition of 'just in case.' She should have called me. My God. I would have taken the kid off her hands so she could get some counseling or whatever she needed to do. Jesus."

"What did the lawyer tell you?"

Vallery grinned. "Oh, it was great. First he tells me, 'Angel, I'm so sorry to be the one to tell you this, but your mother has passed away.' And I'm like, 'Oh my God, was she sick?' And he's all, 'Yes, emotionally she was very sick. She was never the same after Carl's death. She couldn't get over it.' So I'm like, 'Oh, her broken heart killed her?' And I kind of laughed, which was real appropriate, I know. So he says, 'No, she killed herself. She hung herself.' And I'm like, 'Oh my God.' But then I'm like, 'Wait, who is Carl?' And that surprised him. I guess Mom had given him the impression that we were super close or something."

"I can't believe Mom *had* a lawyer."

"Yeah, apparently after she knew she was going to off herself, she got in touch with this guy to get her affairs in order or whatever. I think they used to date. So anyway, he explains to me about Carl and the motorcycle accident and everything. And I'm like, 'Well thank you for letting me know, but I'm not sure I'll be able to make it up there in time for the funeral, money's tight, blah, blah.' And he's quiet for a minute. And then he says, 'Of course there's still the matter of your brother, Collin.' See, by then he'd figured out that if I didn't know about Carl, there's no way in hell I knew they had a kid. I bet he was mad as hell at Mom. He had to explain to me all about the kid and how Mom wanted me to be his guardian or whatever. So I said, 'All right, I'm on my way, but I'm coming from Texas so it's gonna take a while.' And now here I am. I have a meeting with this lawyer guy tomorrow."

"I thought you lived in Colorado."

"I moved to Dallas after college. God, Mom didn't tell you anything, did she?"

I shook my head. "You went to college?"

"Yes, I went to college. That's surprising?"

"Well, the last time you were here, you didn't seem really . . . scholastic."

I hadn't seen Vallery since I was eight years old. She visited one summer during Mom's Dark Days when she'd been too paranoid to work so she somehow got on disability and saw a counselor five times a week. Vallery was fifteen, and her dad sent her to us because she'd gotten out of control. Like Mom could have done anything to fix that. I guess he just needed a break.

Somehow she made a zillion friends her first day in Baltimore, and had a party in our living room every single night for six weeks. It was hard to sleep with all that noise all night long. Mom got pills from her doctor, and she had no idea what was going on. I snuck one of her pills one time and downed it with a glass of grape juice, but it made my arms and legs feel so heavy that I crawled to my bed and slept it off for about sixteen hours.

Vallery rolled her eyes. "Yeah, well I'm twenty-five, Lainey. I grew up. Didn't you? I notice you're not still wearing Care Bears pajamas and picking your nose. Besides, it was just state college, not the Ivy League or anything."

"I wasn't saying I thought you were dumb."

"Yeah, I know. Hey, I do like this house a lot better than the old one. Man, that place was a dump. Whoever Carl was, I guess he set you and Mom up pretty nice."

I laughed. "We even have gas here."

Vallery wrapped up the cheese and dropped the knife in the sink on her way to the refrigerator. "Gas?"

"We didn't at the old house. Mom had it shut off when you were there."

"I don't remember that."

"You don't remember? Mom was afraid of ovens. She

was on disability. Saw a counselor and everything."

Vallery laughed. "You're making that up. That sounds too whacked out even for Mom."

"You don't remember we couldn't cook anything on the stove? We could only use the microwave?"

Vallery looked up at the ceiling and then nodded. "I guess I do remember eating a lot of Hot Pockets that summer." She sat back down at the table. "Where's the kid?"

I shrugged. "Mabel says his grandmother came and got him."

"He has a grandmother?"

I nodded. "Carl's mom."

"Then why did Mom make *me* his guardian?"

I shrugged.

"Why do you think she *hung* herself?"

"I don't know."

"I mean, she has pills out the ass in the medicine cabinet."

I stared at her. "You've been here for twenty minutes and you went snooping through the medicine cabinet already?"

"Yes. Wouldn't it have been easier to swallow a bottle of those and then just drift off to sleep?"

"Is that how it works? You just go to sleep?"

"I don't know. But it seems like it'd have to be more pleasant than snapping your neck."

"I think you suffocate when you hang yourself."

"I don't think so. Anyway, this Mabel lady? She was Mom's friend?"

"Yeah. She lives next door."

"I guess I better go talk to her about this funeral."

"Now?"

Vallery shrugged. "Yeah, why not? Left or right?"

"Left. The yellow house."

"'Kay. I'll be back in a few."

Vallery started for the living room, and then she walked back to me and bent down and gave me a hug. She kissed me on the cheek and walked away.

Alone again.

I sat at the kitchen table and stared at the door to the basement. I walked over and shut it. And then I pushed a chair against it. I knew it was kind of crazy, but I didn't care. I felt entitled to a little absurdity, under the circumstances.

Our basement was one of those nasty unfinished basements with a cold cement floor and bad lighting. The washer and dryer were back in the corner. There were a lot of pipes up by the ceiling. I imagined Mom swinging from a rope from one of the pipes.

Stop thinking about her, I told myself. *Think about happy things. Think about Riley and bunnies and sunshine.*

I pictured me and Riley walking through a field chasing bunnies. I went upstairs to my room and lay on my bed.

I stared up at the ceiling, at my graduation present

from Christine. It was a big collage on poster board. She'd made one for everyone in the Old Crew. In the middle, real big, was a picture of me and Riley sitting together after one of his soccer games, and a bunch of other pictures of us from high school, me and Riley and our friends. Then there were random happy words she'd cut out of magazines. "Fun." "Friends." "Awesome." I hadn't gotten anyone a graduation present. I hadn't even thought about it.

I checked the time and then reached into my bag for my cell phone and called Kara. "Guess who just got to my house."

"Who?"

"You'll never guess."

"I know I won't. Tell me."

"My sister."

"Who?"

"Vallery. My older sister."

"Oh, yeah. Wow."

"Apparently Mom had a lawyer and the lawyer called Vallery and she has to be Collin's guardian or something."

"Wow."

"I know." I looked out the front window at Vallery's Mustang. Where had she put all her stuff? Was she even planning on staying, or would she take Collin back to Texas? Would she even keep Collin now that she knew he had a grandmother who could raise him? Why did she decide to come here at all, after she'd told the lawyer that she didn't even think she'd be able to make it to the funeral?

"I guess I'm staying home tonight," I said. "And apparently there's going to be a funeral. I'll let you know when it is."

For the first time, I imagined Mom's funeral. A ton of people had come to Carl's funeral, and he didn't even have that many friends, so I could only imagine how packed Mom's funeral would be.

"All right," Kara said. "Let me know if there's anything I can do."

I pictured the funeral home full of people, with each and every person making the Poor Lainey face.

"Hey, Kara . . . this is going to sound dumb, maybe, but can you not tell Christine and all of them? About the funeral."

"Oh. Sure. I understand if you don't want a lot of people there."

"Thanks. I'll talk to you later."

I turned on the television. I waited for Vallery to come back, but after an hour she still hadn't. I looked out the window to check if her Mustang was still parked in front of the house. It was. I wondered what I'd do if Vallery went back to Texas just as suddenly as she'd shown up, if Collin went to live with his grandmother, if I was left here in this house all alone.

I called Riley's cell phone and left a message asking

him to please, please, please come over when he got off work.

--·--»≡»»·--

When I asked Riley to spend the night a few days after Grandma Elaine died, he told me he didn't want to because he thought it would look bad. Riley was the kind of guy who wanted to wait until he was married to have sex. Except we didn't wait that long. After two years we knew that we would be together forever and we didn't see any reason to wait until we made it official.

When Riley acted weird about spending the night that first time, I reminded him that we were already sleeping together, and I made him feel guilty about leaving me alone when I was sad. And after he realized that my mom didn't care if he spent the night, and his parents didn't care either, he stopped being uptight about it. He came over whenever I asked him to, even if he had to wake up early for work the next day.

When Riley showed up in my room at ten with an overnight bag, Vallery still hadn't come back.

"Whose Mustang?" Riley asked. "Is he hiding in your closet?"

He winked at me and I rolled my eyes. "You just missed him. He climbed out the window."

Riley took off his jeans and climbed in bed beside me.

"Maybe you can take a ride in it sometime, though."

"Oh, you do know who it belongs to?"

"Yeah. It's my sister's."

He sat up and stared at me. "Your *sister?*"

"Yes."

He grinned, like he thought I was messing with him. "You don't have a sister."

"I do. She lived in Colorado, but now she lives in Texas. Well, she did live in Texas. I guess maybe she's going to live here now. I don't even know. She's Collin's guardian. Maybe. I think."

"Where's Collin? Is he home?"

"No. He's with Carl's mom."

Riley shook his head. "I can't believe we've been dating for almost four years and you never told me you had a sister."

"No, I told you about her. Remember the summer I ate nothing but Hot Pockets?"

"That was her? I thought that girl was your cousin or something." Riley snuggled up to my back. "What's that soap opera you like to watch?" he asked me. "Lainey St. Somebody."

"Hush," I said.

"You should write to them. This would make a good story line."

I'd almost fallen asleep when I heard Vallery come in the front door. A few minutes later she came to my door wearing a Lynyrd Skynyrd T-shirt and flannel pajama pants. I looked at her in the glow of the television. "There you are," she said. "Mabel? Really likes to talk. Oh my freaking God. I'm taking Mom's room. I know that's kind of weird but oh well." Then she turned and walked away.

"So that was your sister?" Riley asked.

"Yup. That was Vallery."

"Nice to meet you!" he yelled after her.

I turned off the television. "Go to sleep," I muttered. And then I was out.

3

THE
FUNERAL

In the morning when I woke up, I felt fine for a second, and then I remembered all over again. The person who had slept across the hall wasn't Mom. The footsteps puttering around the house weren't Mom's. Mom was gone. Vallery was here. I buried my face in Riley's back and fell asleep again until he got up to leave for work.

After Riley left, I stayed in my room. I didn't want to go out and talk to Vallery. I hadn't seen her in *ten years*. What did we have to talk about, besides our dead mother? I kept the door shut, and Vallery didn't bother me.

That afternoon when I heard her leave in the Mustang, I went down to the kitchen to make some lunch. But instead of going to the refrigerator, I opened a drawer and found Mom's phone book. I looked up Carl's mother's number.

I dialed the numbers too quickly and hit a wrong button. The robot voice came on and told me to try again. So I did. Collin's grandmother answered.

"Hello?"

"Hi. This is Lainey. Can I talk to my brother?"

She didn't answer me, but then I heard her yelling for Collin. I waited. Finally he picked up.

"Lainey?" he said.

"Hi, Collin!"

"Hi, Lainey."

"Are you having fun at Grandma's?"

"Uh-huh."

"Are you ready to come home soon?"

"Uh-huh."

"Our sister Vallery's going to bring you home. Grandma and Vallery and the lawyer just have to talk first."

"Uh-huh."

"You know I miss you, right?"

"Uh-huh."

"Okay. I'll—"

But he'd already hung up.

I had no interest in entering Mom's bedroom, but Vallery knocked on my door that night and insisted that I had to help her pick out something for Mom to wear for the funeral.

I looked at Vallery's things piled up in the corner.

She'd brought a red suitcase and three trash bags. It didn't look like a lot of stuff. I wondered what she'd brought and how long she planned to stay. I tried not to look around at anything else. I tried not to think about the fact that we were dealing with my dead mother's clothes. I tried to be cool like Vallery. But it was probably a lot easier to be cool when you hadn't seen the dead woman in ten years.

She hadn't seen Mom wear those clothes. She couldn't picture her in them, walking around the house, playing with Collin, leading one of her groups, making dinner, crying in the recliner after Carl died. Those clothes, to Vallery, were just clothes to be sorted through. It seemed perfectly normal to her that she was rummaging through Mom's things, shoving the rejected outfits into trash bags, picking out the last outfit she'd ever wear. Maybe Vallery would have been the sort of daughter who shared clothes with Mom. But I never went through Mom's closet, never borrowed anything. This felt like an invasion, and I didn't want any part of it.

I let Vallery dig through the closet while I sat on the floor with my back against the bed. I picked up a notebook sitting on the nightstand. I opened it and pretended to look occupied. As I stared at the notebook, I realized what it was. Mom's journal. This certainly constituted a bigger invasion than sorting through her clothes, but I couldn't put it down. Mom hadn't left a suicide note, but maybe she'd written something in here. I flipped to the last page. These could have been the last words Mom had ever written.

Possible new metaphors for life:
flower—blooms, beautiful
river—flows, twists and turns, harsh or calm
storm—harsh and turbulent but then there's
a rainbow
tree—frail sapling but then grows strong

Notes for Mom's workshops. New metaphors for life. Jesus. She spouted off cheesy nonsense, but those women loved her. I flipped back a few pages, but it was all the same sort of stuff. Nothing about Carl or her depression. She must have stopped writing in there months ago.

"What about this?" Vallery said. I put the notebook back and looked at the green dress she held up.

"I guess that's fine."

Vallery turned and looked at it again. "I think I might actually keep this one."

"You're going to keep Mom's dress? You're actually going to wear that?"

"Yeah. So what? It'll fit me."

"But she's dead."

"Lainey, have you ever shopped at a Goodwill? Or bought anything secondhand?"

I ignored her and stared at the row of stuff hanging up in Mom's closet. She set the green dress to the side and pulled a black sweater off a hanger.

"Lainey, answer me."

"Yes, I have."

"Then I hate to break it to you, but you've probably worn some dead person's clothes. Death is the number-one reason why people make donations to Goodwill."

"I'm sure that's a real statistic."

"Well, I'm keeping the dress."

"Okay. Whatever."

Vallery flipped through the clothes. I picked at my fingernails.

"So what were you doing in Texas?" I asked.

"What do you mean, what was I doing? I was living there."

"I know. I mean, did you have a job?"

"Of course I had a job. How do you think I paid my bills?"

I knew I sounded like an idiot, but I just wanted to know something about Vallery, anything about what her life had been like before Mom died. Why did she have to make that so difficult?

"Are you going back?" I asked. I didn't know what I'd do if she said yes. If Riley and I would get the house. If I'd ever see her or Collin again.

"How could I go back, when I have to take care of you guys?"

She wasn't going back. That was good. "You don't have to take care of me. I'll be eighteen soon."

"Oh, right. You'll be able to magically support yourself when you turn eighteen."

"Exactly. So why don't you want to go back?"

"Well, I didn't love it there or anything. I had a job I wasn't too crazy about. I had a few friends. Nothing that I'll really miss."

"You won't miss your friends?"

She shrugged. "I moved a lot, so I have friends all over the place. Dallas is just another place. And I was born in Baltimore, so I guess this is home. Kind of."

"What about all your stuff?"

She pointed behind her at the trash bags. "There it is."

"You didn't have furniture or anything?"

She shrugged. "I let my roommate keep all that stuff."

Vallery pulled a red dress off a hanger. She held it in front of her and looked at it. I looked, too. I remembered that dress. Mom had worn it to a Christmas party we'd all gone to the year before. She'd bought Carl and Collin matching dress shirts and nice new pants. I hadn't wanted to go, but she'd said I could bring Riley, so we went. Mom bought a new dress for me to wear. She picked it out. It was red, like hers.

"That one," I said to Vallery.

"This one?" She tugged at the neckline. "It plunges. Don't you think it might look a little trampy?"

"No," I said.

That night at the Christmas party had been one of the last times I remembered Mom being happy.

I knew from Carl's funeral that a funeral wasn't just the funeral. First they had to lay the dead body out at a funeral home for two days so people could come by and stare at it. And the immediate family had to be there for *hours* on both days, just standing around with the dead body and greeting everyone. And then they had the funeral service and you caravaned to the cemetery and stuck the body in the ground. And then sometimes you even had a party afterward. I really didn't understand why it had to be so drawn out. Who really wanted to be in a room with a dead body for hours at a time, for days? Why wasn't the stupid funeral service enough?

Unfortunately, Lainey Pike didn't make the rules, so Mabel and Vallery arranged for Mom to be laid out for two days at the Lee-Johnson Funeral Home, the same place where we'd had Carl's funeral. I hoped they were giving us some kind of discount for being loyal customers.

The viewing at the funeral home both days was packed. I didn't own much black, so I'd thought for a second about wearing the red dress Mom had bought me for the Christmas party, but then I realized that'd be ridiculous. No one else but Mom would be wearing red. I wore the same black dress that I'd bought for Carl's funeral.

I'd known that Mom had worked with a ton of women, but it was crazy to see them all gathered together like that. All those women who reminded me of the way Mom used to be.

Mom always said she knew exactly how her problems

started. She said her life was happy and great until I was four (which I didn't believe, because she'd already been divorced twice by then). When I was four, she was in a car accident while driving to work with her best friend. Well, that's how she told it. For all I knew it was some random woman she'd picked up at the 7-Eleven. Or maybe it never happened at all. But for the sake of argument, Mom and her best friend were on their way to work when a pickup jackknifed them. Mom had a concussion and the best friend died. That's when she lost half her mind. So she said.

She lost the other half when I was seven. She said we were walking to the store (because after the car accident she hated driving if she didn't have to) and I found a garbage bag at the side of the road. I walked up and kicked it. Mom, for whatever reason, decided to bend down and tear the bag open and investigate. She found a dead body inside. According to Mom. I didn't remember this particular incident at all. She said it was so traumatic that I blocked it from my memory. She said we both cried and cried and we flagged a car down and had them call the cops.

A few months after that, the fear-of-ovens thing kicked in. She'd just dumped her boyfriend and he'd moved out. I don't even remember his name—Daddy Whoever, right? Mom was in the kitchen at the restaurant where she worked and flames shot up out of the oven, and she freaked out. She didn't get burned. Not even close. The chef's eyebrows were singed, but that was the extent of the damage.

A while after that, Mom and Carl met in this support group for crazy people. Not real crazy people like schizophrenics or anything, but dumb people like Mom who were afraid of things like ovens. Carl was afraid of public transportation.

The key to the support group was taking baby steps, and that the whole group be there when everyone conquered their fears. Mom went first. They had Mom turn the gas in the house back on, and that was the first step—Mom just living in the same house with a gas oven. I wasn't allowed to use it, and Mom wouldn't go in the kitchen, so I still lived on Hot Pockets. Then after a week or so of that, Mom and Carl and this other woman and the group leader worked up to just standing in the kitchen and talking. Carl actually acted like he was a little afraid, too, I guess to make Mom feel better about having such a stupid fear. After that, the group leader made dinner in our kitchen for everyone. Then the next week, Mom made dinner. She didn't fall into the oven, and everything was fine. She never relapsed. It was like she'd never had the stupid phobia.

Then they worked on Carl's public transportation nonsense. See, the reason Carl needed to get over his fear of public transportation was that he didn't have a car back then. And without public transportation he really didn't have much of a shot at getting a decent job. I swear to God those stupid fears they came up with were just to get out of going to work every day.

The story of Carl's attempted rehabilitation is long and boring, but in the end, Carl did not conquer his fears the way Mom did. He dropped out of therapy. A few years later, Mom ran into him at work. Since she'd gotten over the oven thing, she'd found a job as a waitress at a buffet. Carl sat in her section one night and they talked a little bit; then he left her a huge tip and his phone number. She didn't have a boyfriend at the time, so things moved pretty quickly after that. I'm pretty sure he was over the public transportation thing by then anyway, but Mom wanted to help him with his anxiety, so he pretended that he'd had some miraculous recovery as a result of her guidance. Mom was so inspired by the experience that she decided to become a life coach and hold her own inspirational group sessions. She started inviting women over at all hours of the day when she wasn't working at the buffet, and she gave them these goofy inspirational talks and had them talk about their stupid problems and write down stuff in journals, and sometimes they did little interventions like Mom had done with the oven.

I could still hear her in my head, standing in the living room, pouring her heart out to those lonely, crazy women.

Picture Mom, a pretty forty-something-year-old woman named Lisa, standing in her living room in blue jeans, a nice shirt, and bare feet. Her hair and makeup are done up nice, like always. There are fifteen women sitting around the living room and dining room. Our living room had a big sectional couch that stretched around two walls, and the dining room was full of chairs too. At first the women used to all fit on our old couch, but when Mom got more popular, we got rid of the dining room table and started eating at the table in the kitchen.

Most of the women are middle-aged. Most of them are overweight. All of them have low self-esteem. It's the first night of group—that's what Mom called it, just "group"—and they're all nervous.

"Can you control the things that happen to you?" pretty Lisa asks them. Some people nod or shake their heads, then look around at one another to see if that was the right answer. Lisa nods at them as she paces back and forth in the living room. "To a certain extent you can. If you don't want to get robbed, you don't walk alone in bad neighborhoods at night. Right?"

The women all nod. They know you shouldn't walk alone in bad neighborhoods at night.

"But that's not enough!" Lisa exclaims. "You can get robbed in broad daylight. You can get robbed in your *home*. Anything can happen to you at any time, anywhere. You *can't* control the things that happen to you. Not completely."

Lisa stops pacing and shakes her head sadly, like she's pondering the unpredictability of life.

The women write this down in their journals. On the first day of group they are all supposed to bring whatever kind of journal they want to express themselves in. Some bring cheap composition books from the drugstore. Most bring expensive hardbound journals.

Pretty Lisa stands in front of them, shaking her fist. "You can't expect life to play fair with your heart"— she pounds her chest with her fist—"or your brain"—she knocks on the side of her head—"or your health"— she places her open palm over her heart. "That's not the nature of the game we call life. You have to recognize the nature of the game and know that you can do your best to make the right choices, but life is going to do whatever the hell it pleases to you anyway. All you can control is how you react to whatever life throws at you. You can shut down or you can soar. And ladies, what are you going to do at the pivotal moment—that moment when you have the choice of a lifetime in front of you? Are you going to fight or are you going to give in? Are you going to shut down or are you going to soar? Well, what's it going to be, ladies?"

"Soar," one of the women mutters, unsure if she was supposed to answer.

"What?" Lisa says, cupping her hand around her ear. "I didn't hear that. I think that might have been the voice of someone who chooses to shut down. I said, what are you going to do, ladies?"

A few of the women start to catch on. "Soar!" they answer.

"WHAT?" Mom shouts back.

"SOAR!" they all scream. And the walls practically shake.

And these women? They paid her a lot of money to do this. After a while Mom quit her waitressing job, and we moved to Ridgely Avenue, where I had a room farther away from the living room and it became a lot easier for me to barricade myself in and ignore her pretend-therapy sessions.

Vallery had said something about Carl and I couldn't get it out of my head. *Whoever Carl was, I guess he set you and Mom up pretty nice.* That was wrong on so many levels, and I felt a little bad that I hadn't stuck up for Mom. Not that she would have wanted me to, anyway. If she had still been alive, she probably would have said, *Oh yes, Vallery, Carl was a wonderful provider. We were all lucky to have him.* When in reality Carl hadn't done a single useful thing.

So no, Carl did not set me and Mom up in anything nice. Mom, shocker of shockers, did that all on her own, thank you very much.

The graduates of Mom's therapy sessions all took her death personally. Mom had taught them to talk about their feelings, so they all felt entitled to come up to me at the viewing and tell me how Mom's death made them feel. They usually started crying. Then they would suddenly realize they were being rude and they'd ask me how *I'm* doing, oh my God, I must be heartbroken. And then I'd say, excuse me, I have to go find my sister. That same exchange was repeated approximately every three minutes with a new woman. The funeral home reminded me of our living room, with all those chairs and couches in random places, and all those distraught women.

Mabel had insisted on sending an obituary to the *Corben Courier*, so I had insisted on something quick and vague:

> *Lisa Ann Snodgrass (née Vallery), 43, wife of the late Carl Snodgrass, died unexpectedly at her home on June 4. She is survived by children Vallery Lancaster, Lainey Pike, and Collin Snodgrass. The family will receive friends at the Lee-Johnson Funeral Home on June 9 and 10.*

I didn't want her to mention the viewing at all, but she insisted we had to.

I hardly recognized any of the faces at the funeral home. That was probably my own fault, since I'd asked Kara to discourage all our friends from coming.

Riley came to both afternoon sessions before he left for work. I wished he'd taken off and stayed with me the whole time, but I didn't want to ask him to. Kara and her parents came the first night. A few of our neighbors were there. Carl's mother didn't come, so Collin wasn't there either. And then, on the second night, with only an hour left to go, my father showed up.

I was on the opposite side of the room, a good distance from the casket. A woman whose name I'd already forgotten rambled on about how Mom had changed her life. I tried to stand so that the woman would block his view of me, but he kept moving around too quickly.

And then he spotted me.

"I'm sorry—" I started saying to the crazy woman. "My sister—"

But by then Dad had reached me.

"Lainey!" he said. He held out his arms like he wanted to hug me. I just glared. He stood like that for a second, and then he went in for the hug anyway.

When I pulled away, he smiled at the woman I'd been talking to, waiting for an introduction. Instead, I held out my hand to her and said, "It was *really* nice talking to you. Thanks for coming." And she took the hint and walked away.

Dad had on a suit. A nice one. I wondered if he'd rented it. I'd never seen him in a suit before.

I wondered why he hadn't bothered to show up until the last hour of the last day.

He looked off toward the casket. "God, how could this happen?" Dad mumbled.

"Um," I said.

"How does she look?"

I shrugged. She was dead; how was she supposed to look? I actually hadn't been anywhere near the coffin. I'd rather picture her alive in the red dress, at Christmas, instead of lying dead in it.

Dad reached into his pocket and handed me an envelope. "It's just a little something for you," he said. I didn't open the envelope but I knew it had to be money. Was a funeral really a gift-giving occasion? Lisa kills herself, and her daughter gets money? Or was this overdue child support? I didn't think he bothered to pay that anymore. "I really wish you'd told me when your graduation was," Dad went on. "I wanted to be there."

Oh yeah. Graduation present.

"Sorry," I said. "Things have just been kind of crazy."

What I really wanted to say was *I invited you to fifth-grade graduation but you didn't bother showing up for that.* Some people expected an infinite number of chances to disappoint you, and it just wasn't fair.

"Liz is sorry she couldn't be here," he said. He didn't explain why my aunt couldn't come, but I got it. Corben was a long way to come from Florida for the funeral of your brother's ex-wife. Dad lived only an hour away, but I was surprised that he had made it.

Dad took my hand and walked toward the casket. I looked around for Vallery or Mabel, anyone who'd give me an excuse to cross the room and get away from Dad.

He stopped in front of the casket and kneeled down on the little bench. I watched Dad and I tried not to look at Mom. And then he started to cry. He folded his hands and bowed his head. It didn't feel right to walk away. After a minute I put my hand on his shoulder. I didn't know what else to do.

4

RETURNING TO MY REGULARLY SCHEDULED LIFE

Riley nudged me on the morning after the funeral. "Back to work today," he muttered. "Better get out of bed."

"Ugh," I mumbled into the pillow.

"What do you want for breakfast?"

"No," I said. "Stay with me."

"You need food."

"I need you." I wrapped my arm around his waist.

"You'll be sorry," he said, and snuggled up next to me. I fell back asleep.

I woke up again to Riley shaking me. "You have ten minutes before you have to be at work," he said, all urgent like. Riley thought being late to work was the end of the world. At his job maybe it was. But at my job I didn't have a boss or any coworkers waiting for me. It wasn't like anyone cared if I showed up a few minutes late.

Riley pulled on his jeans. I looked around on the floor for my nice black pants.

I kept most of my clothes piled up on the floor. Mom thought I was messy and unorganized, but she'd bought me so much stuff that I didn't have any room left in my closet or my dresser. I'd sorted everything into piles. A pile of work clothes in front of the closet. A pile of casual clothes between the bed and the window. The pile on the other side of the bed was Riley's clothes—his shorts and T-shirts and sweaters that he'd left at my house, which I wore until I couldn't smell him anymore; then I washed them and gave them back.

"What?" he asked. "What do you need?"

"Pants," I said. "Black work pants."

He found them and threw them at me. I went to the closet and picked out a clean shirt. Riley watched me get dressed, then I grabbed my purse and we went to the kitchen.

Vallery sat at the table peeling an orange. "Good morning," she said. "Nice shirt, Riley."

Riley went to the counter and opened the loaf of bread. He looked down at his Nirvana shirt. "Thanks." He dropped two slices of bread into the toaster.

"Were you, like, even born when Kurt Cobain killed himself?" Vallery asked.

"Yes," Riley said. He got the butter out of the refrigerator. "But were you even born when Skynyrd's plane crashed?"

I grinned. *Nice one, Riley.*

"I saw them in concert last summer," Vallery said. "That's when I bought the shirt."

"They have, what, one original member left?" Riley asked.

Vallery rolled her eyes and ate her orange. The toast popped up and Riley buttered it, then wrapped it in a napkin and handed it to me.

"I'm going to work," I said. I waved my toast at her.

"Collin's coming home today," she said.

I stopped with my hand on the doorknob. "Oh yeah? That's today?"

"We're having a handoff at the lawyer's office in about an hour."

I smiled. "Good luck with that."

"What?" Vallery asked. "I don't think the old lady will give me any trouble."

Riley and I walked around to the front of the house. Before we got to the gate, we hugged and kissed good-bye. Then I watched him walk to his pickup before I headed over to the Grand Am in the driveway.

I hoped Vallery understood that I was keeping my driveway spot and she could park her Mustang on the street. Our tiny parking pad had never been a problem before. Mom and I shared the Grand Am, and Carl's bike could fit beside it. I had seniority. Vallery might have thought she did because she was older, but that wasn't how seniority worked. It meant who'd been there longest, and that was me and the Grand Am.

Riley waved. I watched him drive away before I tried to start the car. Fortunately it didn't give me any trouble. *Thank God for small miracles*, Mom would have said.

Mom liked to sit way up close to the steering wheel, so I always had to move the seat back when I drove after her. I knew that I'd been the last one to drive the car, but I reached down to adjust the seat out of habit. And the plastic knob broke off in my hand. I rolled my eyes and reached into the glove compartment for my list.

The Grand Am was quite possibly the biggest piece of crap ever. I wished, on a daily basis, that Carl could have crashed the Grand Am instead of the stupid Kawasaki so we could have gotten a new car. But as long as it still ran, there wasn't really a good reason to waste money on a new one. At least according to Mom and Carl. They told me all my complaints were petty, but I kept a list of everything in the glove compartment for Riley. One day he would get around to fixing everything for me.

1. *Windshield cracked.*
2. *Passenger window won't roll down.*
3. *Driver's window completely broken.* (Somehow the window stopped rolling up and down properly and Carl had shoved some wires in there to keep the whole window from falling out. Even with the wires, the window constantly fell open about an inch. If you wanted to put

the window back up, you had to grab the wires, one in each hand, and yank them up.)

4. *Seat belt doesn't work.* (Driver's side, no tension whatever. It just hung there. In the event of an accident it would probably just wrap around my neck and strangle me.)

5. *Air conditioning doesn't work.* (Wouldn't have been such a big deal if the windows rolled down.)

6. *Gas gauge unreliable.* (Acted normally for a while, but when it hit a certain point somewhere below a quarter of a tank, it started going in the opposite direction and if I didn't pay attention, I would think I had three quarters of a tank when I was really dead on *E*. There were plenty of times when Mom gave the car to me on E and I didn't know it so I ran out of gas and had to get Riley to come rescue me with his gas can.)

7. *Interior lights don't work.*

8. P, R, D, N, *and* 3 *don't light up.* (Wouldn't have been a big deal if interior light still worked. At night I was constantly putting it in the wrong gear and backing into poles.)

9. *CD player doesn't work.* (Tape player still worked, though, so Riley bought a bunch of blank tapes and recorded all of my favorite CDs so I could still listen to my music in

the car. Was he the best boyfriend ever, or what?)

10. *Volume control doesn't adequately control volume.* (A lot of the time when I tried to turn it down, the volume would go WAY UP for no real reason, and I had to spin the dial around and around and around before the volume would start to go down again. Very annoying.)

11. *Car sometimes doesn't start.* (This had been going on since the fall, and I'd thought it was reason enough for us to get a new car already, but Carl showed us how to jiggle the battery wires and then try again. He thought he was brilliant for figuring this out. I would have thought he was brilliant if he'd fixed the damn thing. Or bought us a new car.)

I had just enough room at the bottom of the list to add the newest problem with the Grand Am.

12. *Plastic seat adjustor thingy broke off.*

That would definitely be a top priority for Riley.

Corben Mall was just about the crappiest mall I'd ever been to. It was where you went if you needed something right away and didn't want to drive fifteen miles up the beltway to White Marsh. Or you went there if you couldn't drive at all and you had to take the bus, or if you were a teenager and you had to walk or ask your parents for a ride. Really, no one shopped there because they wanted to. They either hung out there when they didn't have anywhere else to go, or they got in and got out.

The mall was anchored on one end by a discount department store and on the other end by a shut-down Ames. Every year there was a rumor about something new opening up there—a Sears or a JCPenney or even a Nordstrom, but it'd been empty since I was a kid.

My kiosk was outside the Big & Tall men's clothing store. It was a big improvement over our previous location right outside the toy store. They kept all kinds of squawking toys outside the store, but the worst was the pig. It walked in circles and oinked. All friggin' day long. Sometimes I walked over and switched it off, but it was only a matter of time before some evil child came walking by and switched it back on again.

Working at the perfume kiosk—any kiosk, really— was the most boring job on Earth. Mall shoppers were leery of the kiosk workers. The scary foreign guys who practically chased you down to get you to try their hand lotion had given us all a bad name. Most people wouldn't make eye contact. And when they did, God forbid you said something friendly, like "Good morning." They'd give you this stupid grin and say, "No thank you," and scurry off. No thank you? Are you kidding me?

The security guards always came by to talk to me while

they were on their rounds, and that broke up the monotony. Corben Mall needed lots of security guards. They had to break up lots of fights and catch lots of shoplifters, and one time there'd even been a shooting in the parking lot.

I also had Rodney from the body jewelry kiosk to keep me from going over the edge. Occasionally I even had customers to deal with. But mostly I just sat on my stool staring off into space. Not the kind of job you would want to have when you had a lot on your mind and didn't want to think about any of it.

As I started up my register, Rodney walked over to me. He looked like exactly the sort of guy you'd expect to sell body jewelry. He had his lip pierced, his left eyebrow pierced twice, a hoop in his nose, and a long bar going through his upper ear. As he walked up, he frowned at me.

"Bob told me what happened," Rodney said. I groaned. He held out his arms for a hug.

Bob was my boss, and I was so glad that Bob had taken it upon himself to spread the news of my mother's death. Rodney had been the one person I'd been counting on to treat me like a normal human being for a few hours. Thanks, Bob.

"It's cool," I said as I hugged Rodney.

He rubbed my shoulder and then walked back to his kiosk. Looking back, he said to me, "Let me know if you need anything."

I wondered why people kept saying that. Like, what would I need? What could Rodney give me that would fix anything?

I opened the cases and straightened out the boxes of perfume, which were already perfectly straight to begin with. It didn't look like anything had even been sold in the last week. Then I stared at my register for a while. I looked around the mall, but there were hardly any shoppers yet. I watched the girl at the handbag kiosk putting on her makeup. Her kiosk was only a little farther away from mine than Rodney's was, but I never talked to her. She'd gone to my high school and we'd taken a remedial math class together sophomore year. Neither of us had actually belonged in that class. Our grades were incredible compared to everyone else's. The teacher posted our averages every week, and the handbag kiosk girl—her name was Gia or Ginny or something—acted like we were competing for the top grade. Which was ridiculous, because it was remedial math. Yet she always got so smug when she had a ninety-eight-point-five percent and I had only a ninety-seven percent. Seriously.

Since I had nothing better to do, I started playing the alphabet game that Rodney had taught me. He had all kinds of games that we played to pass the time on slow days. Normally I would have asked him to play with me, but since he was wearing the Poor Lainey face, I didn't really want to talk to him. And I guessed he wanted to avoid me too, because he'd picked up a book and started reading.

Okay . . . foods. My favorite category.

A. Applesauce. Which I liked.
B. Bratwurst. Which I'd never had.
C. Catfish. Which I'd tried but didn't like.
D. Danish. Which Mom had loved.

"Rodney?" I called over to his kiosk.

He looked up from his book and grinned at me. "Hey, Lainey."

"I'm running to the newsstand. Watch my stuff?"

He laid his book down. "What do you need? I'll get it for you."

"No, I can go. Do you want some Doritos? I'll get you some Doritos."

I walked away before Rodney could keep arguing with me.

I went across the mall to the newsstand and looked at the magazines. I grabbed something with Renée Zellweger on the cover, got Rodney's Doritos (Cool Ranch—I knew what he liked), and went back to my kiosk.

I gave Rodney his Doritos. He thanked me profusely. I read through the magazine twice, putting it down only to help a few customers. And somehow, miraculously, my shift finally ended.

Before I left the mall, I bought a few slices of pizza and some fries and then met Riley at the shop. We ate together in the break room. Since he'd graduated a year ago, he'd been working full-time. I couldn't imagine working full-time at the perfume kiosk, so I still only worked ten or fifteen hours a week. I knew I'd have to find something full-time eventually, but I thought it would be okay to wait until summer was over. Or until people in my family stopped dying.

After lunch I went home, because I couldn't think of anything else to do. I could hear Collin's high-pitched screaming as soon as I got out of my car. Welcome home, right?

I found Vallery in the kitchen with her head down on the table. She didn't look up when I walked in. "You set me up," she said.

"What are you talking about?"

She lifted her head. "You didn't tell me he was like this. I mean, is he *always* like this? Or is he just upset about Mom? Seriously, what's going on here?"

"He has behavioral problems."

"No kidding. And what is he, Mexican? I didn't know Mom dated Mexicans."

"Mom didn't date a Mexican. They adopted Collin. His birth mother is Puerto Rican or something."

"You mean the kid's not even my real brother?"

"Oh my God, Vallery," I snapped. "Just go back to Texas."

"Yeah, right."

I shrugged.

"Why didn't she send him back after she realized how much he screamed? I mean, it's one thing to pop out a kid like that and be stuck with him. What was wrong with her?"

"You don't just send a kid back. And you know, you're basically doing the same thing."

"No, this is different."

"How?"

Vallery looked off toward the living room. We listened to Collin scream. I wondered what I would have done if I was Vallery. I wasn't sure if I'd give up my whole life to come back to Baltimore and take care of a kid I'd never even met. Didn't even know existed. Actually, I was pretty sure I wouldn't have done it.

"This is family," Vallery finally said. "You don't turn your back on your family."

"Right." How could she have felt any kind of loyalty to Mom? She hardly knew her.

"So. This is what he does? He screams?"

"Sometimes. He is five, you know."

"This isn't normal."

"I never said he was normal."

"I brought him home from that lawyer's office two hours ago and he hasn't stopped screaming, not for a goddamned second. I thought maybe he was hungry, and I asked what he wanted for lunch, but he just screamed in my face."

"I'll try to talk to him."

I went to Collin's room. He was lying on his back on the bed, kicking the wall and screaming as loud as he possibly could. I stepped around the toy cars and trains and LEGO blocks and action figures and made my way to the bed.

"Hey, Collin," I said.

(High-pitched screaming.)

I lay down on the bed beside him and put my feet up on the wall. "Want some lunch?"

(More screaming.)

"So you met our big sister Vallery? She's pretty cool, huh?"

(Screams. Kick, kick, kick against the wall.)

"Did you have fun at Grandma's house?"

(Screaming suddenly stopped. He shook his head.)

"Grandma's kind of mean, huh?"

(Kick, kick, kick.)

"Are you hungry? I already ate lunch. I had pizza and french fries with Riley. But I'll make you a sandwich if you want."

"I don't WANT a sandwich."

"Well, tell me what you want."

"I want you to GO AWAY."

"Not gonna happen."

(Kick, kick, kick.)

"Want to hear about my day?"

(Collin shook his head.)

I told him anyway. I started with breakfast and told him about work, and my customers, and every little thing that happened to me. By the time I was done, he'd stopped screaming and kicking altogether. That was a trick I'd learned from Riley a while ago—just start talking about your day or some other random thing. For some

74

reason it shut him up. I don't know why.

I rolled off the bed and walked toward the door. Behind me, I heard Collin roll off the bed too. "Lainey," he called after me.

I stopped at the doorway and turned. "Yeah?"

"I'm HUNGRY."

"Okay," I said.

We went to the kitchen, where Vallery was still sitting at the table. She and Collin looked at each other but neither of them said anything. I opened the cabinet and took out the peanut butter. I looked back at Collin.

"Collin, tell Vallery you're sorry for being bad and busting her eardrums."

"No."

I slammed the peanut butter down on the counter and turned to give him The Look of Doom. I'd picked that up from Carl, unfortunately.

Collin glanced over at Vallery, then back at me. "I don't remember what to say."

"Say, 'Vallery, I'm sorry for being bad and busting your eardrums.'"

"Vallery, I'm sorry for being bad and busting your eardrums."

Vallery nodded. "Apology accepted."

"No more screaming," I said as I opened the bread. "Promise?"

"No more screaming," Collin repeated. "Promise."

Collin was good at repeating things. He wasn't,

however, good at having any idea what he was agreeing to, so I knew he'd break that promise in less than an hour.

I finished making his sandwich. "TV?" I asked. He nodded. I carried his sandwich into the living room and put it down on the coffee table in front of the television.

I walked back into the kitchen. "He'll probably be good for about twenty minutes," I said to Vallery. "Maybe you should take advantage of it and go take a nap or something."

She stared at me like I was crazy. "I'm pretty sure I'm not going to be able to do this every day."

"Every day won't be this bad. I don't even remember the last time he screamed like that." That was only because I hadn't been around him in a week, but Vallery didn't need to know that.

"So what kind of problem does he have? Like ADD?"

"Maybe," I said. "He's been diagnosed so many freakin' times, I can't keep it straight. There's the ADHD. And they think he has attachment disorder. And sometimes they put him on the autism spectrum. Autism is a spectrum, apparently. It's not just one thing."

I opened one of the cabinets and pulled out Collin's file. Even though he had just finished kindergarten, Collin already had more paperwork on him than I'd amassed in my entire public school education. I dropped the papers in front of Vallery.

"IEPs, doctors' reports, psychiatric evaluations."

"Are you going to pull out the stuff on Collin or do I have to find it myself?"

"It's *all* about Collin."

Vallery laid her head down on top of the file. "I can't do this."

"You can leave," I said. "It's not like there's a law saying you have to keep him."

Vallery sat up and crossed her arms. "And leave you two alone? I don't think so."

"I'm just saying. If you're going to bitch and complain about him the whole time, maybe you shouldn't be here."

"Oh, Lainey. Jesus Christ. I was just being dramatic. If our crazy mother could take care of this kid, I can too."

I shrugged. "Okay."

"It's just going to be more challenging than I thought. No big deal."

Vallery opened the file and started reading through the papers. I went into the living room to clean up after Collin's lunch.

I was pretty sure that if I'd been in Vallery's position, I'd already be on my way back to Dallas.

That night around ten, I lay in my room and listened to Vallery try to put Collin to bed. I'd already told her that Collin didn't sleep by himself, but she seemed to think I was lying.

"Collin, you stay in this bed. It's bedtime, all right?

We'll have playtime again tomorrow."

As soon as Vallery shut his door, I heard Collin jumping on the bed and laughing.

Then Vallery opened the door again. "Collin! Lie down!"

This happened about ten times before I finally went out into the hallway.

"Val, he's not going to sleep in his bed alone. You have to let him sleep with you."

"Seriously?" she asked. She glared at me. Behind her, through the open door, I could see Collin jumping on his bed.

"I already told you that. Right, Collin? Where do you sleep?"

"Mommy's bed."

"Mommy's bed," I repeated to Vallery.

"Where's Mommy?" he asked.

"Heaven," I said. "Remember? She had to go be with Daddy."

Fortunately, I didn't have to give him that first Mommy-went-to-Heaven talk. Mabel and Carl's mom covered that before Vallery brought him home.

"Do you want to go sleep in Mommy's bed with Vallery?" I asked Collin.

"No," he said.

"Okay," I said to Vallery. "I'm going back to my room. You just have to pick him up and take him to bed with you."

I shut my door. Vallery called Collin's name. Collin screamed.

It wasn't funny, but I shoved my face in my pillow and started laughing.

5

HOW WE ENDED UP
WITH COLLIN

The thing about Mom was that she really loved all of her boyfriends even when they were absolute scum. Well, she loved them for a while. And then they cheated on her or forgot to put the toilet seat down for the hundredth time, or did something else to make her mad, and she kicked them out. Sometimes they got annoyed with her first and left on their own, but not often.

So at the beginning I couldn't tell that Carl was any different from the others. But after a while I realized she didn't get annoyed with him, didn't nag him, and you could look at her when she was around him and tell she thought he was something special. I spent a whole lot of time trying to figure out why. This was my best guess: It was because of the way they met, in therapy. He was all vulnerable and broken like she was, and when she looked at him, she saw someone who would understand her and sympathize with her. What I saw was a lazy guy who sat on the recliner all day while Mom busted her ass at the buffet to pay for our house and food and everything. And when she got home every night, she kissed Carl and looked at him like he was a god or something. Then she started dinner and straightened up and I knew that, for some reason, she was happier than she'd ever been. Honestly, it drove me kind of crazy. I hadn't understood why she'd been miserable before, but it was even harder to understand what had changed.

One day after they'd been together awhile, Mom finished making dinner and then told me to come to the table. I usually ate in my room, so it was weird that Mom suddenly wanted to "eat like a family." Half the time I didn't even eat the same thing they were having. If Carl didn't like something, she wouldn't make it, but if I didn't like it, I was just being stubborn. After the plates were on the table, before Mom had even picked up her fork, she looked at Carl and said, "I want to have a baby."

There was a big long silence after that when neither of us had any kind of reaction at all and Mom and I just stared at Carl.

I tried to picture Carl as a father. He wasn't bad to me at all, but he'd never been especially fatherly. There was that time I'd gotten a splinter in my hand and he'd used Mom's tweezers to pull it out. I was crying and he'd told me, "It'll only hurt for a minute. Hush. It's okay." He could have said something a lot worse, or he could have not helped me at all. That was nice enough. But he never asked me how my day was and we didn't do anything together except watch TV, and that didn't count because we didn't talk.

I waited for him to refuse or to laugh in her face, and I figured that this, finally, would be the night she fell out of love and dumped him. Instead, Carl pushed his chair back and walked over to Mom's side of the table. He hiked up his jeans and then bent down on one knee and took Mom's hand.

"Lisa," he said, "will you marry me?"

Of course he didn't have a ring or anything. But Mom started bawling and kept saying, "Yes, yes, oh yes! Oh God, yes!"

Carl stood up and Mom stood up and they hugged and Mom jumped up and down. "We'll have a baby," he told her. "We'll have as many babies as you want."

Mom cried and Carl held her. And I was invisible anyway, so I took my plate and finished my fish and macaroni and cheese in my room.

━━◆━━

Vallery and I had both been accidents. Mom had married Vallery's dad right out of high school when she was seventeen but they hadn't been planning on having kids for a few years. Then she found out she was pregnant. Their relationship didn't last very long after Vallery was born. She'd only been dating my dad for a few months when the same "oops!" happened again. So it was kind of ironic that when Mom actually tried to get pregnant, she couldn't do it.

For months all they talked about in the house was her stupid uterus. Her groups had a special prayer time for her at the end of every session to support her in her pro-creation goals. After a year it still hadn't happened, and someone in her group suggested that maybe she should look into foster care because there were so many poor children in the world who needed a good home.

Not long after that, Mom saw an ad in the *PennySaver* for therapeutic foster parents. I think the word *therapeutic* is what got her. Unfortunately for Mom, *therapeutic* was the polite way of saying that the kids had serious prob-lems, and the kids who came to stay with us were way beyond anything Mom and Carl had been prepared to deal with. For someone who loved helping people, Mom didn't have too much patience for the kids.

The first boy was about thirteen and got sent home from school the first day for threatening another kid with a knife. Mom said no thank you and sent him back to the agency. The next boy was polite and did well in school, but one night I woke up to find him standing beside my bed and staring at me. I cried and begged Mom to send him back, but she didn't want the agency to think she was a flake. It wasn't until Carl backed me up that she agreed to get rid of him. Then she decided maybe she'd have better luck with girls. They sent us a girl, but she was psy-chotic. She never actually did anything, but the way she talked about wanting to hurt the other kids at school was so disturbing that we couldn't take it. Mom tried to talk to the girl about her feelings and even had her join one of the groups. But then the other women in her group said she made them kind of uncomfortable. Eventually Mom gave up and sent her back.

After that, the agency thought Mom and Carl might do better with a younger kid. That's when they sent us Collin.

It was a disaster from the second he stepped into our house. He hadn't been there for more than ten minutes before he pulled off all his clothes and peed on the television. Carl smacked him, even though you're not really allowed to hit foster kids, and then Collin screamed for two hours. Mom put his clothes back on and tried to hold him and rock him, but he struggled out of her arms and ran and hid in his new room.

"You can't treat the poor boy like that, Carl," Mom said to him. "He's been neglected. He needs love."

That's what Mom told us over and over. *He just needs love.*

I guess Mom was drawn to Collin for the same reason she was drawn to Carl. He was messed up and really needed help. But just like Carl, Collin didn't seem to get any better either.

Mom took him to all sorts of specialists to have him diagnosed and evaluated. She was never happy with anything they told her. I'm not sure what sort of answer she wanted, but she never seemed to get it.

Collin spent every second of the day with Mom when he wasn't at school. She thought if she just spent enough time with him, he'd eventually feel bonded to her and all his problems would be solved and he'd start behaving and be normal.

"What if they take him away from me?" Mom asked me sometimes.

"I don't think they will, Mom," I said to her.

"What if they think he's not making enough progress?"

I thought that the agency was probably just happy that Mom had finally found a kid she wanted to keep. And I didn't think they'd be able to find another family who wanted to deal with Collin, anyway. But I couldn't tell Mom that. She was too paranoid. Collin had already been taken away from one mother who couldn't help him, so what was stopping the agency from taking him away from her, too?

Just after his fourth birthday they decided to adopt him. Well, Mom did, and Carl went along for the ride. That was another way Carl was different from Mom's other boyfriends: He didn't tell her what to do, and he didn't get in her way. The process was a long one and involved lots of paperwork and lots of interviews—we even had to get fingerprinted and have background checks—but they went through all of it. They gave up the support of the agency, financial and otherwise, just so Mom could be sure that no one could ever take Collin away from her.

And then she left him. It just didn't make any sense to me.

For the last two years or so, Mom had cried a lot less often. I stopped finding her slumped in the kitchen or hiding under the covers when I got home from school. She smiled all the time, and I knew she was finally happy. I thought it was because of her groups, because she'd found something she was good at, and because she had Collin. I thought Carl the freeloading bum was a weird addition to her new life. I didn't realize he was the foundation for it.

But it was Carl all along. He was the reason she stayed optimistic and didn't cry. He was the reason she started those groups to help other people. He was the reason she got Collin and tried to be a good mother.

And then he was gone.

And then there was nothing.

6

THESE ARE THE PEOPLE I CALL MY FRIENDS

Kara called me at work the next morning. "Christine wants to have a reunion dinner with the Old Crew."

It had been only a couple of weeks since graduation, but of course Christine wanted to have a reunion dinner.

"When?" I asked.

"Tonight at Lobster Larry's."

"Tonight?"

"Lainey! Come on. It'll be fun."

"How will it be fun?"

"You'll get to see me."

"I can see you without Christine and all her jock friends."

"Please?"

I sighed. "All right. We'll be there." I answered for myself and Riley. We were the kind of couple that had been together so long, our friends didn't call us up and say, "Come to a party; bring your boyfriend too." If you invited one of us, you were inviting both of us.

The Old Crew was how I'd met Riley. Kara joined the volleyball team in ninth grade, and that's when she became friends with Christine and all of Christine's friends. I'd been Kara's best friend for years and wasn't about to let her ditch me for a bunch of jocks, so I latched onto their group. The Old Crew also consisted of a bunch of guys from the boys' soccer team, including Riley and Christine's boyfriend, Wallace.

When I got home from work that afternoon, I found a note from Vallery on the kitchen table. Actually, it was more like a calendar, with her name and my name written on alternating days.

I went into the living room and found Collin on the floor watching cartoons and singing his favorite jingle, the one for Sparkly Clean dish detergent.

"Enjoy your feast—then cut the grease! CUT THE GREASE!" He loved the jingles that rhymed.

Vallery lay on the couch behind him with a wet washcloth on her face.

"Hey, Collin," I said. "How was your day?"

"I had a Bad Morning," he said.

"What happened?"

He shrugged.

"But you're having a Good Afternoon?"

He nodded. "I shut my fucking mouth and had lunch. Like a good boy."

I kissed him on the forehead. "You know that's a bad word."

"Vallery said it."

"Don't say it again. Okay?"

He nodded. I eased myself up on the couch by Vallery's feet.

"How was your day?" I asked Vallery. I was kind of being sarcastic, since I already knew it had been awful.

"Screw you," she mumbled. "I've heard that stupid jingle seventy-five million times."

"Aren't you going to ask how my day was?"

"You work at the *mall*. I know how your day was."

I reached over and yanked the washcloth off her face. "What's up with the note on the table?"

"I think we should have a schedule. You keep Collin one night and I'll keep him the next night; otherwise I'm not going to get any friggin' sleep."

"That sounds fair."

"So you agree to it?"

I nodded. "Sure. You've really had a bad day, huh?"

"I'm still adjusting."

"Well, I'm here now, so why don't you take a break? Get out of the house or something?"

"Are you serious?" she asked.

"Yeah. Go get something to eat or take a walk or whatever. We'll be okay."

Vallery sat up and kissed me on the cheek. Then she grabbed her purse and headed out to the Mustang.

"Where's Vallery?" Collin asked.

"I don't know. Going back where she came from?"

"Really?"

I shrugged. "No. Probably not."

I figured Vallery wouldn't come back anytime soon, and I was right. When Riley came over to pick us up for dinner, Vallery still wasn't home. Unfortunately, Collin having a Good Afternoon was no indication that Collin would have a Good Evening, and I was really worried about taking him to the restaurant.

"I have Collin," I said to Riley when he walked in, "so we should take the Grand Am."

"Vallery go back to Texas?" he asked.

I grinned. "I made that joke earlier."

He sighed and shook his head. "Guess I need to step up my act."

Riley put Collin's shoes on and we went out to the car. I tossed the keys to Riley and helped Collin into the backseat. When I tried to cross the seat belt over his booster seat, he smacked my hand away.

"Collin," I said, and gave him Carl's Look of Doom. "I need to buckle you in."

"No." He yanked the strap away from me.

I yanked it back. "You need to let me buckle it. We're going for a ride."

"No."

"Fine. Fly out of the car. See if I care." I slammed the door and started to climb into the passenger seat.

"What are you doing?" Riley asked. "That's not safe."

"Then you buckle him in."

Riley shook his head and twisted around in his seat. "Come on, Collin. We're going for a ride. We need to be safe."

I sat in the front seat and rolled my eyes as Riley coaxed Collin into sitting still while he buckled him in.

"You just have to know how to talk to him," Riley said as he turned back around. I rolled my eyes again. I'd just tried *the same thing* and it hadn't worked.

Riley turned the key. Nothing happened.

I sighed. "I'll get it." Riley popped the hood, and I jumped out of the car and jiggled the battery wires.

Collin sang along with the radio the entire way to Lobster Larry's. I kept switching stations, trying to find something he didn't know so we could get a moment of silence, but he seemed to know every word to every song ever recorded. Ever.

Riley parked. I got out and opened Collin's door.

"Play Baby?" he asked as I unbuckled him.

"All right," I said. When Collin wanted to play, usually that meant he was in a good mood and he wouldn't start screaming. Usually. I had no desire to deal with a screaming kid in a restaurant, so I picked him up out of the car and carried him on my hip like he was a baby.

Since we got there late, the Old Crew already had a table. Christine hadn't been expecting Collin, and there were only two extra seats. It didn't matter anyway since

Collin had to sit on my lap. Like a Baby. Whatever. Fine.

Christine jumped up and hugged me. It had been only two weeks, but she was already fatter than at graduation. "Fatter" probably wasn't the proper terminology to use, since she was pregnant. But Christine was kind of chubby even when she wasn't pregnant. "I'm so sorry," Christine whispered in my ear.

"Not now," I whispered back. I absolutely didn't want any displays of sympathy there at Lobster Larry's.

I sat down next to Christine, with Baby Collin on my lap. Christine tried to say hi to him, but he had his head buried in my boobs and wouldn't answer her.

I waved at Kara sitting on the other side of the table. She was wearing a mechanic's button-down shirt that said DEAN over her hot-pink tank top.

"Who's Dean?" I asked.

She looked down at the shirt and rolled her eyes. "Nobody," she said. She shot Christine a look, so I guessed they'd already had this conversation. "I bought this from the thrift store."

"To give the illusion that she has a hot mechanic boyfriend," Christine added.

"It's just a shirt."

For as long as we'd been friends, Kara had never had a real boyfriend. She'd been on a few dates, but that was about it. Christine was firmly convinced that Kara was a lesbian. Until I started dating Riley, she'd thought Kara and I were a couple.

There hadn't been a tremendous turnout for the reunion dinner. Kara sat between Joe and Owen. Joe had been on the soccer team with Wallace and Riley. Owen didn't play soccer, but he had dated a girl on the volleyball team with Kara and Christine. After Owen and the girl broke up, everyone at the lunch table liked Owen better, so he stayed and she left. Claudia and Jamie, both volleyball alumni, sat on the other side of Owen. There was a guy I didn't know next to Jamie. Probably her boyfriend. Christine had a strict rule against extraneous girlfriends and boyfriends at Old Crew events, but no one really paid much attention to her.

The waitress came and took our drink orders and dropped off a stack of small plates. The plates at Lobster Larry's were all different colors, and Christine rearranged them and passed them out so that they were in order of the colors of the rainbow. We studied the menu. The waitress brought a basket of biscuits. I fed one to Collin. Kara whipped out her cell phone and called her mother to consult her on what she should order for dinner. "What was that thing I liked when we came to Lobster Larry's that one day?" she asked. "Was it the popcorn shrimp?"

Riley was already deep in conversation with Jamie's new boyfriend. I nudged Christine and pointed to Kara on her cell phone.

"Jeez, did she call her mom again?" Christine asked. We both laughed.

I felt like it was my turn to talk. The obvious thing to

do would be to ask her how the pregnancy was going, but every time I did that, she just went into way too much detail and grossed me out. Before I could think of something polite to say, Christine spoke again.

"So you're raising Collin now?" she asked.

"Um, no."

"I can't believe you didn't invite us to the funeral."

"I, uh, didn't send out invitations or anything."

"We all would have been there for you. Kara made it sound like you didn't want us there."

"Sorry. Next time I'll send out a group email."

Christine glared at me. She didn't know how to deal with my sarcasm. "Anyway, your mom didn't leave him to you? You're almost eighteen."

"He's not a piece of jewelry or something."

Collin squirmed on my lap. His hand gripped my stomach.

"So who'd she leave him to?"

I sighed. "My sister."

Christine's eyes widened. "You have a sister?"

"Yes, I have a mysterious sister no one's ever heard of before who's suddenly back in town. Just like on a soap opera. Call me Lainey St. James, okay?"

"I don't watch that show. I like *Days of Our Lives*."

Collin's grip on my stomach tightened.

I stroked his hair. "Baby Collin," I whispered, "you're hurting Lainey."

He slid out of my lap and disappeared under the table.

Christine looked down at the floor. "Do you think he was listening?"

I shrugged. "He was sitting right here."

"I guess he's pretty upset."

"It's Collin," I said. "He's usually upset."

"But he's like an orphan now."

"Jesus Christ, Christine," Wallace interrupted. "Can you talk about something else?"

I tried to catch Wallace's eye to whisper a thank-you to him, but he didn't look back up from his menu.

⸺ ⸢⸣ ⸻

Our food came. I'd ordered chicken strips as usual, and french fries for me and Collin to share. I bent down and pulled up the tablecloth. "Come up and eat some chicken?" I asked, but I knew he wouldn't.

He shook his head. He'd found a toy car on the floor, and he drove it up and down the table legs.

"You want to eat down there?" I asked. He nodded. I slipped him chicken and french fries under the table. And that's how we got through dinner. You didn't expect Collin to behave like a normal kid. You adapted.

Of course we couldn't just leave when we were finished eating; we had to sit and "catch up" for another hour, like we hadn't spent the whole dinner doing that. At one point Riley switched seats with Claudia because she wanted to talk to me. Fortunately she didn't want to have an awkward conversation about my mother. Instead, we had an awkward conversation about this new cosmetics

95

company she worked for. She tried to convince me to have a "beauty party." I knew I wouldn't, but I told her I'd think about it, and she gave me a business card. Then she went around to the other side of the table to sit next to Kara and presumably have the exact same conversation.

At the end of the night, Collin didn't want to come up from under the table, so we said our good-byes from our seats. Joe and Claudia left first, then Owen, then Jamie and her boyfriend. As I bent down under the tablecloth and tried to convince Collin that he'd love to go home and watch endless amounts of TV, Kara walked over to our side of the table and raised her carry-out container. "I got the apple pie à la mode for my dad," she said. "I have to get home before it melts."

She bent down and waved at Collin. He ignored her. Riley bent down and started talking to Collin. Kara and I hugged. "Thanks for coming out," she said, and then she left.

Thanks for coming out! That had been what all of Mabel's church friends would say to Mom whenever Mabel dragged her anywhere after Carl died. Like they had to acknowledge what an effort it had been for her to leave the house, and practically congratulate her for it.

I wasn't getting like that, was I?

No. I wasn't. I'd never liked hanging out with all Kara's Old Crew friends anyway. Kara knew that, so she had thanked me for coming out anyway. That wasn't weird. I wasn't weird.

Riley's coaxing didn't work on Collin either, and he finally reached under the table and pulled him out.

"NO, NO, NO, NO, NO!" Collin screamed as Riley carried him from our table to the door. Every single person in Lobster Larry's looked up and watched us walk out.

We'd parked next to Christine's van. As Riley fought to buckle Collin in, Christine pulled me aside.

"Thanks so much for coming out tonight," Christine said.

"Yeah. Thanks for inviting us."

"You sure have your hands full, huh? Is Collin going to camp or a playgroup or anything over the summer?"

"He's doing some enrichment program at the school. But that doesn't start for a while."

"Well, if you ever want to go on a playdate," she said, and made a pretend telephone out of her thumb and pinky, "call me. Some of the girls in my moms' group have kids Collin's age."

"Uh, thanks," I said. As I got into the car, I shivered at the thought of taking Collin on a playdate with Christine and her other teen mom friends.

When we got home from Lobster Larry's, the Mustang was back. Parked in the driveway.

Riley helped Collin out of his booster seat, and I went upstairs to Vallery's room. She was in bed watching TV. I leaned against the door. "So where'd you go?"

She held out her hands. "Got my nails done."

"Very nice. Your car is in the driveway."

"Good. That's where I left it."

"We're lucky we found a spot on the street."

Vallery shrugged.

"Do you not care at all?" I asked.

"About what?"

"Parking in my spot."

"I thought it was a first-come, first-served thing. Anyway, you're getting Collin to sleep tonight, right? Because it's pretty late."

"Are you serious? I had him all night! I had to take him out to *dinner.* Do you know how much of a nightmare that was?"

"Well, I had him all *day.* And I gave you a copy of the schedule. You didn't have any complaints about it earlier."

"But Riley was going to spend the night."

Vallery smiled. "There's room. You have a queen."

I left Vallery's room and slammed the door on my way out.

"Riley?" I called.

"In Collin's room," he yelled back.

Collin and Riley both sat on the floor, building LEGO towers. Collin loved to stack them as high as he could before the whole thing toppled over and snapped in half.

"Collin's going to sleep with me tonight," I said. "Vallery made up some kind of stupid schedule. If you want to go home, I won't be mad or anything."

Riley shrugged. "I'll stay. You ready for bedtime, Collin?"

"No," Collin said. He didn't even look up from his tower.

"You don't mind?" I asked Riley.

"Not at all."

"Okay, Collin. Five minutes till bedtime."

"No!" That time he did look up.

"Yes," I said.

"No!"

"Yes! Four minutes!"

I got up and went to Collin's dresser. I wasn't sure where Mom kept his pajamas. On the rare occasions when I'd needed to dress him, I'd grabbed something Mom had just washed and folded and left in his laundry basket in the basement. I opened a few drawers until I found them. I pulled out his Spider-Man pajamas. His favorite. I knew that much.

"Spider-Man pajamas?" I asked.

He shook his head.

"Yes."

"Five more minutes!"

"More like *two* more minutes."

"FIVE MORE MINUTES!"

Riley reached up for my hand. I dropped the Spider-Man pajamas on Collin's bed and helped him up. "Why don't you go get ready for bed?" Riley asked. "I'll help Collin."

"Yeah?" I asked.

He kissed my forehead and then pushed me toward the door. I knew I should have told him that it was my brother, my problem, but instead I smiled and walked away. He was much better at this than I was, and we both knew it.

7

THE SNOW GLOBE

When I woke up the next morning, Collin was gone. I walked halfway down the stairs, saw him sitting on the couch watching cartoons, and then climbed back into bed with Riley.

"Are you supposed to get up with him?" Riley asked. He rubbed my back. "Or is it Vallery's turn now?"

"I don't know. I checked on him. He's watching TV."

"I have an idea."

"Oh yeah?"

"Mmm-hmm. You're gonna get up and scramble some eggs and make some sausage and maybe whip up a stack of pancakes. And I'll go out in the yard and fix some of the stuff on your list. Then I'll come in and we'll all have breakfast. Won't that be nice?"

"I have a better idea."

"What's your idea?"

I wrapped my arms around Riley. "Let's just go back to sleep."

"Laine. We gotta get up and do something. We can't just stay in bed."

"I can. It's my day off."

"We'll sleep for ten more minutes. Then we'll get up and do what I want. Deal?"

"Two more hours?"

"Lainey."

"Fine."

An hour later I stood by the stove flipping pancakes with a spatula. After Riley discovered that we didn't really have any useful tools in the garage (as if Carl ever did anything mechanical), he came back inside and started heating up the precooked sausages in the microwave. I'd sent Collin upstairs to jump on the bed and wake Vallery up. She'd been mad at first, but the smell of breakfast won her over and she trudged into the kitchen and started popping slices of bread into the toaster.

Riley set the table and filled four plates with food. I went into the living room, picked up Collin, and brought him to the table. I sat him in his chair and scooted it in.

He grabbed at the eggs with his hand.

I picked up the fork and gave it to him. "You're not a baby. Use your fork."

He held the fork in his right hand and used his left hand to pick up pieces of scrambled egg. Whatever. I sat down between Collin and Riley and started my breakfast. I was just finishing up my toast when Collin leaped up from the table and ran into the living room.

"Collin!" I yelled. "Finish your breakfast!"

"Let him go," Vallery said. "It's kind of gross to watch him eat."

I shrugged. "Whatever."

"Thanks for cooking."

"It was Riley's idea."

"What time do you work today?"

"I'm off."

"Good."

"Why?"

"I have an interview."

"For a job?"

Vallery looked at me like I was stupid. "Yes, for a job."

"Why?"

"Uh, maybe because I had to quit my old job to come to Baltimore and live with you goofballs."

"But who's going to keep Collin if you get a job?"

"We'll have to coordinate our schedules or whatever. You can start working more afternoons and evenings."

"I can't work more afternoons just because my sister says I have to work more afternoons. Bob doesn't have many people who can work mornings. He really depends on me."

Okay, I was exaggerating. And Riley worked a lot of later shifts anyway, so I really didn't have much reason to want to work during the day. Except I didn't want Vallery to tell me what I was going to do. And I didn't want her to go get a job and leave me alone with Collin every day.

"I'm sure Bob would understand if you talked to him," Riley said.

I ignored Riley and shook my head at Vallery. "I don't think you should get a job. You're Collin's guardian. That means you're supposed to be here to take care of him."

"Okay, then I guess you want to start paying the mortgage and the gas and electric and—"

"Yeah, I can afford that."

"Exactly. Someone has to pay the bills, Lainey. If you want to go work full-time, knock yourself out. Otherwise I'm going to need you to help me out."

"What about the money?"

"What money?"

"Isn't there money? Didn't Mom leave us money?"

Vallery rolled her eyes. "No. Are you kidding me?"

"No, I'm not kidding."

"There was a little money, but that went toward the funeral."

"Lainey," Riley said. I knew he wanted me to shut up. I ignored him.

"Fine, get a job," I said to Vallery. "I don't care."

"Jesus Christ. Do you want to know what your problem is?"

"No, I don't."

"You're such a spoiled little kid. But we're not

little kids anymore. We're grown-ups. And when you're a grown-up, you have to pay for things you don't necessarily want to pay for. It's not all clothes and take-out food and CDs anymore."

"No one asked me if I wanted to be a grown-up," I mumbled. I took my plate to the sink, and then I went back and grabbed Collin's. Vallery kept talking, but I flipped the garbage disposal on and I couldn't make out anything she said.

Everyone left after breakfast. Vallery got dressed in a black and gray business suit and went for her interview. Riley insisted on taking Collin to the park. I stayed home and cleaned because I couldn't remember the last time anyone had wiped down the counters or mopped or vacuumed. After I'd made decent progress, I lay on the couch and turned on *Heartstrings*.

Riley and Collin came back halfway through. Collin ran through the living room carrying the toy car he'd found at Lobster Larry's. He made obnoxious noises and drove the car up the railing as he went up the stairs.

Riley sat down on the couch beside me. I didn't acknowledge him until the commercial break.

"Sorry about breakfast," I said.

He shrugged. "I don't think I'm the one you should apologize to."

I went back to not talking to him until *Heartstrings* went off. After the credits rolled, he took the remote.

"No talk shows," I said.

"All right. Can you go check on Collin?"

I went to Collin's room and watched him ride the toy car up and down his bedpost; then I went back to the living room. On the television, a woman in a blazer with a big fake smile held up sheets of stickers.

"What the hell are you watching?" I asked.

"It's scrapbooking. My mom does this."

"Oh, like pictures? Like a photo album?"

"Yeah. You take your pictures and put them in the scrapbook, then you decorate it and stuff. My mom's are really nice."

I watched the woman smear glue all over the back of a picture and then slap it down on a piece of yellow-and-pink striped paper. "What's with the crazy paper?"

"I don't know. It's just to make it look nice."

I reached for the remote.

"Lainey, I want to watch this."

"Why?"

"To get ideas. I think we should make one."

"Why?"

"For Collin."

"I guarantee you, Collin will not care about a bunch of pictures and stickers and crazy paper."

"You don't know that. He should really have something to help him remember—"

"Drop it, Riley."

"Fine."

After Riley left for work, I went back to cleaning the kitchen. Vallery came home from her interview and went straight to her room before I even had a chance to ask how it was. Then I heard the crash.

I ran up to my room and found Collin crouching on top of my dresser.

"COLLIN!" I screamed. "What the hell did you do?"

I grabbed his arm and yanked him down. His head smacked against the door as I pulled him out into the hallway. He cried. I dragged him to Vallery's room and shoved him in. Vallery sat on the bed pulling off her pantyhose.

"It's your turn!" I yelled at her. "So watch him!"

I went back to my room and looked at all of the stuff he'd knocked off my dresser. I picked up my bottles of perfume and lotion and threw them back in their basket. I made a pile of papers and ticket stubs and receipts. Then I started picking up the pieces of the Elaine Pike Memorial Shrine. After she died, everything my grandmother ever gave me found its way onto the top of my dresser. Every greeting card. Every little note. Every little gift.

I picked up the angel statue. The keychain from Disney World. The cards. A shopping list from when she stayed here after Carl died. And then I touched a shard of glass. I felt the carpet. Wet. And it sparkled with glitter.

"No," I said. "Oh, *come on*." I felt the carpet, pricked myself with more shards of glass, and then finally found the broken snow globe underneath the dresser. The little angel was still attached to the base.

"Jesus Christ, Collin!" I screamed. "You know you're not supposed to be in my room!"

I picked off the few jagged pieces of glass that hadn't already broken off. I rubbed the little angel's head and put it back on top of my dresser. Then I got back down on my knees and picked the rest of the glass out of the carpet.

As I walked into the hallway, Vallery came out of her room and followed me down to the kitchen. "What did he do?" she asked. "He's hiding in my closet banging his head against the wall."

I showed her my hand. My palm was spotted with drops of blood. And glitter. She looked at my bloody, sparkling hand and shook her head in confusion.

"He broke my snow globe," I explained.

"Oh. That sucks."

"My grandmother bought it for me when I was a baby. It's, like, the oldest thing I own."

"Jeez," Vallery said. "I'm sorry."

And she probably was sorry that I was upset, but she obviously didn't get it. Didn't understand how upset I was, or why. I didn't want her to see that I was crying, so I dropped the glass into the trash can and went to the sink to wash my hands. I could just make out the *thud thud thud* of Collin smacking his head against the wall. Vallery sighed and turned to go back to her room.

My hands shook as I dried them with a towel. Mom was always getting rid of my old toys and clothes, practically as soon as I'd outgrown them, but I'd always held on to that snow globe. And now parts of it were in the trash can. In my carpet. Embedded in my hand.

I walked upstairs past Vallery's room and heard her calling to Collin. I heard the *thud thud thud* of his head bouncing off the wall. Collin knew he was in big trouble—that I'd been mad enough to hurt him—but he didn't get why. Vallery knew I was upset, but she didn't understand how I felt. And in that moment I realized that nothing that mattered to me meant anything to either of them.

Riley came over after work with shopping bags full of stuff. He dropped them on my bedroom floor and smiled at me.

"Riley, what's all that?" I asked, although I kind of already knew.

He bent down and held open one of the bags. I walked over and looked inside. Paper. Lots of crazy-colored paper. "My mom gave it to us so we can get started on Collin's scrapbook."

"I thought I said—"

"If you don't want to help, I'll do it myself. I know he'll love it."

I lay down on my bed.

"Well, knock yourself out. That kid doesn't appreciate anything."

"Will you show me where the family pictures are, or do I have to find them myself?"

"Hall closet," I said. "In one of Carl's old shoe boxes. That's how much we treasure our memories around here."

Riley shook his head and left my room. He came back with the shoe box and sat down on the floor and started unloading his plastic bags.

"Look at all these scissors," he said, opening a canister. "I wonder why she gave me so many." He stared at a pair with yellow handles and then tried them on a sheet of white paper. "Oh, it does fancy cutting. Look, Lainey."

He held up the paper. The edges were scalloped.

"That's nice, Riley."

He tried another pair of scissors. "Look at this one."

I hardly glanced at him. "Yeah, cool."

He sighed and wiped his hair out of his face. "You don't care at all, do you?"

I looked at him sitting on my floor surrounded by all that crazy paper. Why did I have to be mean? He was just trying to do something nice. "Of course I care. Come here."

Riley put the scissors back in the canister and climbed up on the bed. "I just want to do something nice for him."

"I know." I kissed him.

"Hello," he said.

"Hello," I said.

Riley lay down with me.

I kissed his neck and slid my hand down his chest. I bit his earlobe and reached down to rub the front of his shorts.

He pulled away and laid his head on my stomach.

"Your stomach's making funny noises," he said.

"What was that?" I asked.

"What was what?"

"I was getting friendly and you moved away from me."

"I just wanted to lie down with you."

"No. You're being weird. What's wrong with you? Am I keeping you from your paper cutting? Fine, I'm sorry. I don't want you. I don't want to touch you. Go. Get off my bed." I tried to push him off me.

Riley sat up. "It's just—I remember after your grandmother died."

I turned away from him. "I don't want to talk about people dying."

"You didn't want me to touch you. Remember?"

I did remember. The first time he kissed me after I found out about Grandma Elaine, I ran to the bathroom and cried. And every time after that I pulled away. Finally he asked, "Are you afraid that she's up there watching or something?" And I nodded. And he told me he was sorry. And we didn't have sex again for a month.

"I don't feel that way now," I said to him. I tried to kiss him again, but he turned his head.

"Well, I do. I don't want to do anything right now. I feel weird."

"Come on, that's silly."

"It wasn't silly when you felt that way. Why is it silly now?"

Because she wasn't your *mom* is what I wanted to say. But I didn't say anything. And after a while Riley slid back down onto the floor and started trying out the rest of the scissors.

I turned on the television and flipped through the channels until I came to a sitcom I'd seen a few times. I watched it, but I didn't laugh at any of the jokes.

"You rearranged your dresser," Riley said. He pointed a pair of scissors with hot-pink handles. "And your—what happened to your snow globe?"

That's all it took. I started bawling. Riley dropped the scissors and got up on my bed.

"Oh honey," he said. He hugged me. "Did it break?"

I nodded. "This is what you wanted," I choked out.

"Huh?" he asked. "I didn't break your snow globe."

I shook my head. "Collin broke it."

"Was it an accident?"

I nodded. "You've been waiting for me to cry," I said. "You want me to be normal."

"You're normal. I know you're normal." Riley rocked me and rubbed my back. "It's okay. Cry if you want to cry. Don't cry if you don't want to cry. It's all right."

"I'm not crying for her," I said.

"Who?"

"My mother."

"Okay."

"I miss my grandmother. And he broke my snow globe!"

"I know. But it was an accident. Right?"

I thought about the last time I'd seen Grandma Elaine, the day I dropped her off at the airport. She told me not to pay to park, so I dropped her off at the curb. I helped her find a cart for her luggage, and then I left her there.

I should have paid the few dollars to park.

I should have carried her luggage myself.

That would have been twenty more minutes I had with her.

I pushed my face into Riley's shoulder and cried.

8

THE DREAM AND
WHAT IT DOESN'T MEAN

I paid attention to my dreams because of Mom, like a bad habit I'd accidentally picked up. She had the women in her groups write down their dreams in their journals and interpret them every week.

"What do you think the snake represents?" Mom would ask one of the women. Lots of women dreamed about snakes.

"Maybe my husband," the woman would guess. That was usually the right answer.

Mom would nod. "Yes, I think it could be your husband. And when you consider the snake as a symbol of your husband, how can you relate that back to your waking life?"

Mom could interpret their dreams to mean absolutely anything. One woman who had the snake dream decided to divorce her husband and go back to nursing school, because that's what Mom told her the dream meant.

She bought me a fancy leather-bound journal for my fifteenth birthday. "Write down your dreams," she said to me.

"I don't dream," I told her.

"Everyone dreams!" she said. "Write it all down. The dreams you have when you're asleep and the ones you have when you're awake."

"Okay," I said. But I most definitely rolled my eyes.

I actually did try a few times, but I felt stupid about what I'd written, so I tore the pages out and threw them away. I still had the journal somewhere in my closet, but I couldn't remember anything I'd ever written in it.

For the first time since she'd died, I had a dream about Grandma Elaine that I actually remembered. She and I were at Dad's house visiting. It wasn't a real house he'd ever lived in—just one of those dream places. There was a creepy man sitting in a recliner. Sometimes he looked like Carl and sometimes he looked like a stranger. I didn't like the guy in the recliner, so I took my paper dolls out to play in the yard.

The paper dolls were something I'd really played with when I was a kid. Mom would never buy me the paper dolls I wanted from the drugstore, but when we got back home, she'd draw me a paper doll family on a piece of notebook paper, and I'd name them and cut them out. I kept them all in a Ziploc bag. I lost them when I was about twelve, a long time after I'd stopped playing with them.

In the dream, my paper dolls were blowing into the street, and my father came outside and we ran to catch them. As I grabbed the paper dolls and shoved them into the bag, I recognized their faces.

After we'd rescued the paper dolls and secured them in their plastic bag, we went back inside. The creepy man gave me a funny smile, and suddenly I wanted to leave, so I decided to pretend Grandma Elaine was sick and needed to go to the hospital.

"What hospital do you need to go to?" I asked her. I went over to where she was sitting on the couch and I put my arms around her, like she needed to be held up.

Grandma Elaine mumbled something that I didn't understand. Then suddenly her body felt heavier in my arms, and I realized that she *was* sick and we really did need to get her to a hospital.

I held on to her. "What hospital?" I asked again.

"Michaela Davis," Grandma Elaine mumbled. "Michaela Davis."

And then Collin climbed over me, kneeing me in the stomach, and I woke up. I opened my eyes in time to see Collin run out of the room.

Riley rolled over and smiled at me. "Good morning, sunshine. Don't rush. You don't have to be at work for two more hours."

I rolled over onto my elbow and looked at him. "I

had a weird dream," I said. I explained about the paper dolls, the creepy guy in the recliner, Grandma Elaine, and Michaela Davis. I didn't know anyone named Michaela Davis. I didn't know why that name would pop into my dream, or why it would stick with me after I'd woken up.

"What do you think it means?" Riley asked.

I shrugged. "I don't know who Michaela Davis is. I'm pretty sure it's not a hospital."

"I'll go home and Google it while you're at work."

"All right."

"Go back to sleep."

"I have to go watch Collin."

"He'll be a good boy and watch TV," Riley mumbled. And then he was asleep again.

<hr />

After Grandma Elaine died, I had a lot of crazy thoughts. I thought maybe this would be like *Heartstrings*, and she'd show up at my front door one day explaining that the evil Santiago Villanova had faked her death and held her hostage, but now she was free. Whenever our land line's caller ID showed a Florida area code, my heart skipped a beat, but it was usually a telemarketer, sometimes my aunt, never my dead grandmother. I waited for her to appear in my dreams and send me a message, but it didn't happen, and I didn't know what kind of message I wanted her to send me anyway. A lot of times I woke up remembering that I had dreamed about her, but I couldn't remember the dreams. Since the Michaela Davis dream was the first dream that I could remember vividly, I wanted it to mean something. I thought it *had* to mean something.

Riley called me at Perfume World a few minutes before he had to go in to work. "Here's what I got on Michaela Davis," he said. "There's a musician and an actress named Michaela Davis. They might be the same person but I'm not sure. There's also a student at Bowling Green State University—she has a really obnoxious website. Then there's a disc jockey for a classic rock station in Wisconsin. There's a character in this book called *Another Day*—"

"Wait," I said. "We have that book."

"You do?"

"Yeah. That must be what it means."

About a year ago Mom had read *Another Day* and then had all her groups read it—even bought them all copies to keep. She begged me to read it until I finally gave in and started it, but I never finished. I hadn't remembered the character's name. I didn't remember very much about the book, period.

"So what do you think it means?" Riley asked.

I shook my head. "I don't know."

When I got home from work, I went into Mom's bedroom. Well, Vallery's. As Vallery settled in, she'd packed more of Mom's stuff in boxes and trash bags and shoved them into the closet, and more of her own stuff ended up on the floor. She took down Mom's pictures—a print of a clown that she'd loved for some ridiculous reason, and a picture of a sad Indian she'd bought because Carl liked it and said he was part Indian, though I think he was lying, or maybe he had a great-great-great Indian grandfather, but I bet everyone in America had a great-great-great-somebody who was Indian. Vallery didn't put anything in their place. The walls were bare and there were two little holes where the nails had been.

I didn't see the books piled up on the floor under the window anymore, so I looked around and found them stacked up in the closet. I scanned the titles until I found *Another Day*. I pulled it out of the pile, and the other books toppled over but I didn't pick them up. I grabbed the book and ran back to my room.

I sat on my bed and looked at the cover—a close-up of a woman's face with the silhouette of a different man on each one of her cheeks. I tried to remember what the story had been about. I tried to remember Michaela Davis and figure out what my grandmother had been trying to tell me in my dream.

Nothing came to me. I opened the book, and something fluttered to the floor.

I stared down at the small piece of paper that had landed between my feet. A note? Why would Grandma Elaine leave a note for me in one of Mom's books? I closed my eyes and picked it up.

Then I opened my eyes slowly and looked at it.

It was a receipt for a Slurpee from the 7-Eleven. The

date was smudged off.

I laughed and rolled my eyes and then picked up the phone and called Riley.

"Did you find the book?" he asked.

"I found it."

"So any idea what the dream means?"

"Well, this piece of paper fell out, and I thought that it might be something important. But it just turned out to be a receipt from the 7-Eleven."

"Huh. That's kind of a letdown. Why do you think it was in there?"

"I think it was just my bookmark. I started reading it a few years ago."

"You don't think it means anything?"

I crumpled up the old receipt and tossed it at the trash can. "Absolutely nothing."

There was a knock on the front door that afternoon while I watched my taped recording of *Heartstrings*. I'd started taping it every day so I could fast-forward through the commercials.

I ignored the knock. No one I had any interest in seeing would be randomly knocking on my door in the middle of the day. If it was Mabel, she would have just walked in after the first knock.

There was another, louder knock at the kitchen door. I got worried that all this knocking might wake Collin. After Vallery had left for another job interview, Collin had fallen asleep on the floor in his room while playing with his LEGOs, but it was Vallery's night to keep him, so I didn't care if he napped. And then I heard the door creak open.

"Hello?" a woman's voice called out.

"Uh, who's there?" I yelled, and walked to the kitchen, holding the remote control in front of me like it might protect me from an intruder. A little woman with a ridiculously long braid down the middle of her back stood by the kitchen door.

"Oh! I wasn't sure if anyone was home," she said.

"Then why did you walk into my house?" I asked, still holding up the remote, although I doubted this woman posed any real threat. She was a little younger than Mom, thin and demure-looking, dressed in a red blouse, white shorts, and white sandals. She *could* have been a black belt in karate, but probably not.

"Are you Vallery?"

"No. How do you know Vallery?"

"I had a few questions about her mother's . . . business."

It was funny how quickly gossip traveled. Two months ago no one in Baltimore had ever heard of Vallery Lancaster, and now people were sending this woman to Vallery instead of me with questions about Mom.

"What about it?" I asked. "I'm her other daughter. I can help you."

I knew the polite thing would have been to offer the

woman a seat and a glass of lemonade, but I let her stand there awkwardly by the door. I still held the remote up like I might hit her in the face with it at the slightest provocation. I had to tell Vallery that we should start locking the doors.

"Well, I'd been taking sessions with her last year. And of course I think it's such a *tragedy* what happened to her. We were all praying for her to get through it, but I guess the Lord had other plans. Anyhow, I loved your mother like a sister and I want to carry on her memory."

I shrugged. "Okay."

"I want to continue her work. I want to inspire women the way she inspired me. I want to teach like she teached."

Taught, I thought, but I didn't correct her. "Well, you can teach whatever you want."

The woman smiled. "I'm glad you feel that way. I came here to ask if your mother left anything behind. Any new lessons or speeches, any words of wisdom she jotted down? I have my notes from the sessions I attended, but I thought maybe she had left other things behind that might be helpful to me."

I knew Mom had left notebooks. At least one, but probably a lot more than one. But I shrugged. "I really have no idea."

"I understand those writings would be precious to you, so I'm prepared to write you a check for any amount that you think is appropriate. Maybe you could take a look through her things and let me know what you find?"

"I can look around. I'm not sure there's anything here, though."

"I remember she often had a blue binder with her. Maybe you remember seeing her with a blue binder?"

"I can check."

"Journals, computer files, just anything you can find. I'll leave you my number."

I found a pen and paper, and she wrote it down.

"All right," I said. "I'll let you know if I find anything."

The woman left and I stood there in the kitchen holding her number. *Deborah*, she'd written. Deborah wanted to be just like my mother. She wanted to buy my mother's notebooks and computer files. I looked at the clock. Vallery had been gone for over an hour. She'd be back soon.

I went upstairs to Collin's room and nudged him with my foot.

"Nap's over," I said. "Vallery will be home soon."

I went to Mom's/Vallery's bedroom and stood by the door. I heard Collin clanging his LEGO bricks together. I went back to the closet where I'd found *Another Day* and looked through the boxes where Vallery had been throwing Mom's stuff.

I found a stack of composition books full of Mom's handwriting and the blue binder that the Deborah woman had mentioned. I looked through the rest of the room—twice—to make sure I hadn't missed anything.

I took Mom's stuff back to my room and sat on the bed and looked at the pile. *Any amount that you think is appropriate*, the woman had said. What would she agree to, though? Certainly not thousands of dollars. Maybe a few hundred.

A few hundred would help with the apartment Riley and I wanted to get.

I wondered what Vallery would have done, how much money she'd want in exchange for Mom's lifework, the only thing she'd ever been good at. Vallery would have called Deborah back already. No, Vallery would have checked for the notebooks before she let Deborah leave the house.

But for some reason it wasn't that simple for me. For some reason I stuck her phone number inside one of the notebooks and then I slid the notebooks, one by one, underneath my mattress.

⋅⋅ ▰✦▰ ⋅⋅

Later that night I crawled out of bed and went to the kitchen. I looked through the refrigerator to see what we had. Milk? Probably sour. Crystal Light lemonade? That was Vallery's—better not to touch it. Then I knew what I wanted: a Slurpee. I put my shoes on and grabbed my wallet.

I drove to the 7-Eleven on Corben Avenue. There were new ads in the window for hot dogs. The hot dogs on the posters were enormous, but I knew the real hot

124

dogs rolling around on the warming rack were practically as thin as my fingers. When I got inside, I realized I didn't have any cash. I went back outside to the ATM.

The prompt to enter your PIN popped up, and I froze. What was my PIN? The four-digit code that I'd punched in a million times had suddenly fallen out of my head. I stood there with my fingers hovering over the buttons. Which looked familiar? Four, maybe. There was definitely a nine in there. Somewhere. I hit a few numbers that looked right. No good—the machine beeped at me. I tried another combination of numbers. And then I felt a hand on my shoulder.

"I wouldn't suggest trying again. If you enter your PIN wrong one more time, it's going to keep your card."

I stared at the man with his hand on my shoulder. He wore an olive-green camouflage coat and had longish brown hair and a scruffy beard. For a second I thought he was a homeless person, but then I doubted a homeless person would speak coherently or know much about the ATM.

"How do you know?" I asked. I took a step back and he let his arm fall to his side. I glanced back at the 7-Eleven to see if there were people inside to hear me scream and come to my rescue if he tried to abduct me. But I couldn't see anyone. The huge hot dogs blocked my view.

"I forgot my PIN one night and it kept my card," he explained.

"Oh," I said. I hit a button and the machine ejected my card. I shoved it in my purse real quick in case he wanted to rob me. Not that it would do him any good to steal my bank card, since I couldn't tell him the PIN.

"You'll have to go to the bank tomorrow and get them to issue you a new PIN. It's a huge hassle, though. They have to call some home office and then you have to wait for it to come in the mail, which takes about a week."

"I'm sure I have it written down somewhere. You know, when they first sent it to me in the mail."

He grinned. "You kept that? You were supposed to memorize it and destroy the evidence."

"Yeah, well, it's a good thing I didn't." When he smiled, I realized he wasn't actually as old as I'd first thought. Probably just a few years older than I was. The beard just made him look thirty. And a little crazy. But that grin changed everything.

"What brings you out at this hour, anyway?" he asked. "You work the night shift?"

"No, I just really wanted a Slurpee."

"And now you can't get any cash."

"Nope."

"Well, let's go," he said.

"Where?"

"Inside. On me."

"I don't know," I said.

"Oh, come on!" He threw his hands up in the air. "You've already spent five minutes out here talking to me. We'll just walk in and I'll pay for your Slurpee and we'll go our separate ways. Tell me how that's dangerous."

I shrugged. "Okay. But when I remember my PIN, I'll hunt you down and pay you back."

"Fair enough." He held the door open for me, and we walked inside and headed for the Slurpee machine. I filled my cup with piña colada. He mixed all six flavors into his. Kara and I used to do that with fountain sodas back in middle school, when it was the cool thing to do. It was called a Suicide. I don't know why.

We went up to the register, and the cashier put her romance novel facedown on the counter and rang us up. He paid and we went outside. He sat down on the curb in front of the pay phones, right next to the big NO LOITERING sign.

"No loitering," I said as I sat down beside him.

"They only frown upon loiterers on skateboards. We're cool."

He held his Slurpee out toward me, and I thought for a second that he wanted me to take a drink.

"Cheers," he said.

"Oh." I tapped my cup against his.

We sat there and sipped our Slurpees. He kept stirring his with the straw. I didn't feel like grasping for topics of conversation and he didn't start any, so we just sat there and watched the cars on the street, and the occasional customer turn into the 7-Eleven parking lot. Finally I heard *slurp slurp slurrrrrrrrrp*, and he was finished. I swallowed the last few sips of mine, and we stood up and tossed the empty cups in the trash can.

"Thanks for the Slurpee," I said.

"No problem."

He stood by the front of his car. I stood by the driver's door of the Grand Am. Now he was supposed to ask for my phone number so I could keep him up-to-date on the PIN situation, and arrange to pay him back when I had cash again. But he just stood there and smiled.

So I said, "See you around," and got into the Grand Am. He waited for me to back up, and then he opened the door to his car and waved as I drove off.

9

DUMPSTER DIVING

"**I** think Collin's dying," Vallery said when I got home from work the next afternoon.

"What's wrong?" I asked.

She pointed at him, sleeping beside her on the couch. "He's lying down and being quiet. And the TV isn't even on. He hasn't made any noise all day."

I went up to Collin and put my hand on his forehead. "He has a fever, Val. Just give him some Tylenol."

"Are you sure he doesn't need to go to the doctor or anything?"

"No. Only if he starts crying about his throat or his ears or something. He'll be fine tomorrow. Today, just enjoy it."

"Enjoy it? That's twisted, Lainey."

"Well, haven't you enjoyed your quiet morning?"

"No. I've been worried."

I went into the kitchen. I dug through the cabinets and found the cherry-flavored children's Tylenol. "Rock, paper, scissors," I said, walking back into the living room.

"Huh?"

"One, two, three, shoot!" I yelled. Vallery threw rock. I threw paper. I covered her fist with my hand. "I win." I handed her the medicine. "Have fun with that."

I walked up to my room, waiting for Collin's screaming to start. At the top of the stairs I looked back. Vallery held Collin up and poured a capful of the medicine into his mouth. I kicked myself for not giving him the medicine this time, when he was too knocked out to complain. Vallery would keep score. Next time, when he would surely be in a terrible mood and want to fight, it would be my turn to do it.

<hr>

Collin fell asleep in his own bed a little after nine o'clock. Vallery ran into my room and gave me the thumbs-up sign. "He's still out. You know what this means?"

"What?" I asked.

"Margaritas," she said, and ran down to the kitchen.

<hr>

"What we're celebrating," Vallery said as she carried two margaritas into the living room, "is that I got a job. They called today and offered me the position."

"Why didn't you tell me?"

"I'm telling you right now."

I took the margarita glass from her. "I'm sorry I was such a bitch about it before."

She shrugged. "It's okay."

"Well, congratulations. What are you doing?"

"Some kind of secretarial work."

"Sounds great."

"Don't make fun. Everyone lied to you when they told you a college degree was the ticket to a great career and successful life. Mine, thus far, has failed to help me in any way whatsoever."

"What was your degree in?"

"American studies."

I laughed. "What's that supposed to prepare you for?"

Vallery shrugged. "I don't know. It seemed like a good idea at the time. All my classes were really fun."

"Riley and I are going to start at the community college in the fall," I said. "He took a year off so we could take a few of the same classes and graduate together."

"You guys are disgusting, do you know that?"

I nodded. "I know."

"So you're going to get married."

I shrugged. "I guess."

"You guess? You have the rest of your life planned around him and you haven't talked about getting married?"

"He hasn't asked me yet, but I guess we will."

"You're awfully young to be settling down."

"We've been together almost four years."

"Have you ever even had another boyfriend?"

I shook my head. "Not really."

Vallery whistled. "Brave young girl."

"I love him."

"I'm sure you do."

"Did you have a guy in Texas?"

"Huh?"

"Like a boyfriend."

She shrugged.

I grinned. "That wasn't supposed to be a hard question."

"Well, there was a guy for a while. I could never settle down like that, though. There's too much out there to sample."

"That's a nice way of looking at it."

Vallery finished the last of her margarita and went into the kitchen for a refill. "I bet," she called to me, "when you go into a restaurant, you can look at the menu and pick exactly what you want. I can't do that. No way. I make up my mind and then I see what someone else orders and it looks good to me, and I want to have it." She came back in and sat down next to me on the couch. She carried a bunch of envelopes in her hand. I gave her a questioning look but she kept talking. "That's why I love buffets. It's not because I want to gorge myself, you know? I just love it that there's no room for error. Meat loaf turns out to be a bad choice? Dump it in the trash and go back for the chicken. You can't do that in real restaurants."

"What are you holding?"

She looked down at her margarita glass.

"The envelopes?" I asked.

"Oh! Right." She waved them toward Collin's room. "This kid is having a birthday."

"I know." My birthday actually came before Collin's, but if Vallery didn't know that, then I wasn't going to tell her.

Vallery nodded. "Apparently his grandma has planned some hoopla at her place." She held the envelopes up and shook them in my face. "We're supposed to pass these out to—get this—his friends. Does this kid have friends?"

"Well, he's starting camp next week," I said. "Maybe he'll make some new friends."

"Camp?"

"Yeah."

Vallery slapped my leg with the envelopes. "No one tells me a goddamned thing around here!"

"Sorry. I forgot about it too, but then we got a letter in the mail a few days ago. I left it on the table for you."

"I didn't see it. Is it, like, sleepaway camp?"

I shook my head.

"Damn it."

"It's at his school. It's actually almost just like school but we call it camp to make it sound more exciting."

"Okay. Well, I can drop him off on my way to work if you pick him up."

I shrugged. "Okay."

I was on my second margarita and Vallery was on her third when Riley showed up with his overnight bag.

"Where's Collin?" he asked, looking around the living room. "It's after his bedtime."

"That's why he's in bed," Vallery said.

I giggled. After two margaritas, anything amused me. I got the giggles under control and explained, "He's been sick."

Vallery raised her glass. "Margarita bucket is in the kitchen. Help yourself."

"No, thanks." He eyed me and then sat down in Carl's old recliner.

Riley didn't like it when I drank—and I didn't do it often, because when I did I always got myself in trouble. It's not that I was an angry drunk like some people (ahem, Christine). It seemed like drinking only amplified whatever mood I was already in. If I was feeling happy and flirty, drinking made me too friendly and too flirty. If I was kind of in a pissy mood, drinking made me knock-down-drag-out angry.

I'd probably embarrassed Riley at every party we'd ever been to, but two incidents were especially bad. The first was at Jamie's birthday party sophomore year. I had a little too much on an empty stomach and ended up getting in a fight with a girl from the basketball team who I thought had been checking Riley out. She wasn't, and she was a lot bigger than I was anyway, so even if she had been, I should have kept my mouth shut. Not one of my brighter ideas.

The second time was at a party junior year. I kissed a guy. Right in front of Riley. Again, not one of my brighter ideas.

I hadn't finished the margarita, but I took my glass to the sink.

"We're going to bed," I said to Vallery as I walked back into the living room.

She held up her glass. "One more for the road?"

I went back to the kitchen, filled her glass up, and put the bucket back in the freezer. When I went back to the living room, Vallery stood and reached for her margarita. I shook my head. "Let me carry it," I said. "It's really full."

Riley took Vallery's arm and led her up the stairs to her bedroom. The margarita sloshed over the sides of the glass as I slid my hand along the wall and walked toward the stairs.

When Riley let go of her, she flopped down onto the bed. I set her glass on the nightstand.

"Hugs!" she said. I hugged her, and when I stepped back she reached for Riley. "I love you guys," she said.

"We love you too," I said, rolling my eyes. At least she was a happy drunk.

I followed Riley across the hallway to my room.

As soon as the door shut behind us, he started.

"What do you two think you're doing?"

"Calm down. We just had a few drinks."

"What about Collin?"

"What about him? He's asleep."

"Okay, let's say he woke up with a really high temperature and needed to go to the hospital. You and Vallery are drunk. Vallery can't even walk straight, and you hardly can either. Who's going to drive him there?"

I smiled and then kissed him on the cheek. "You."

He didn't smile back. "What if I wasn't here?"

"Jesus Christ, Riley, that's why they invented ambulances."

"I just wish you two were a little more careful. I mean, you're *parents* now. You're *responsible* for him. I don't think you're taking this seriously."

I flopped down on the bed. "I get so sick of listening to you talk sometimes."

"You get sick of listening to me talk because you know I'm right."

I shook my head and rolled onto my back. "No, I'm just sick of you. You're smart and perfect and I'm just so irresponsible. Sometimes I can't even stand to look at you."

"God, please just go to sleep. I hate it when you're like this."

"Remember that guy at the party?" I asked.

"No."

"You remember. Junior year. That guy."

"My junior year, or your junior year?"

"Mine. Duh."

"I don't know what guy you're talking about."

"That guy I kissed. At the party."

Riley frowned at me. "Why are you bringing this up?"

"I just wanted you to know, I really wanted to kiss that guy. Like, really. I'm glad I did it. It's nice to sample stuff, you know? Like a buffet? You shouldn't just get stuck with what you order."

"God, Lainey. What makes you *say* these things?"

"You should have broken up with me then."

"Why?"

"I'm a bad girlfriend. I don't deserve you."

"Lainey."

"We should break up." I covered my face with my hands.

He touched my shoulder. "You don't mean that. It's the tequila talking."

"I do mean it. I don't want to go out with you. You're too good."

He nudged me. "Scoot over. I'm going to sleep."

I rolled over to the edge of the bed. I fell asleep before Riley even finished taking off his pants.

That night I dreamed about the Slurpee guy.

We were in bed together, cuddling, watching a movie. He wore boxer shorts and that camouflage coat. When I woke up, I still remembered the way his body had been curled around mine, the way it had felt in the dream when he'd rested his hand on my hip. As I lay there in bed the next morning thinking about Slurpee Guy with Riley's arm wrapped around me, I couldn't help but realize that the feeling I had when Riley touched me and the feeling I'd had in my dream weren't the same at all.

The night before came back to me in slow motion. Telling Riley we should break up. Tucking Vallery in. Talking about food.

I always ordered chicken. Always. Chicken strips if they had them, or a chicken sandwich if they didn't. I'd been doing that for years. I didn't like buffets. Mom had worked at too many buffets. I'd always been embarrassed every time we had dinner there and she knew all the people clearing plates and refilling the food.

I looked at Riley sleeping with his face resting against my arm.

Why did you come over last night? I thought. I hadn't asked him to. Usually I loved it when he came over and surprised me.

Usually I didn't dream about half-naked strangers.

I liked to pretend that Riley and I had always been disgustingly happy, but we'd actually broken up for a few months during my sophomore year. It was in the fall, so it didn't interfere with his junior prom or our birthdays, and we still spent Christmas together because we weren't ready to tell our families. It was easy to forget afterward that it had ever happened.

But it had. And it had happened because I dumped

him to go out with Grant, who sat next to me in art class. And I wanted to go out with Grant from art class because I'd had a sexy dream about him.

I didn't know why I'd had that sexy dream about Grant. I'd never thought about him in that way before. But after the dream, I wanted him. I told myself it was a stupid crush and it would go away, but for weeks I pined after stupid Grant. So finally I picked a fight with Riley, we broke up, and I dated Grant.

After a few weeks I realized I didn't like Grant all that much, and breaking up with Riley made my social life really awkward (plus I missed him). I dumped Grant and got back together with Riley.

Dumping Riley was the dumbest thing I'd ever done.

I stroked Riley's hair. His eyes flickered open. He blinked a few times and then smiled at me.

I couldn't leave Riley again. He was perfect, even though I hated that sometimes. You didn't leave a perfect guy. Well, not unless you were Mom.

I hadn't thought about that guy in years, the one perfect guy Mom had dated, the only one I'd really liked. I couldn't even remember his name. He wasn't all that good-looking, but he could cook and he was super nice and he treated Mom and me like queens. Mom only went out with him three times. She didn't like the way he was going bald, or the funny shape of his nose, and besides, some better-looking guy from work had asked her out. I hated her for dumping him. He could have been the perfect father. He definitely wouldn't have driven a motorcycle off the highway and broken her heart.

And I wasn't going to be like that. Yeah, I got annoyed with Riley sometimes. But only when I knew he was right. He knew what was good for me. *He* was good for me.

I hated buffets.

I loved chicken.

I loved Riley.

It's not like I was ever going to see Slurpee Guy again, anyway.

As I stumbled up to my kiosk later that morning, Rodney grinned at me and walked over.

"Rough night?" he asked.

"Too much tequila," I mumbled. "I think this is what a hangover feels like."

Rodney was no stranger to spending mornings hungover in the center of the mall. He immediately went on a newsstand run and brought back Gatorade and Excedrin (for me) and Cool Ranch Doritos (for himself). I drank half the bottle of Gatorade, popped a few pills, and then sat on my stool and stared off into space for who knows how long.

I almost didn't recognize Christine when she walked up to the kiosk swinging a bag from the maternity clothes store. It looked like she'd gained another twenty-five pounds since the Old Crew reunion dinner.

"Hey there, Miss Lainey," she said with a big smile. Of all Kara's jock friends, she was the one who'd always tried the hardest to be my friend even though I usually never hung out or talked to her if Kara wasn't around. Since she'd found out Mom died, she'd been calling every few days to check on me. I only answered the phone about twenty percent of the time. I couldn't tell if she felt bad for me or if she was just excited that someone else in the Crew had a kid. Even though I didn't, really.

"How's it going?" I asked.

"Not bad. Guess what!"

"What?"

"We're getting an apartment!"

"Really? Wow." I'd always assumed Riley and I would be the first ones to get our own place. We should have been.

"Yeah, I know! Crazy, huh? Anyways, we were thinking about going Dumpster diving tonight if you and Riley want to go."

"I thought you didn't do that anymore," I said. Christine hadn't invited us Dumpster diving in forever. She and Wallace used to go just about every week and dig food out of the grocery store Dumpsters and pick up anything else they thought they might be able to sell at the flea market. After she got pregnant, she decided Dumpster diving was disgusting and wouldn't let Wallace do it anymore.

"Yeah, well, we're going to need new furniture for the

apartment, so Wallace figures if we start now, we might be able to find some good stuff by the time we move in."

I nodded. "Yeah, okay. We'll come."

"Sweet. We'll pick you up around midnight, 'kay?"

I nodded and Christine strolled off.

After I told Vallery I wanted to go out that night, she decided she had plans.

Well, she said she had them all along.

Whatever.

If Collin would just fall asleep, then I could carry him out to the van when Christine and Wallace showed up. He'd sleep through the whole thing. But of course Collin did not just fall asleep after I changed him into his pajamas and dragged him into bed with me. After I got tired of reading him the same Dr. Seuss book seven times, I let him watch TV. When I got up to go to the bathroom, he ran into his room. It didn't seem worth the effort to drag him back, so I let him play and checked on him every few minutes. He'd thrown all his pillows and sheets and clothes and toys on the floor. He was evidently playing some sort of game where he couldn't touch the carpet. He hopped all around the room to get from his dresser to his bed to his closet and back again. He sang the dish detergent jingle over and over: "CUT THE GREASE!"

When Riley got there, I was back in my bed. I'd turned the TV up louder so I couldn't hear Collin.

"Shouldn't he be settling down?" Riley asked. "Where's Vallery?"

I shrugged. "She went out. I told her we were going out with Christine and Wallace but she left anyway. She's pretty hell-bent on that schedule she came up with."

He looked at his watch. "We're supposed to go out with Christine and Wallace?"

"They want to go Dumpster diving," I explained. "And look for new furniture. They're getting their own apartment."

Riley nodded. "That's cool. You're going to take Collin out at ten o'clock at night?"

"No, they're not getting here until midnight."

"When's Vallery coming back?"

"I don't know. She'll probably come back at six in the morning, just so I have to keep Collin all night."

"You're seriously going to take Collin out at midnight?"

I shrugged.

"He's five years old, Lainey."

"He'll sleep in the van."

"I don't think this is a good idea."

"I don't think it's up to you."

Riley stood in the doorway and stared at me. *What are you doing?* I asked myself. *Stop fighting with him.*

"Well, I don't think I'm going," Riley said.

"That's fine," I tried to say in a friendly way. But then I added, "I don't remember inviting you."

"You specifically said that *we* were supposed to go out with Christine and Wallace tonight."

I shook my head. I was out of control. I had no idea why I was being such a jerk. Maybe Collin's obstinacy had rubbed off on me.

Riley sighed. He came in and sat next to me on the bed. "Lainey, I don't know what to do anymore."

"About what?"

"You."

"What about me?" I asked, like I didn't know.

"Honestly?"

I nodded.

"Honestly, you're being a huge bitch. I'm just trying to help you, and you don't appreciate any of it. I know you're going through a rough time—"

"Shut up, Riley."

"Lainey, no, let's talk about this."

"I don't want to talk about anything."

"Lainey, come on."

"Shut up, Riley. Just shut up."

Riley stood up. I looked away from him. He stomped down the steps and then I heard the front door slam shut behind him.

A moment later Collin appeared in my door. "Indoor voice!" he shouted, and then he ran away.

＊＊＊

Christine drove and Wallace sat shotgun. I was in the backseat between Owen (starting to nod off) and Collin (wide-awake). There were Cheerios crushed into the floor and seats and there were fast-food bags everywhere. Christine shared the van with her mom and had tried to convince me that I should leave Collin at her house, but I liked her mom too much to do that to her.

It was trash night in Christine's neighborhood, but we knew we wouldn't find much. The trash in nicer neighborhoods was much better.

Riley took me to see the Baltimore Symphony Orchestra once when his dad got free tickets from work. We made one wrong turn, and suddenly we were on a street full of strip clubs and drug dealers. It didn't make any sense to me that such debauchery would be one wrong turn away from the symphony. Fortunately things weren't like that in Corben; you had warning that you were driving into the ghetto. So we slowly drove through the slums and worked our way to the neighborhoods with better trash.

"Where are we going?" Collin asked.

"Just driving around," I said.

"McDonald's?"

"No."

"Yes."

"Collin, you're not hungry."

"We can stop if you want," Christine said.

"No. He's not hungry."

Collin started to cry.

"I've got a Fruit Roll-Up," Wallace said.

I leaned forward and took it from him. "Thanks."

"Sure."

I gave it to Collin and he stopped crying. He held it out to me. "Open please," he said.

I shook my head. "You can do it."

That would keep him occupied for at least five minutes.

As we drove, Wallace and Owen jumped out a few times to inspect something on the curb, but after an hour we hadn't had any luck, so Christine drove to the apartment complex to show us their new place. Of course, it was nearly two in the morning, and we could only look at the outside. Collin's head was turned away from me. I thought he'd fallen asleep, but I didn't want to look and risk waking him up.

"You should check the Dumpsters," Owen suggested. "I bet they have five or ten around here."

"Good call," Wallace said. He looked back at me and Owen and nodded with approval. "Very good call."

At the second Dumpster they found a few prospects and set them aside as they dug around. I slid up to the front seat next to Christine. I glanced back at Collin and his eyes were shut, thank God. He looked all sweet and angelic, the way kids only look when they're asleep.

I hadn't done any actual diving and I was feeling pretty worthless. The least I could do was make conversation.

"So," I said to Christine, "how's it going?"

She shrugged. "Fine. We've got a billion things to do

before the move. It's crazy."

"It happened pretty quickly. I didn't even know you were thinking about moving."

"Well, Wallace wanted to and I didn't really care too much. But he started looking at apartments and we found this one for really cheap. We couldn't turn it down."

I nodded. "Cool" was all I could think of to say.

"Riley didn't want to come out?" she asked.

I shrugged and hesitated a little too long before I said, "He was tired."

Christine looked at me. "You have a fight or something?"

"Not really."

She reached over and touched my shoulder. "You know, I'm here if you ever want to talk. About anything. About boyfriends or raising kids or anything." She put her thumb and pinky up to her ear and mouth. "Just call me."

I nodded. "Thanks, Christine."

Wallace came back up to the door and I moved back to my seat. "Let's ride down a few more streets," Wallace said. "I'm feeling lucky."

Christine drove out of the apartment complex, and we drove up and down streets until we found trash piled up on the curb.

"End table!" Wallace called out when we were halfway down the block.

"Hush," Christine said. "Collin finally fell asleep."

"End table!" Wallace whispered.

Christine pulled over to the curb, and Wallace and Owen hopped out. They inspected the end table. Out of the corner of my eye I saw someone walking toward the curb.

I didn't think Dumpster diving was technically illegal. And if it was, it shouldn't have been. I mean, it was trash. But some people didn't see it that way. When we used to go real Dumpster diving behind the supermarket, we always brought a few cardboard boxes along so we could tell anyone that we were moving soon and looking for empty boxes. If people came along and saw you taking food—even from a Dumpster!—they just assumed you were doing something wrong.

I turned to look at the guy approaching the curb. He wore a bathrobe and slippers and carried a trash bag. He dropped it by the curb, glanced at Wallace and Owen, and then lifted his hand in a polite wave. Just before he turned and walked back toward the house, I recognized his scruffy face and long hair.

"Slurpee Guy," I said aloud. The windows were tinted (by Wallace in an attempt to make the van look more hip; instead they were spotted with air bubbles), so I knew he couldn't have seen me.

"What?" Christine called from the front seat.

Collin stirred beside me. "Nothing," I said. Collin's head bobbed around for a second, and then he rested it on his shoulder and snored a little.

I'd seen him again. That had to mean something, right? That couldn't just be a stupid coincidence.

Don't see signs, I told myself. Sometimes things happened and they didn't mean anything. Sometimes a dream was just a dream. A coincidence was just a coincidence.

Forget about it. Don't be Mom.

My ringing cell phone woke me up early the next morning. Too early—and I didn't even have to go to work. I looked at the caller ID and saw Riley's name. I hit the "reject" button and sent him straight to voice mail. I knew I'd had a terrible attitude, but that wasn't any excuse for him to call me a bitch.

I got out of bed and found Vallery in the kitchen. "If Riley comes by, don't let him in," I said.

"Have a fight?"

"Just don't let him in." I went around and checked that the doors and windows were all locked. Not that I really thought Riley would resort to crawling in through a window.

Vallery followed me into the living room. "Collin's asleep in his own bed." She pointed at her watch. "And it's after eight A.M. Please tell me how you managed that. Is he still sick? I thought you said he was better."

I thought about lying, but then I decided to go for the truth. "I took him Dumpster diving last night. He didn't fall asleep in the van until around two. Then when we got home, I carried him in and he didn't wake up, so I left him in his bed."

Vallery nodded. "I'm not even going to ask what you mean when you say 'Dumpster diving.'"

"All right," I said. I went to my room and got back in bed.

⸻

I napped most of the day, which turned out to be a stupid idea. At eleven that night I sat in bed wide-awake, and for the first time I wouldn't have minded watching Collin. At least it would have given me something to do. I could still hear him in Vallery's room, reciting his favorite TV commercials every few minutes. Finally I slid out of bed and got out the shoe box of pictures that Riley was storing under my bed along with his crazy scissors and scrapbook papers.

Mom's peak picture-taking years were the first few years of Vallery's life, and then again when she got Collin. The in-between years, the Lainey years, hardly exist. I came across a few pictures of me that my second-grade teacher took and sent home. Some Polaroids of us that one of her boyfriends had taken. A few pictures from one Christmas when I was ten. But mostly Baby Vallery and Little Collin.

I put the pictures away and slid the shoe box back under my bed.

Due to sheer boredom, I pulled one of Mom's notebooks out from under my mattress. I opened to a random page and began to read.

Be the change you want to see in the world,
Ghandi says.

"Ghandi?" Yeah, okay.

Accept responsibility for your action. Acknowl-
egment of your mistakes is the first step toward peace
for all. Apologize and make amends.

I could think of a few people who should take that
advice. Dad, for example, wanting to act like a real dad
now but never bothering to apologize for being a jerk.
Maybe I should have Mom's words of wisdom published
and pass copies out as Christmas presents.

> *Don't ever go to bed angry.*
> *Being kind is better than being right.*

I slammed the notebook shut and shoved it back under
my mattress. Mom's Book of Clichés made me nauseous.

I reached back under my bed and dragged out a stack
of papers. I pulled up my trash can and threw out magazines, pay stubs, school papers. And then I found a letter
from my bank with that familiar four-digit code I'd somehow managed to forget.

I put my shoes on and decided that now was as good a
time as any to go to the ATM. Not having cash sucked.

I drove to the 7-Eleven, got my money, and wandered

around inside for a while. I walked every aisle twice and flipped through about fifteen different magazines. Then I noticed the cashier glaring at me. I grabbed one of the magazines and took it up to the counter to pay.

It wasn't until I walked out to my car and I looked around the parking lot that I realized what I was doing, why I'd chosen to loiter at this particular 7-Eleven. I wanted to see him again. Slurpee Guy.

But it's hard to accidentally run into someone when you're trying to do it on purpose.

I got in the Grand Am and drove to the diner. I didn't even know if Kara was working, but as I stood by the PLEASE WAIT TO BE SEATED sign, I spotted her red hair. She saw me from across the room and waved me over.

"Can't sleep?" she asked.

I shook my head.

I sat in one of her booths, and she poured me coffee. "I'll come sit with you when I have a minute," she said, and then walked over to another table.

I looked out the window at the parking lot and saw a flash of headlights. I realized that if Riley went by my house and saw my car gone, I was so predictable that he'd know exactly where to find me. He'd come in and find me sitting here. He'd get down on his knees and apologize. And it would be good enough for me. I'd apologize too. We'd hug. He'd buy me an omelet.

As the car parked, I daydreamed that it might be Slurpee Guy instead. He couldn't sleep either. He'd been thinking about me. He'd gone to 7-Eleven too, but I'd left right before he got there. By chance he drove to this diner. He'd see me sitting here alone and he'd come over. I'd tell him about my PIN. We'd catch up. I'd buy him an omelet.

God, that ridiculous dream. I couldn't get it out of my head. I thought about Slurpee Guy in his underwear, spooning me. It wasn't even real, but it played in my mind over and over and over.

The bell rang as the door of the diner opened. I turned. Slurpee Guy coming to formally make my acquaintance? Riley coming to reclaim me? I wasn't sure who I wanted it to be.

Of course it wasn't either of them. An older couple stood in the doorway, no one I knew, looking a little weary. They'd probably just stopped for something to eat before they got back on the road and finished driving to wherever it was they really wanted to go.

10

ON THE VERGE

Riley left ten messages on my voice mail before I finally decided to call him back. His tenth message said, "It's almost your birthday. I need to know what you want to do. If you don't tell me, I'm just going to plan something crazy."

I'd been trying really hard to ignore my birthday.

"Riley," I said when he answered the phone. "Please don't plan anything. I don't want to do anything."

"You don't want to go out anywhere?"

"No."

"You don't want to see me?" he asked.

I hesitated.

"Lainey?"

Of course I missed him. I knew I was supposed to be with him forever, that we weren't supposed to stay mad at each other.

"I want to see you."

"So we're finished being mad?"

"You were mad?"

"No. But you were mad."

"I'm sorry."

"I'm sorry too. I shouldn't have said those things."

"It's okay. I deserved it."

"Lainey. A man should never talk to a woman that way. I was a complete jerk."

"It's all right. Do you want to come over?"

"Sure," he said. "Give me like ten minutes."

After we hung up, I felt good for about a minute and then I felt a little sick to my stomach.

I didn't want to think about my birthday, because my birthday made me think of my mother. I knew that was dumb. My birthday should have been all about me. But all my happy memories of my mother seemed to happen on my birthday.

On my birthdays I got to eat what I wanted and do what I wanted, and Mom wouldn't tell me no. I wore a tiara and Mom called me Queen Lainey.

On my sixth birthday I wanted a Care Bears marathon. Mom went to the store and bought all the VHS tapes she could find, and we sat on the couch in our pajamas and watched them all day long, only taking a break to watch *Heartstrings* with Grandma Elaine.

On my seventh birthday I wanted to race go-carts

because I'd seen them on TV and become obsessed with them. I also asked that Daddy Steve leave for the whole day. Mom didn't like it, but she said, "Okay, Lainey, it's your birthday." I heard him get out of bed and leave around eleven thirty the night before. I heard Mom yell, "Oh, get over it, Steve, it's her birthday!" and then the door slammed shut behind him. The next night I heard him come home a few minutes after midnight.

On my eighth birthday I wanted to do over Christmas because Christmas the year before had really sucked. Daddy Steve had gotten drunk and ruined everything. Mom got the boxes of decorations out of the hall closet. We put up the fake tree and decorated it with lights and ornaments. I climbed up on a chair and stuck the angel on top. Mom wrapped my birthday presents and we left them there all day while we baked cookies and drank cocoa. Of course I said that Daddy Steve had to leave for the whole day again. Except that year he didn't come back. He'd left Mom a few times before, so it wasn't all that surprising. But a month later she met Daddy Jerry, and he was a thousand times better than Daddy Steve—so when Daddy Steve begged Mom to take him back, she had enough sense to say no.

On my ninth birthday Mom went to camp with me. It wasn't a real camp—just a day program through the rec council. We played games and took art and dance lessons and sometimes had guest visitors, like the woman who came from the petting zoo. Mom went with me to art class, and I showed her the painting of a chameleon that I was working on. We ate lunch together in the cafeteria. She played tag with us on the playground. That night I wanted to bake a birthday cake instead of buying one from the store, and I asked Daddy Jerry to help. That made Mom happy.

On my tenth birthday Mom asked what I wanted to do, and I said that I wanted french toast for breakfast and then I wanted to go to the beach. We went out for breakfast, and then we changed into our bathing suits and got in the car and drove for three hours.

Back then I didn't understand the concept of the off-season. The only times we'd ever been to Ocean City had been in October or March, when the prices weren't jacked up, when the whole place wasn't swarming with people. For the first half hour I walked around scowling, but then Mom grabbed my hand and said, "Isn't this great, Lainey? It's like all these people came to the beach to help us celebrate your birthday."

We swam in the ocean and then we made an ugly sand castle. I wanted chicken nuggets for lunch, and we had to walk to three different restaurants to find some. We kept trying because it was my birthday. Any other day we would have gone to the first restaurant, and Mom would have said, "For God's sake, Lainey, just pick something on the menu or I'm ordering for you."

On my eleventh birthday we went to a bunch of different museums. That was the year they put me in the smart classes in school, and I was trying my best to be more cultured. Mom read the little plaques by all the paintings and acted very interested. Then we had sundaes for dinner, because I said so.

My twelfth birthday was my first birthday after I met Kara. We had an all-day slumber party with Mom, watching movies and reading magazines and playing truth or dare.

On my thirteenth birthday Kara and I had a crush on the guy who worked the shoe counter at the bowling alley, so Kara, Mom, and I went bowling for his entire shift. We ate pizza and got two pitchers of soda. As we walked across the alley to return our shoes, Kara whispered, "I dare you to tell him it's your birthday." When we got up to the counter, I handed him back my shoes and said, "It's my birthday." He smiled and said, "Happy birthday." And then Kara and I ran away squealing.

On my fourteenth birthday we went back to Ocean City, and Kara came along. We walked the boardwalk and sat on the beach and pointed out cute guys. Mom got in on it too, even though she had Carl at home. We laughed a lot.

On my fifteenth birthday things were different. I'd been dating Riley for a couple of months. He knew my birthday was coming up and he wanted to take me out. So when Mom asked me, "Have you thought about what you want to do for your birthday this year?" I said, "Oh, Riley's taking me somewhere." We had Collin by then, so I don't think Mom really wanted to take me out anyway.

I've already forgotten what Riley and I did on my birthday that year, or for the next two years. We probably had dinner or saw a movie or went out with some of our friends. One year he played his guitar for me and sang. He didn't like his singing voice, so he never sang for anyone except me.

My birthdays with Riley didn't stand out because with Riley, every day I could count on him to keep his promises and to care about doing what I wanted to do. But Mom? With Mom it was an annual event.

— ❦ —

My eighteenth birthday started out pretty painlessly. I woke up before anyone else and went to work. Rodney didn't know it was my birthday, so he couldn't make a big deal out of it. Kara and Christine called me using the three-way feature so they could sing "Happy Birthday" to me at the same time. I could hear Wallace in the background on Christine's line singing too.

When I walked out to the parking lot after work, I saw Riley leaning against the Grand Am. I wondered what he was doing at the mall in the middle of the day, and then I noticed the roses. He actually had a dozen roses. I groaned.

"Riley," I said as I walked up.

"What?" he asked with a smile. "It's just flowers. They're pretty. See?"

I took the flowers from him. "Thank you." They were pretty now, but in three days they would be wilted and dead. I hated when he bought me flowers. Who wanted to receive a present that was going to die?

"I gotta get back to work. But I'm going to pick you up at seven tonight. Okay?"

I nodded.

I laid the flowers on the passenger seat, and on my way home I called Kara and told her about the flowers so she could remind me how sweet Riley was. It wasn't that I didn't already know, but for some reason listening to Kara swoon made me feel really good.

"Happy birthday!" Vallery turned around and yelled as soon as I walked in the door.

"How did you know?" I grumbled. I walked past her into the kitchen and found a vase for the roses.

"That's a really stupid question," she said. She got up off the couch and followed me. "So what are you and Riley doing tonight?" she asked.

I shrugged. "I don't know. Dinner, I guess."

"Apparently, your friends are coming here for cake afterward. Riley just informed me of this an hour ago."

"If that was supposed to be a surprise," I said to Vallery, "you just ruined it."

"Wouldn't you rather be warned?"

I nodded. "Yeah. Thanks." My friends coming over for cake definitely hadn't been what I'd had in mind when I'd said I wanted to stay in. And who were my friends, anyway? Just Riley and Kara? Plus Christine and Wallace?

Plus the entire Old Crew? Why couldn't Riley listen to anything I said?

— ——◆——— —

When we pulled up in front of Riley's house for dinner that night, the house looked dark and empty.

"Where is everyone?" I asked.

Riley grinned. "Did you think I was inviting you over for dinner with my whole family?"

"Yes." I sighed but he didn't notice.

He led me to the dining room. The table had already been set for the two of us. Riley's mom kept two fancy candles in the middle of the table that were never lit, but tonight they were.

"What's for dinner?" I asked.

"Spaghetti with meatballs, salad, and garlic bread."

"Smells good," I said.

"Just give me a few minutes to heat it up."

I scratched the tablecloth with my fingernails and waited. The tablecloth was new—the Carters usually didn't eat with one on the table. Riley hummed as he stirred the spaghetti. I tried to ignore him.

I knew something was wrong. Not with Riley, but with me. It was my birthday, and my boyfriend had gone through the trouble of getting rid of his family, making me a nice dinner, and organizing a surprise gathering of my alleged friends. Yet I was so irritated, I had to bite my tongue to keep from biting his head off. Something was definitely wrong with me.

161

Just act normal and get through dinner, I told myself. *Then tell Kara all about it, and she'll tell you what a great boyfriend you have, and you'll get out of this funk and be normal again. Eventually.*

Riley carried two plates over to the table. He smiled at me. I smiled back, and I wondered if he could tell the difference between my fake smile and my real one.

After dinner Riley carried our dishes to the sink and then stood beside the dining room table, looking at me. "We still have forty-five minutes to kill," he said.

"Until what?" I asked, playing dumb.

He grinned. "Your surprise. We have *forty-five* whole minutes."

He held out his hand and pulled me up. We walked down the hallway to his room. If I'd been paying more attention, I would have noticed that look in his eye and realized what it meant. Instead, I looked at my watch and wondered what was on television.

But then as Riley pulled me down onto his bed, I realized what he had in mind. It had been almost a month since we'd done anything more than kiss, and obviously he'd stopped being concerned that my mother was spying on us from Heaven.

"Oh," I said. "Oh."

"What?" Riley asked.

"Uh . . ."

He looked closely at me. "You're still not comfortable with it?" he guessed.

"I don't know," I said. Like I'd been the one who hadn't wanted to do it in the first place.

"You don't know?"

I shook my head.

He sat up and put his arm around me. "We can talk about it, if you want."

"No," I said quickly.

"Lainey, you don't have to pretend that you're not hurting."

"There's nothing to talk about. Jesus Christ. Can't you ever listen to a single thing I say?"

"I do listen. But I know you better than that."

"You don't know me at all. God."

"Lainey. Come on. What are you talking about?"

I couldn't help it. All of the words I knew I shouldn't say came tumbling out of my mouth. "Well, if you knew me at all, you'd know how I feel about roses, and you'd know that you're the one who loves spaghetti, not me, and you'd know it drives me crazy how you're so damn full of yourself all the time."

Riley didn't say anything for a minute. He was smiling. A tight smile. His fake smile. "Lainey, I've had about enough of this. Really."

I nodded. "Me too."

"You've had enough of . . . what?"

"This. You."

"Trying to be supportive and understanding? Right. Okay."

"That's exactly what I mean!" I shouted. "Even when I tell you that you do something wrong, you insist that you do everything right. Your ego is *enormous*."

"I'm honestly not sure how much more of this I can handle."

"You're not sure how much *you* can handle? Jesus, Riley. Are you just trying to dump me before I dump you?"

He turned to look at me. "Is that what we're doing here?"

I sighed.

"All of a sudden. On your birthday."

"It's not all of a sudden. I've been fed up for a while."

"Why didn't you say anything?"

Because I don't want to be my mother.

Because it's crazy to obsess about someone you're never going to see again.

Because I'm supposed to be with you.

"Well, your timing is excellent," Riley said before I could figure out how to respond. "There are about two dozen people waiting at your house for cake and ice cream. And we're going to show up and act normal. Okay?"

I said okay.

⸺ ❦ ⸺

Riley's ability to fake happiness amazed me. He helped me cut the cake and pass out plates, and then he mingled and talked and made everyone laugh. I actually thought he'd stopped being mad at me, until we ended up alone in the kitchen at one point. I smiled at him—a weak smile, but at least it was a real one—and he glared at me and turned away.

I didn't even bother to fake a smile after that. At least half a dozen girls pulled me aside and asked if I was okay. I mumbled something about allergies and they all looked like they didn't buy it, but they all nodded and asked if I needed some Claritin. My father called in the middle of all that. I let him go to voice mail.

Riley was the last to leave. Not because he wanted to stay around me that long, but to keep up his charade. I walked him to the front door. I'd wrapped up three pieces of cake in aluminum foil for him to take home to his family.

"Guess I'll see you around," he said. Like he didn't care at all whether he actually saw me around or not.

"Guess so," I said. I closed the door.

<hr/>

Our street was along Corben's annual Independence Day parade route, which was mostly inconvenient because we couldn't park our cars on the street that day, and it made me popular with the Old Crew. They all liked to watch the parade from my yard and use our bathroom. But this year no one showed up. Everyone had already found out about me and Riley, and obviously they were going to shun me and stay friends with him.

Collin hated the fourth of July because of all the loud noises (which was ironic, since he loved to make loud noises), and Vallery hadn't seen the parade since she was a kid, so we turned on the TV for Collin and then sat out on the porch. Vallery lasted halfway through the procession of antique fire engines; then she rolled her eyes and declared, "This is the same as I remember it," and went inside.

I sat on the porch alone and watched the fire trucks, the marching bands, the Boy Scouts, the veterans.

Kara came by at one point and sat on the porch swing with me. "When are you guys getting back together?" she asked.

I sighed. She'd already asked me at least seventeen times since she'd found out. I hadn't told her. I guess Riley had, or he'd told someone and they'd told Kara.

"I don't know," I said.

"You know you guys are meant to be together."

"I know."

She rolled her eyes like I was the most ridiculous person she'd ever met. Which I probably was.

"I just want to be alone," I said. "You know. On my own."

Kara nodded. "I get it. Well, I better get back. I'm supposed to bring Christine a hot dog."

As Kara walked away, a shiny Camaro drove past along the parade route. The balding man sitting in the back of the car waving to the crowd looked kind of familiar. I checked out the sign on the side of the car.

Lee-Johnson Funeral Home.

And then, as the Camaro passed by a group of kids

sitting on the curb, the old man tossed out a handful of Tootsie Rolls. The kids jumped up and ran for the candy.

I didn't know if I wanted to laugh or cry. I stared at the bald guy's head until the car turned the corner, and then I took my orange juice and went inside.

⸻

On Tuesday everyone started something new but me. Vallery came down to the kitchen dressed in her black and gray suit.

"You're wearing that same suit?" I asked.

"Huh?"

"You wore that to the interview."

"Did I?"

I nodded.

"Crap." She went back upstairs and came down a minute later wearing black pants and a gray shirt.

"Very different," I said.

"Oh, hush."

I got Collin dressed for camp while Vallery ate her cereal; then I packed his lunch. When I went back into the living room, Collin was half naked.

"Jeez, Collin!" I yelled. "What did you do with your clothes?"

He ignored me completely. Like I expected anything more.

⸻

I ate breakfast. I took a walk. I watched *Heartstrings*. I started to straighten up my room, but I got tired of that pretty quickly and took a nap instead. If I hadn't dumped Riley, I probably would have gone to the shop to have lunch with him. Instead, I ate half a bag of stale potato chips. I left early and stopped by 7-Eleven for a Slurpee. When I picked up Collin, he cried because I hadn't brought him one too. I let him have mine.

When we got home, I found a note from the teacher in his take-home folder. "I am so excited to work with Collin this summer. I can tell he is a very special boy. However, he needs to be reminded to keep his hands to himself."

I figured I'd let Vallery handle that one, but when she got home, she only wanted to talk about her job.

"They didn't train me on anything except what to say when I first answer the phone," she said as she crashed down on the couch beside me.

"Oh yeah?"

"Yes. And the phone rang all day long. I'm not even kidding. And it took me half the day to figure out how to transfer people. I kept hanging up on them."

"It'll get better," I said. "The first day is always rough."

"It won't get better," she promised me. "I can already tell."

I nodded. "That's the right attitude."

On Wednesday I worked. I played the alphabet game with Rodney. I sold four bottles of perfume. Then I left the mall and picked up Collin from camp. I got there a few minutes early and passed out birthday-party invitations to all the kids from camp. I had two left. I could give one to Mabel. Who else would want to attend Collin's birthday party? Christine, maybe. If she didn't totally hate me for dumping Riley.

As I drove home, I pulled the teacher's note out of his folder and read it to him. "'Collin needs to stay focused during group activities. We all like Collin and want him to be our friend.' Do you hear that, Collin?"

"Yes."

"You have to stay focused when you're doing group activities. You can't wander off or make noise or anything. Okay? You have to listen and follow directions."

"Okay."

Like that little chat would do any good.

Vallery's second day at work wasn't much better than her first.

"How many people did you hang up on today?" I asked when I heard her come in.

"On purpose or accidentally?"

I shook my head. "Vallery."

"What! Not many."

On Thursday I worked again. Alphabet game. Six bottles of perfume sold. Picked up Collin.

The note: "Please review sharing, taking turns, and respect for others."

Vallery went straight to the bathroom and took a bubble bath when she got home. When I asked about her day, she just rolled her eyes.

On Friday I didn't have to work but I wished I did, because I'd had a stupid dream that I couldn't shake. My dreams suddenly had this annoying way of setting the tone for the rest of my day. Or longer. Like that stupid dream about the Slurpee Guy.

In this dream I was taking a drive with Vallery. We were in the Grand Am but she drove. It was a beautiful night. Lots of stars. Lots of trees and hills.

Eventually we stopped at a hotel. But it wasn't actually a hotel. It turned out to be a mental institution, and Vallery was checking me in.

I wanted to explain that I didn't really belong there, but I was afraid to talk to anyone. They showed me to my room, and then a girl came to my door and invited me to join a group session downstairs. She told me if I wanted to come, I had to write down my feelings. Then she asked me if I wanted to read what she'd written. I didn't, but she was crazy so I told her I would. She handed me a watermelon. She had written her feelings on the watermelon.

I didn't want to go to group and talk to a bunch of crazy people. What if my mom led the group?

I didn't want to leave my room, period, but after a while I got hungry. I ate the watermelon, rind and all.

And then the girl came back to my room on her way

to group. She asked if I'd read her feelings. I didn't know how to tell her that I'd eaten them. So I ran.

In the light of day that all sounded really silly, but I'd felt a little nauseous and on edge ever since I'd woken up. To distract myself, I started cleaning. I wiped down and straightened up the whole house until the only thing left to do was the laundry. And I wasn't doing the laundry. Absolutely not. I'd done one load of laundry since my graduation—at Riley's house. Since then I'd just let the clothes pile up on my floor. I hadn't run out of clean clothes because I'd started wearing some of the things that Mom had bought for me that I'd never thought I would wear.

I drove to Collin's school that afternoon wearing a frilly turquoise skirt and a white blouse with poufy sleeves. Even though I'd rather be in jeans, the nicer clothes normally made me feel at least a little pretty—but I hadn't washed my hair in three days, and my legs hadn't been shaved in a while, so I mostly felt gross. I looked like I'd done a half-assed job of impersonating someone else.

As I got closer to Collin's school, I started wondering about the note the teacher would send home. What would be wrong with Collin today? It wasn't like he always had the same problem—if that was the case, maybe we could try to fix it. Oh no, not Collin—he has a different problem every day. Or maybe there were so many things every day that the teacher just picked one at random every afternoon, because if she wrote down everything that he needed to do differently, she'd never get it all down on paper.

God, Collin, why can't you just be normal?

And then I started to shake. I couldn't tell at first because the car itself always shook so badly that my hands and arms vibrated just from holding the steering wheel. But then I felt it throughout my whole body. My stomach tightened. And then I knew I was on the verge.

One time when I was seven or eight, Mom and I came home and she went to the refrigerator, stared inside for a few seconds, and then slumped to the floor and burst into tears.

I went up next to her and put my hand on her shoulder. "What's wrong, Mommy?" I asked, because that's the sort of thing I would have done back then.

"Oh, Lainey, I'm on the verge," she said, and wiped her eyes. "I just wanted a turkey sandwich. Just a goddamned turkey sandwich. Is that so much to ask for?"

"Daddy Steve ate the turkey for lunch yesterday," I whispered, like I was tattling. "We have ham. I can make you a ham sandwich."

Mom leaned her head against the open refrigerator door, dangerously close to getting mustard in her hair. Daddy Steve was a slob and never bothered to shut the lid on anything. "I just wanted the turkey. I had my heart set on it. But it's all right. I've been on the verge all day. I'll be all right."

"What's 'on the verge' mean?" I asked.

She held my hand. "It means Mommy thinks she's

almost ready to completely lose it." she explained. And then she stood up and stared into the refrigerator for a few more minutes before she wiped her eyes and took out the ham and made herself a sandwich.

When I was a kid, I always wondered what big terrible thing had happened to upset Mom. But as I got older, I realized it's not one thing that threatens to put you over the edge. It's the culmination of all the little things. Working a sucky part-time job at Corben Mall. Not being able to help your sister with the bills. Having a whack job for a brother. Having a dead whack job for a mother. Wearing frilly, poufy clothes because you can't go down to the basement and do laundry. Breaking up with your perfect boyfriend and having no idea if that was the right thing to do.

You get enough of that adding up and it puts you on the verge of completely losing it.

I wanted to turn the car around and drive away. First I'd sell Mom's notebooks to Deborah. Then I'd find a cheap little apartment somewhere, anywhere, far away. I could forget about responsibility and whack jobs and love and Slurpees and everything else. At least for a little while.

Of course I didn't turn around. I pulled into the elementary school's parking lot and waited for the dismissal bell and braced myself for the note.

Honestly, I doubt the Grand Am would've even made it past the state line.

11

FORTUITY AND ADVENTURE

Sometimes the cool thing about working at the mall is that your friends always know where to find you. But most of the time, the sucky thing about working at the mall is that your friends always know where to find you.

Riley showed up on Monday. Rodney shook his finger at me. "Rutabaga," he said before he walked back to his own kiosk.

"Inside joke?" Riley asked.

"We were playing the alphabet game."

He nodded. "Don't know what that is, but okay."

"So," I said. Riley'd gotten a haircut. It hadn't been that long since the last time I'd seen him, but the new cut made it feel like more time had passed. I wondered if I looked exactly the same to him. No, my hair probably looked dirtier.

Riley looked down at his feet. "Listen, I understand

that we broke up, or we're taking a break or whatever, and that we need some time to let things cool off, but my company picnic is this Saturday, and I was really hoping that you still want to go. It would mean a lot to me if you could just pretend to like me for about an hour. It'd be really cool if you could do that for me."

What would it really matter if I went to one more picnic with him?

"I guess," I said. "I'll go."

He smiled. "Really? Great. I'll pick you up around noon."

He hesitated for a second and then kissed me on the cheek. I didn't smile back at him; I looked at my perfume case. He hesitated for a moment and then walked away.

I didn't want to watch him walk away, because I didn't want him to see me watching if he turned back around, but I couldn't help it. The girl at the handbag kiosk waved a flyer at him, but he kept walking. Then he stopped and smiled. I wondered if he remembered her from school.

I imagined the conversation they were having.

Hello, sir! We're having a super-duper sale today! Perhaps you'd like to purchase a handbag for your special lady friend?

Riley handed the flyer back to her and shook his head.

Oh, no thank you. I no longer have a special lady friend. She actually turned out to be a real bitch.

I slept in on Friday and didn't get up until I thought Vallery and Collin had already left. But when I stumbled down the stairs in my pajamas, I found Vallery and two strange guys sitting in the living room. I stopped at the bottom of the stairs and stared.

The strangers wore khaki shorts and polo shirts. Vallery sat in a chair across from them, looking at some kind of brochure on the coffee table.

And then I took a good look at the guy in the blue polo shirt. He'd trimmed the beard a little, but it was him. The Slurpee Guy. In my living room.

"Uh," I said, by way of greeting.

That certainly wasn't what I wanted to say. I wanted to yell, "Oh my God, it's you!" I imagined I'd have a similar reaction if I woke up one morning to find the actress who played Lainey St. James sitting on my couch. She'd be familiar to me, but she'd have no idea who I was, so I couldn't scream and let on that she meant anything to me. I knew he wouldn't remember. He was probably just a nice guy who bought Slurpees for all the girls who forgot their ATM code.

The Slurpee Guy stood up and held out his hand. I walked over and shook it. The other guy stood up, and we shook hands too.

"I'm Eric Blankenship," Slurpee Guy said. "And this is my partner, Frank Cooper. We're here today to offer you the finest selection of bestselling national magazines at rock-bottom prices."

Of course he didn't remember me. I tried not to feel slighted. I knew that our past relations existed only in my head. He'd bought me a Slurpee. That was it.

But then as he sat back down on the couch, he winked.

Well. How about *that*.

I smiled and kneeled beside the coffee table and looked down at the brochure.

"These are really good prices," Vallery said.

"Rock bottom," I agreed. "Shouldn't you be at work?"

She shrugged. "I'm tired. Collin was making me nuts this morning, so I called and told them I had to take him to the doctor. They completely understood. This kid thing is really convenient sometimes."

"That's very responsible, Val. You haven't even been there two weeks."

"Oh, shut up. I'm not taking off the whole day. Anyway, I'm going to get *Cosmo* and *Glamour*. Or maybe *Redbook*. Yeah, *Cosmo* and *Redbook*."

"We're actually running a special today," Eric said. "When you buy three, you get one free."

"Sweet," Vallery said. "Lainey, you can pick one."

I felt Eric's sneaker rub against the back of my foot. I glanced up at him, but he looked down at his paperwork. I thought it had been an accident. But then he did it again. I wondered what magazines he subscribed to.

"How about *Newsweek*?" I suggested.

"*Newsweek*? You're kidding me."

"What? It's informative. It'll balance out the trash you're getting."

She shook her head. "What kind of eighteen-year-old girl are you?"

"You said I could pick one."

"Fine, but that's all you get. I'll take *Cosmo*, *Redbook*, and *Glamour*, and you can get your *Newsweek* for free."

"That's generous of you."

"It really is."

Eric handed us the order forms and two pens.

"Do you really need all this information?" I asked Eric. "Phone number and email address and everything?"

"It's not necessary to process your order," he said. "But it's certainly encouraged."

"All right," I said. And I winked at him.

⋆⋆ ═╬═ ⋆⋆

Eric and Frank left. Vallery left for work. I lay on my bed and looked at the phone. It didn't ring. I got in the shower. As I rinsed the conditioner out of my hair, I heard the phone ringing.

I grabbed a towel and ran to my room.

"Hello?"

"So, Miss Lainey Mae Pike, why do you keep popping up in my life?" Eric asked.

"Oh no, you have it backward," I said. I tried to wrap the towel around my wet hair. "You keep popping up in mine."

"Is that right?"

"Yes. First you started chatting me up at the ATM, then you kicked yourself for not getting my number, so you started knocking door-to-door, pretending that you're selling magazines."

"Just so I could find you?

"Uh-huh."

"The magazines are a ruse?"

"Exactly. I didn't leave my glass slipper behind, so you improvised."

"What about my partner, Frank?"

"He's a friend you enlisted to lend credibility to your ruse."

"You have me all figured out, huh?"

"I do."

I could feel my heart beating. I wondered how long it'd been since I'd felt like this. Actually excited about something. Six months? Longer?

"Just for the record, you *were* hinting that I should call you, right?"

I laughed.

"I'm serious! I have a bad habit of taking things the wrong way. Usually with disastrous results. Now I tend to be a little too cautious sometimes."

"It's okay. You didn't take it the wrong way."

"How freaky is it that we ran into each other again?"

"Well, Corben's not that big."

He sighed. "I pegged you for having a greater love

of fortuity and adventure. I must admit I'm a little dis-appointed."

"Okay, you want fortuity? I've got something for you."

"What's that?"

"I saw you again. Before today but after the day at 7-Eleven."

"Oh yeah? Where?"

"I shouldn't even tell you this. It's embarrassing. But anyway, it was trash night. You came out at about two in the morning in your robe and slippers, and there were two guys digging through your neighbor's trash."

Eric laughed. "Yeah, I remember that. Which guy were you?"

"I was sitting in the van."

"And you didn't get out and say hi?"

"I thought it would have been kind of awkward to hop out of the van and strike up a conversation, under the circumstances."

"Well, we could have avoided the entire magazine ruse. Besides, I don't judge. If you want to pick through trash, go for it."

"I don't pick through trash. But my friends are getting their own apartment."

"You said that with such confidence that I almost believed it made sense."

"They need furniture. You should see some of the stuff they picked up. People throw away anything."

"We're a wasteful society. I'm glad there are people in the world like your friends who believe in recycling and reusing. Anyway, you know where I live?"

"Kind of. I remember the neighborhood."

"Then why don't you come on over?"

Eric lived in the basement apartment in his dad and stepmom's house. I'd been right about the beard being deceiving—he was only twenty-one. The apartment was basically one room—the kitchen area to the left, a futon and TV straight ahead, and the tiny little bathroom to the right. There were stacks of DVDs and CDs everywhere, but I didn't recognize most of the titles.

"Nice digs," I said.

"Don't tease." He'd changed out of the polo shirt into a brown tank top. "It's not much, but it's home."

"I wasn't joking. I'd love to have my own place. Even if it is *this* small."

He grinned and poked my arm. "You said you wouldn't tease me."

"Those words never came out of my mouth."

"You're right." He took my hand and led me over to the couch. "So you live with your family?"

"I live with my sister. And we have a brother too."

"Older, younger?" Eric clicked on the television but muted the volume.

"He's five. Almost six."

Eric whistled. "Wow. Way younger."

"Yeah, we take care of him. And trust me, he's a handful."

"So your parents . . . ?"

I hesitated, but not too long, before I smiled and told him my parents were dead. Not exactly true, but close enough. And if I acted all cavalier about it, he'd think it'd happened a while ago, that I didn't need a pity party.

"You're like *Party of Three* now."

I nodded. "Exactly." I decided I should keep talking before he asked any more questions. "You didn't go to high school around here, did you?" He would have been a senior when I was a freshman, and I didn't recognize his face.

"Nope. I lived with my mom in Indiana and went to high school up there."

"And you sell magazines."

"For now, for the summer. During the winter I'm a ski instructor up in PA. Or I will be. I still have to go up there and apply."

"Ah, you're multitalented."

"I am. What about you? What do you do, besides tend to your young sibling?"

"I sell perfume at the mall." I laughed. My job suddenly sounded ridiculous.

"That's cool," Eric said. "That must be awesome for people-watching." He grinned. I got the impression that he did think it was cool. Actually, I got the impression that no matter what I did, Eric would have found some way to spin it so that it seemed cool.

"Question," I said.

"Shoot."

"You like me."

"That's not a question. And it's also awfully forward."

I hit his arm, but not too hard. "No, I'm serious. You called. And then you invited me over. You must like me, right?"

He turned to me and grinned. "Okay, I'll show my cards first. Yes, I suppose you could say that I like you. I find you attractive. I find your personality intriguing."

I rolled my eyes. "Did you like me the first time we met, at the 7-Eleven?"

He nodded. "Yeah. You were cute, funny, all frazzled with the ATM."

"And you bought me a Slurpee. So I figured you liked me."

"Yeah."

"But you didn't get my number or anything."

"I know."

"Why not, if you liked me? Didn't you care that we might not ever see each other again? Oh, wait a minute . . . do you have a girlfriend?" I looked around the apartment, like maybe I'd spot a bra or some tampons, some evidence of a girlfriend.

He touched my knee. "Chill," he said. "No girlfriend. And you?"

I shook my head. "No girlfriend. And no boyfriend anymore, either."

"Ah, that's what I was waiting for. You to dump the boyfriend."

"No, I'm serious."

"Well, I was waiting for a sign."

"A sign."

"Yeah, a sign that I should ask for your number. You didn't give me anything, so I didn't ask. Of course, I kicked myself afterward. But I knew if it was meant to be, I'd find you again. And I did."

"How'd you find me?"

Eric smiled. "I had a dream about you last night."

My eyes felt like they bugged out of my head. I hoped Eric didn't notice. "Really?"

"Totally. I dreamed that you were walking down your street. I could see the corner, the street signs. I knew I'd find you there in one of those houses, so Frank and I grabbed our brochures and order forms, and we set out to sell some magazines."

I wondered if I should tell him about my dream, but then I noticed the smirk, and a wicked look in his eye. "Are you messing with me?"

He laughed. "Yes. I'm sorry. I didn't think you'd believe that."

I smacked his arm. Harder this time.

"But seriously, it was fate," Eric said. "And then you winked at me, and that was my sign."

"Yeah, well, you started the winking."

"It was a small risk. If you weren't receptive, I could have just pretended I had something in my eye."

"That would have been smooth." I put my hand on Eric's knee. "What kind of sign are you getting now?" I asked.

"Mmm," he said. "A good one."

I rubbed his thigh. "How good?"

"Really good," he murmured. He leaned in and kissed me.

His beard scratched my face, but I didn't mind. Riley couldn't grow a beard yet. He tried once, and the guys on the soccer team laughed at him until he shaved.

Oh, for God's sake, stop thinking about Riley.

So I kissed Eric and thought about how this day had gone from completely ordinary to completely bizarre. How Slurpees and trash and magazines kept bringing us together. Fate. I knew that dream had meant something. There was no such thing as coincidence. Mom had been right about that much.

Eric pulled my feet up onto the futon and we both lay down. He kissed me from my forehead down to my fingertips, and then back up to my mouth. I knew I had to get Collin soon, but I couldn't make myself tell Eric I had to leave.

"Your hair smells good," he whispered before he bit my earlobe. I probably hadn't gotten all the conditioner out before I ran for the phone.

Eventually I stopped thinking altogether. I lost track of time.

But then as Eric gnawed on my neck, I looked over his shoulder at my watch. I had to leave. Right now.

"I gotta go," I said.

"What?" he asked. "Why?"

"My brother. I have to go get him." Eric moved and let me get up off of the couch. "How's my hair?" I asked.

He shrugged. "I don't know."

"I mean, is it sticking up or anything?"

"It looks fine to me."

I walked to Eric's tiny bathroom and combed my hair with my fingers. And then I noticed the red mark on the inside of my arm, right above my elbow. It was nearly the size of my fist. I poked it and discovered that it also really hurt.

Eric came up behind me and put his hand on my waist. "See, I told you it looks fine."

"Look," I said, and held out my arm. "How did you do that?"

He shrugged. "I bit you a little."

"No kidding. That's going to bruise. Why did you *bite* me?"

"You were *there*. I thought you liked it. I'm sorry." He made a stupid puppy-dog face. I rolled my eyes and kissed him.

"I really do have to go right this second. What am I going to do about this?"

Eric walked to his closet. He came back with a plaid button-up short-sleeved shirt. He slid it on over my black tank top and then stepped back and looked at me.

"I really like this look on you," he said.

"Shut up."

"I'm serious. It's hot."

I rolled my eyes. "I gotta go."

Eric walked me to the door. I kissed him again—quick on the lips.

"You're walking off with my shirt," he said to me as I stepped outside. "This means you have to see me again."

The day Riley re-asked me to the picnic, I'd picked out what I would wear—a green sundress with spaghetti straps. It was cute, but more importantly, it was clean. I dug through my closet that night, trying to find something to wear in lieu of the dress. I didn't have anything decent to wear on top of it. Eric's button-up wouldn't cut it. I owned lots of nice sweaters, but nothing that was summer-appropriate and the right length to cover up the godforsaken bruise.

"You have to keep Collin," I finally yelled out into the hallway to Vallery.

"When do I ever say, 'Lainey, you have to keep Collin even though it's not your turn to keep Collin'?"

"I have to go to the mall and buy something to wear to Riley's company picnic."

Vallery came to the door. "I thought you were broken

up. Or fighting. Or whatever you kids do these days."

"We are. We're broken up. But I promised I'd go to this picnic with him."

"You have tons of clothes. You're telling me you don't have anything in there that you can wear?"

I sighed. "I'm having an issue."

"What issue?"

"I'll show you, but I don't want to talk about it."

"All right."

I pulled up the sleeve of Eric's shirt. The bruise had turned bright purple and it still hurt.

"Holy shit. What did you do?"

I just stared at her. I must have looked guilty, because Vallery grinned. "Or should I be asking who?"

"It's not what it looks like. I just need something to cover it up."

"Did he tie you up?"

"No, Vallery. God."

"Fine, don't tell me. Anyway, we're about the same size. I'll see if I have something." She disappeared into her room. She came out a minute later with a pink tank top, a pink lacy shirt with three-quarter-length sleeves, and a jean skirt. "If you don't like this outfit, then you're insane and I refuse to help you anymore."

I took it from her and tried it on. The lacy shirt covered my bruise, but I wouldn't be uncomfortably hot. And it was cute. Not that I wanted to look cute for Riley, but I didn't want to look *not* cute.

I walked out into the hallway and did a stupid little spin for Vallery.

"Perfect," she said. "But remember to give it back. And don't wash that shirt with your clothes. It needs to be washed separately."

"Jeez, Val, I'll take care of your clothes."

"You better."

"Thank you!" I yelled as I slammed the door shut.

———————

I adjusted Vallery's jean skirt as I walked out to Riley's car on Saturday afternoon. It fit, but it was a size smaller than I usually would wear. And shorter.

"You look nice," Riley said as I climbed into his pickup. "New outfit?"

"Vallery let me borrow it."

He smiled at me, probably thinking I'd wanted to look nice for him and I'd begged Vallery for help.

I looked at the Frisbee on his dashboard. "Why are you bringing that? You know I'm no good at Frisbee."

He shrugged. "Maybe someone else will want to play."

"Why are you bringing me if you're not even going to spend time with me?"

He squeezed his eyes shut. "God, Lainey, don't start already."

"Watch the road."

"Do you want me to take you back home? I don't want to fight all damn day. It's not worth taking you if

189

you're not even going to try to have fun."

"I want to go," I said. "I already got dressed. Let's just go."

We drove to the park and walked to the pavilion where Riley's company had gathered. The park in Corben was kind of filthy. There was a lake or a pond or something there, but you'd never want to swim in it, and they had signs up saying that you shouldn't. There were playgrounds, but I wouldn't want to play on them, either. Homeless people or stupid teenagers probably peed on them. God, that was such a Mom thing to think. She was always telling me that when I was a kid. *Don't play on there, Lainey. Someone probably peed on it.* Like people actually went around peeing on playground equipment for fun.

We stood in line for food. I reached for a hamburger, but Riley tapped my arm with his paper plate. "There's chicken over there," he said.

"I want a burger."

"Why?"

"Because I do."

"Okay. Whatever."

Riley grabbed two bottles of Coke, and I followed him to a table. We sat down across from his friend Rob.

I bit into my hamburger. Rob smiled and waved at me. I waved back.

"Old Mrs. Byrd came in again yesterday," Rob said to Riley.

"Already? What's her problem now?"

"The head gasket."

"And I bet that's our fault."

"Of course it's our fault. We live to sabotage that woman's car."

"Why would she think we *want* her to keep coming back?"

I zoned out while they talked about work. That was something I definitely wouldn't miss: hanging out with Riley's friends and coworkers. Then as I chewed my last bite of potato salad, Riley took my plate and carried it to the trash.

"Frisbee?" he asked, walking back up to the table.

"I'm game," Rob said. He snatched the Frisbee from Riley and ran off toward the field.

"Laine?" Riley asked.

"You know I'm not going to play."

"I know. But I figured I should ask."

"What am I supposed to do?"

"I'll only play for a few minutes. Vinny's girlfriend is around here somewhere. You should find her and say hi."

"I don't know Vinny's girlfriend. I don't even know Vinny."

He stopped smiling. "You met them at the Christmas party. We sat with them all night."

"I absolutely don't remember that."

He rolled his eyes and looked toward Rob. "Well, I'll

be back in a few minutes."

I went and got a plate of chips just to have something to do. I sat back down and watched Riley and Rob play Frisbee. After a few minutes, another guy ran over and joined them.

And then a blond girl who looked vaguely familiar sat down across from me.

"Hi!" she said. "I'm Kimberly. It's nice to see you again. We met at the Christmas party."

"Oh, yeah," I said. "I'm Lainey. Nice to see you again." Like she didn't already know who I was. I was sure Riley had gone up to Vinny and begged him to ask Kimberly to go over and talk to his antisocial killjoy girlfriend. Ex-girlfriend. Whatever. Had Riley told all of them that we'd broken up?

"Where'd you get that shirt?" Kimberly asked. "It's supercute."

"Thanks," I said. "It's my sister's."

"You have a sister? You're so lucky. I always wanted a sister, but I just have two brothers."

"Yeah, it's . . . great."

"Do you still live at home too?"

"Yeah."

"That's cool. I'm only twenty, but it seems like everyone I know is in this big hurry to like move out and live on their own. And I'm like, Why? I have the rest of my life to live on my own and pay tons of bills and everything."

I nodded. "True."

"Do you and your sister, like, share everything?"

I knew she was talking about clothes and shoes and nail polish or whatever, but I thought about Collin. "Yeah," I said. "We do."

"You're so lucky."

Lucky. Right.

I looked past Kimberly and saw Riley trotting back over. Thank God.

⁕

Riley parked in front of my house and turned the truck off. "Is now a good time to talk?" he asked.

"What do you want to talk about?"

"What's going on with us."

"So what is going on with us?"

"Jesus Christ, Lainey. Okay, I've been talking to my mom about our situation. She was pretty young when my grandma died, and she's been trying to help me understand what you're going through and how you're feeling. And I really do want to understand, Lainey. I'm sorry I said you were being bitchy. That was really insensitive of me. I really want to understand, and I really want to help you."

I shook my head and looked out the window. "I don't need help. I don't *want* help."

"It's okay if you're feeling sad. You don't have to hide it from me. It's okay to be emotional around me. That's what I'm here for."

No, I thought, *you're here to be absolutely perfect and*

make me feel like crap.

He took my hand. "I know you're sad. It's normal to be sad."

"Well maybe I'm not normal, okay? Because I am not sad. And my mom has nothing to do with what I said to you on my birthday."

"Lainey, come on."

He let go of my hand and rubbed the steering wheel. I picked at the seam on Vallery's skirt.

"You know, I don't need you to give me permission to feel any certain way."

"I know, Laine. Jeez. That's not what I was trying to say. I just want to help."

"Well, don't scream at me. That doesn't help."

"I'm sorry. You're just so damn stubborn. It frustrates me and then I say things I shouldn't say."

"*You're* the stubborn one. Obviously I just want to be left alone right now. Obviously I don't want you around."

"That's really what you want?"

I nodded.

"Fine. Can I go inside and get my stuff?"

I nodded again. We got out of the truck. I went to the kitchen and rearranged the cups in the cabinet and waited until I heard Riley come back down the stairs and close the front door behind him. Then I went upstairs to my room.

The deodorant and extra toothbrush that he kept on

my dresser were gone. The DVDs that had piled up on top of the television were gone. He'd taken his pile of clothes. I felt under the bed. He'd taken all the scrapbooking stuff. And the shoe box. My ex-boyfriend had jacked my family pictures.

Whatever. It wasn't like there were many of me anyway.

As I pulled my hand back, I felt a piece of paper and I pulled it out. It was one of our 1.4 million grieving pamphlets.

I opened it up and looked at the stages of grief that I'd already read about a million times. My eyes went straight to the section on "anger." I felt like it was written in big red flashing letters. I felt like there was an arrow and a sign saying YOU ARE HERE.

Yeah, I was angry. That was no big secret. Actually, I wasn't sure "angry" even began to cover it.

12

KING
COLLIN

Someone tapped on my window, and I nearly peed my pants. I looked over and saw Eric's face on the other side of the glass.

I went over and opened the window. "What the hell are you doing out there?"

Eric smiled and climbed in. "Wanted to see you."

"And you're sneaking in my window at midnight? What are we, thirteen? Did you climb my *tree?*"

He kissed me. "You liked it, didn't you?"

"Well. It was certainly more interesting than ringing the doorbell. Or calling first. Or making real plans."

"I have this insomnia thing," he explained.

"Me too, apparently."

Eric kicked off his shoes and climbed in my bed. He held out his arm, and I slid in beside him.

"We could have a real date tomorrow. What are you doing tomorrow?"

Tomorrow was Collin's birthday party.

"Oh, tomorrow? I'm hanging out with Kara."

"You told me about her. Hold on. She's . . . the red-head."

"Good job."

He grinned. "I'm such a good listener. So what are you and Kara doing tomorrow?"

"Shopping. Girl stuff. You know."

He nodded. "That's cool. That movie where Sandra Bullock drives a bus just came on, if you want to watch."

I shrugged and handed him the remote.

I couldn't believe I'd lied to Eric about my brother's birthday party. But if I'd told him about it, he might have expected me to invite him. And if he came to the party, there'd be way too much to explain. I'd have to explain Collin being half Puerto Rican while Vallery and I were plain old white. I'd have to explain why Collin's grandmother wasn't my grandmother, or Vallery's grandmother, and why she wasn't Puerto Rican either. I'd invited Christine—what if she actually came? I'd have to introduce her to Eric. And would I introduce him as my friend, or my boyfriend? We hadn't talked about that yet. We'd hung out every other day for the past week, but we hadn't had a real date yet. He came over to my house once during the day, but I had to leave for work, so he only stayed for about an hour. I'd been back to his place, and we'd spent a lot of time cuddling on his futon, and he'd made me soup on the hot plate in his tiny kitchen. Did that make him my boyfriend? I had no idea. When Riley asked me to be his girlfriend in ninth grade, he'd decorated my locker with balloons and written me a note on a heart-shaped piece of construction paper. I couldn't picture Eric being so explicit.

My cell phone rang. Eric was closer, so he reached for it and checked the caller ID.

"It's the redhead," he announced. "Speak of the devil. Want me to answer it?"

"Nah. She probably just wants to confirm our plans or whatever. She'll leave a message."

"Is she an insomniac like us?"

"Kind of. She works the night shift."

"Oh yeah, the diner."

"Yeah."

"We'll have to go sometime."

"Definitely."

The phone beeped. Kara had left a message. I had no idea why she'd really called, but it was kind of miraculous that the phone rang just in time to back up my lie.

I knew it was ridiculous to lie to Eric. But whatever we were doing, we didn't have to make it that complicated.

When Collin woke up the next day, I gave him a crown I'd bought for him at Walmart and explained to him that it was his birthday so he was king, and Vallery and I would do whatever he wanted. He ran to his room and came back with his blue baby blanket and had me pin it around his shoulders like a cape. He also wanted to wear his pajamas all day. Then he declared he wasn't taking a bath. I'd anticipated that much, so I'd given him a bath and washed his hair the night before.

"What do you want to do first, King Collin?" I asked.

"Donuts," he said.

So we drove to Donny's with Collin in his pajamas, blanket, and crown and got a box of original glazed donuts.

I'd never met Donny, but I always imagined him as some kind of pimp. All the girls who worked there were pretty enough to be models, and they boxed donuts and poured coffee in short pink dresses with matching frilly aprons. But the donuts were truly awesome.

"I better get a crown and donuts on my birthday," Vallery said as we ate at a tiny table in the corner.

"You will," I assured her. "When's your birthday?"

"Are you *kidding* me?"

"No. How should I know?"

"Jeez. September tenth."

"I'll put it on my calendar."

Vallery ate one donut, I ate two, and Collin ate seven. We took the last two home in case he got hungry later.

"He's going to barf," Vallery said in the car on the way home.

I shrugged. "He can barf if he wants to. It's his birthday."

⊷ ⋅⋖⋗⋅ ⊶

My bruise was considerably faded but still a nasty puke green color, so I wore a tank top and Eric's shirt. We'd invited Mabel to Collin's party, and she came along with us to Collin's grandmother's house. Even though we took the Grand Am, Vallery drove. It reminded me of the dream about the mental institution. Mabel sat in the front seat, and I sat in the back with Collin.

"Present please," Collin said.

"It's up to Mabel," I told him. Mabel's present was the only one in the car. Vallery and I hadn't gotten anything yet. She'd thought I'd bought a present and I'd thought she had.

"I get what I want. It's my birthday."

"I said Vallery and I would give you whatever you wanted. Mabel doesn't have to."

"Mabel, please, please, please?"

Mabel turned in her seat and smiled. "Why, yes, Collin, because you used very good manners." She passed the present back to Collin, and he tore it open. It was a LEGO set.

"Awesome!" he screamed, and shoved the box at me. "Open please, Lainey."

"Collin, let's wait until we get out of the car. You don't want to lose the pieces."

"Lainey, please!"

"As soon as we get out of the car."

Vallery pulled up in front of Collin's grandmother's house. Collin's grandmother lived north, closer to Towson, in a medium-sized house with an enormous backyard (at least compared to ours) and a two-car garage. I always wondered how Carl had ended up down in Corben. I wondered if he was raised there and then his mom saved up and moved out, or if he'd been raised in the big house but then grew up to be a lazy bum, and Corben was all he could afford.

"Time for your party!" I said to Collin. I patted his leg. "Are you excited?"

Collin looked at the house and shook his head. "King Collin would rather go to Disney World."

Vallery turned in her seat and smirked at me. "Well, Lainey?"

I'd always known never to ask for anything extravagant, because I didn't want Mom to have to tell me no. It was more fun to entertain the idea that I could actually go to the Eiffel Tower if I wanted to, but I'd really rather go bowling. Who wanted to spend ten hours on a plane on your birthday?

"You should have put that request in a little earlier," I said to Collin. "Disney World is really far away. Besides, there are no presents at Disney World. But there are presents at your party."

"More presents?" he asked.

I nodded. "Let's leave the LEGOs here and go get more presents?"

Collin grabbed my hand. We walked around the side of his grandmother's house. And as Vallery pushed open the gate to the backyard, and we saw the crowd of strangers gathered there, Collin froze.

"Holy crap," Vallery said. "Who *are* all these people?"

I tugged on Collin's hand. "Come on," I said.

"No." Collin eyed the crowd. "Where are the presents?"

"I don't know—probably on a table somewhere. Let's go find them."

Vallery touched my arm and leaned over to whisper in my ear. "Deal with him. We'll go in and tell the old bat that we're here."

Vallery and Mabel walked in. The gate shut behind them.

I turned to Collin and straightened out his cape. "Collin, are you ready to go to your party?"

"King Collin wants to go play LEGOs."

"But it's *your* party, Collin. Everyone's waiting for you."

"No party!"

"Collin, let's go."

"King Collin says no!"

I couldn't argue with that. It was his birthday. And it wasn't in the spirit of the birthday tradition to argue with the birthday boy.

"You really don't want to go in and see everybody?"

He shook his head so hard that I was worried it might break off from his neck and fly away.

"Is it because there are a lot of people?"

He nodded.

"Okay, we'll play LEGOs in the car. Let me go tell Vallery."

Collin crouched down in the bushes, and I went through the gate. As I walked across the yard, I looked around to see if I spotted any little kids, anyone he might go to camp with, anyone we might possibly know.

I found Vallery and Mabel by the dip. "He wants to play in the car for a few minutes," I said. "He's too scared to come in."

"Oh, poor Collin," Mabel said.

"This party was a dumb idea," Vallery said.

I shot her a dirty look.

"Not that I don't think he deserves a nice party," she explained. "But he's . . . you know. Why would you want to invite fifty people over to witness Collin have a meltdown?"

"Exactly. So we're going to go play LEGOs for a few minutes."

I went back around to the side of the house and found Collin where I'd left him. I took his hand and pulled him to his feet, and we walked back to the car. We climbed into the backseat, and I opened the box of LEGOs.

"What are you going to make?" I asked Collin.

He studied the pieces in his hands. "Birthday robot," he decided.

Collin started building his birthday robot, and I tried

to keep all the pieces on the seat. It was hot in the car—even after I rolled the back windows down—and I took off Eric's shirt and threw it over the seat. I wondered how I would get everything fixed now that I'd broken up with Riley. It'd probably be cheaper to buy a whole new car. Not that I had money for either.

Someone banged on the hood of the car. I turned around and was face-to-face with Collin's grandmother.

"You two need to come inside," she said with her nose wrinkled. She wore a yellow shirt with a watermelon on the front and matching yellow shorts. The brightness of her ensemble hurt my eyes.

I got out of the car. "He's scared. He doesn't know any of those people. I'm giving him a few minutes to calm down."

"It's only family. And you're already *late*."

I leaned in and looked at Collin. "Do you want to go get more presents?" I asked.

He narrowed his eyes at me.

"I'll stay with you," I promised. "I'll hold your hand."

He shrugged.

"Let's leave the LEGOs."

Collin nodded and put his robot down on the seat. As he slid out of the car, Collin's grandmother gasped. "Now what in the hell is he wearing?"

"His pajamas," I said.

"And a blanket? Oh, for Christ's sake. Come on in the house."

I didn't really want to, but Collin didn't fight me when I took his hand, so we followed her into the living room. Collin's grandmother had one of those houses with pristine white carpeting and furniture that looks too antique and expensive to actually sit on. Collin's grandmother disappeared. I pulled Collin over to the couch and we sat down. She came back a moment later and handed Collin a present wrapped in shiny blue paper with a bow on top. "Here's your first present, sweetheart. Happy birthday." And then the old bag *glared* at me.

Collin tore open the present and then stared. He held a white polo shirt in one hand and khaki shorts in the other. I pictured him selling magazines door-to-door with Eric and Frank. I laughed. Collin's grandmother shot me a dirty look.

"Clothes?" he asked.

"You have other presents," I told him. "Grandma just wants you to put these nice clothes on for the party."

Collin looked at them and shook his head. He dropped the outfit on the floor with the discarded wrapping paper. "No," he said.

"Collin, you'll look very nice in that outfit," I said.

"No. Batman pajamas."

"Collin, put the damn clothes on now," his grandmother snapped.

I turned and glared at her. "Don't talk to him like that," I said. "It's his birthday. If he doesn't want to wear the damn clothes, he doesn't have to." I took Collin's hand,

and we stood up. "Let's go get the rest of your presents."

His grandmother grabbed his other hand and yanked him away from me. "Collin, you're putting these clothes on for your party. I don't care if you like it or not. You can't run around in your pajamas and a *blanket* all day."

And then Collin screamed. He kicked his grandmother in her leg and ran up the stairs.

"Collin Snodgrass!" she screamed. "Lord almighty." In a flash of yellow, she ran up the steps after him.

I picked up the clothes, folded them, and set them on the couch. I crumpled up the wrapping paper and walked down the hall, hoping to find the kitchen, where I'd hopefully find a trash can.

And then I saw a familiar face staring back at me from one of the picture frames on Collin's grandmother's wall.

Carl's face. Carl's young, smiling face. He was much younger there than he'd been when I'd known him. He was probably only eighteen. And handsome, actually, before he'd gained fifty pounds and lost most of his hair.

Who could have known then that one day that handsome young man would turn out to be a lazy unemployed freeloader?

Who could have known then that one day he'd take a dive off the highway and end up as roadkill?

I thought about Carl's mother. I wondered what she felt every day when she walked past this picture. I wondered what she felt when she looked at Collin. Could she somehow see Carl in his six-year-old, half-Puerto-Rican face even though he wasn't actually Carl's biological son?

I started to shake. On the verge? You bet.

I opened a door at the end of the hallway. Fortunately it turned out to be a bathroom. I sat down on the toilet. I closed my eyes and saw Carl's face.

Why cry over Carl now? I never did before.

I sat there on the toilet with my hands pressed against my eyes until the tears stopped and I had myself under control. I splashed some water on my face and opened the bathroom door. When I stepped into the hallway, Collin's grandmother stood there. "He's locked himself in the upstairs bathroom," she said, then turned and walked off.

We were great guests. Come over, act rude, then lock ourselves in the bathroom.

I went upstairs and knocked on the bathroom door. "King Collin, it's Lainey. Can I please come in?"

He started kicking the door.

"You don't have to put the new clothes on. You can wear your Batman pajamas and your cape and your crown, and we'll go get the rest of your presents and go home. Okay, King Collin?"

"No!"

"Okay, well stay here, all right? I'll be right back."

I went out to the backyard to find Vallery. It was definitely her turn to deal with this. Instead of Vallery, I spotted Christine and Wallace. They were too far away to intercept me, so I just waved and kept walking. Then someone grabbed my arm. I turned. Riley.

"Why . . . ?" I asked. How many times did I have to break up with him?

"You invited me," Riley reminded me. I'd told him about the party, obviously. But that had been before.

I sighed. "You know what? Now isn't a good time. I have to go get Vallery."

He reached out and grabbed my hand. "Laine, what's wrong?"

I wanted to walk away, but instead I let it all spill out. "Collin's spazzing out. His crazy-ass grandmother didn't like his pajamas, so she started screaming at him and telling him he has to put on this stupid outfit that she bought for him. And he got pissed off and now he's in the bathroom screaming and kicking the walls. I need to find Vallery and Mabel so we can get out of here."

Riley grinned. "You let him wear pajamas to the party?"

"It's his birthday!" I screamed. This had always worked out fine when Mom did it.

"Calm down, okay? I'll go talk to him."

"No. We're leaving. I'm getting Vallery and Mabel, and we're kicking the door in and going home."

"You can't leave. Just let me try to talk to him."

"Fine," I said. "Whatever."

I found Vallery and Mabel talking to a bunch of women I didn't recognize. Vallery broke away from them and came up to me.

"We may have to make a run for it," I said. I filled her

in on what had happened inside.

"Riley's in there with him?" she asked. "Are you two back together?"

I glared at her. "No."

"Well. All right."

We watched the back door and waited. Finally Riley and Collin walked out of the house, holding hands. Collin had changed into the outfit his grandmother had bought for him. His face was red and he trembled a little, but when he saw the presents table, he smiled.

"Crisis averted," Vallery whispered.

I walked over to Collin and Riley, but as soon as I got there, Collin ran off toward the presents. I stood there alone with Riley.

"What did you do?" I asked.

"Just talked to him." He reached out and stroked my arm, right above the elbow. "What happened here?" he asked.

I looked down at my bare arms, at the nasty yellow bruise, almost completely faded. I'd forgotten to put Eric's shirt back on when I got out of the Grand Am. And of course Riley would notice.

I watched Collin tear into a present. His grandmother ran across the yard, holding her camera.

"I was bitten," I said.

"I thought he stopped doing that a long time ago."

I shook my head. "It wasn't Collin." I shook off Riley's hand and walked across the yard toward my brother.

13

THE INCIDENT

Before she died, Mom filled out Collin's papers for summer camp and put me down as the backup emergency contact person. On the day of the incident, they couldn't contact Mom since she was dead, so they called me at work.

"We've had an incident," his teacher said. "And I'm having trouble getting in touch with . . . your mother? Lisa Snodgrass? Could you come pick Collin up from camp?"

"Lisa's dead," I said. "What's wrong with Collin?"

"I'd rather discuss it when you get here. He'll be requiring medical attention."

"What? Well, take him to the hospital."

"This isn't the sort of situation we deal with."

I imagined Collin bleeding to death and the stupid teacher at camp backing up slowly and then going to the office to look up my phone number and call me to come get him.

"Is he hurt?" I asked. "Broken? Bleeding? What?"

I noticed Rodney staring at me from his kiosk.

"He . . . Collin has gotten a crayon stuck in his ear."

I laughed. "A crayon? Are you kidding me? Jesus."

What? Rodney mouthed. I picked my pen up off of my register and held it up to my ear. Rodney shrugged.

"We don't find this amusing, Miss Pike. It's proving to be a large distraction."

"Jesus, it's a freaking crayon. Did you try to pull it out?"

"Of course we tried to pull it out. It's stuck. He needs medical attention."

"Is he in pain?"

"No. He's playing quietly."

I didn't believe that for a second.

"Okay, well, I'm at work. I can't come get him right now."

"As I said before, we need someone to come immediately. Perhaps I should call . . . Mr. Carter?"

"Riley?" I asked. "Riley Carter?"

I hadn't realized Mom had put him down as the other emergency contact. I mean, I knew she had during the school year. She'd used Mabel and Riley since I was still in school too. But for the summer session I thought she'd changed it to me and Mabel.

211

"Yes, Riley Carter. Is that all right?"

"Don't call Riley," I said. "He's out of town. What about Mabel?"

"I'm sorry, I don't know a Mabel."

"Mabel White. She's our neighbor."

"She's not on my contact list."

"That's okay. I can call her for you."

"I can't let him leave with someone who isn't on my list."

"Oh my God. Well, listen. I'm going to call my sister. Your list is very outdated, but she's Collin's guardian. She has papers and everything. Would *that* be acceptable?"

There was a long pause. "That's fine. I'll give her the forms when she arrives. Please tell your sister this is very urgent."

"All right."

I hung up and dialed Vallery. She hadn't even wanted to give me her work number and address in case of emergency, but I'd insisted.

"It's a great day here at Parker Associates. This is Vallery speaking. How can I help you?"

"Are you kidding me?" I asked. "That's seriously how they make you answer the phone?"

"Well hello, Miss Pike!" she said in her fake friendly voice. "What can I help you with today?"

"We have a situation. Collin got a crayon stuck in his ear. The teacher is freaking out and wants someone to come pick him up."

"I'll call you right back," she whispered, and then hung up on me.

Rodney walked over. "What's going on?" he asked.

"My brother got a crayon stuck in his ear," I explained. Rodney stared at me for a second and then started laughing. I laughed too, and then the kiosk phone rang.

"It's a great day here at Perfume World!" I exclaimed. "This is Lainey speaking. How can I address your urgent olfactory needs?"

"You know what?" Vallery yelled. "I don't have time for this bullshit!"

"They let you talk that way at work?" I asked. "And so loudly?"

"I'm on my cell phone outside in the parking lot. And I'm *only* out here to call you back. I am not leaving work. I am not picking up that kid in the middle of the day because he has a crayon in his ear. Why don't they just pull it out?"

"That's exactly what I said, but apparently it's in there pretty good. The teacher thinks that only a dedicated team of the best surgeons at Johns Hopkins will be able to remove it."

"Lainey, I am not laughing. But I'm glad you think this situation is amusing, because *you* are going to take him."

"Uh, no, I'm not."

Vallery groaned. "If it's not urgent enough that they need to rush him to the hospital themselves, then I don't think it's urgent enough that *either* of us should miss work to get him early."

"If you tell your boss that Collin needs to see a doctor, then he has to understand."

"Lainey, I just took off to take him to the doctor!"

"No you didn't! That was a lie!"

"It really doesn't matter at this point. Look, there are two reasons why you're going to be the one to deal with this. First, they called you, not me."

"Actually, they called Mom first. Should we just wait to see if she's going to get him?"

Vallery sighed. "My second reason is that you pick him up anyway. This really has nothing to do with me."

"Vallery, I can't leave! If you leave, you have other people there to cover for you. I have *no one*. I can't leave here for another hour."

"Then wait an hour. I don't know what to tell you."

"Oh my God. I can't believe you're doing this to me."

"I don't have a choice. If I keep missing time, they're going to fire me. It's still my probationary period. And if I get fired, are you going to—"

"Okay, fine. I'll take care of it." I slammed the phone down.

I looked at the schedule under the register. Yasmin worked the afternoon shift. Yasmin was cool—she wouldn't rat on me if I had to leave early. To go to the *hospital*.

I had to go, right? It had to hurt.

I walked over to Rodney's kiosk. "I have to go pick him up," I said, rolling my eyes.

"I'll watch your stuff," he said.

I looked at my watch. "It's a whole hour."

"It'll be okay. I'll cover for you."

"Thanks, Rodney."

I made sure the keys were inside the desk drawer, and then I walked off. The handbag kiosk girl smiled when she saw me coming.

"Thirty percent off!" she said. "Today only!"

I held my purse up to show her that I didn't need a freaking handbag.

"Take a coupon," she called after me. "And come back later?"

I kept walking.

"Does it hurt?" I asked as we sat there waiting. Collin shook his head and accidentally whacked the crayon against the chair. His little lips quivered like he wanted to cry.

I'd taken him to the urgent-care center, which handled stuff like crayons in the ear, but not anything major like broken bones or heart attacks or profuse bleeding. The closest real hospital was in the city, and I didn't exactly know how to get there. The urgent-care center would be good enough, though. And probably cheaper, since that's where the poor and homeless people went.

"Jeez, Collin, why would you do that to yourself?

Why would you want to stick a crayon in your ear?"

"I didn't!"

"You didn't?"

"No!"

"Collin, I know you're lying. There's a crayon sticking out of your head. Right now."

"Zach did it!"

"Zach stuck the crayon in your ear?"

"No!"

"Okay then."

"Zach *made* me!"

"He *made* you."

Collin nodded.

"Is that the truth? Remember, God is watching."

I couldn't believe I'd just said that. Sometimes when I dealt with Collin, it was like my mother had temporarily possessed my body and I had no control over the things that came out of my mouth.

"Zach made me do it!"

If you spent enough time listening to Collin's lies, you could detect a slight difference in the way he spoke when he was actually telling the truth, or at least thought that he was. And for some reason, I believed him then. I didn't know why this Zach kid would make him stick a crayon in his ear, but I believed that it had happened.

"All right," I said. "I believe you."

He dropped his head. "Mrs. Young didn't."

"People aren't always going to believe what you say

even when you're telling the truth."

"Not fair."

I put my arm around Collin, being careful not to bump the crayon. "I hate to break it to you, but life is never going to be fair."

<hr />

The receptionist found some coloring books in the back and brought them out for Collin. I thought it was kind of funny, with the crayon in his ear and all. But no one else picked up on the irony, and I felt dumb for laughing. When Vallery showed up after work, Collin was lying on the floor under the chair, coloring.

"I can't wait to see how much we get billed for that," she said as she crossed the waiting room and sat down beside me. "You know, his grandmother is cutting us off."

"What do you mean, cutting us off?"

"She's been giving us money every week for Collin."

"She has?"

"Yes. But she's super pissed about his birthday and she said she's not cutting me any more checks. I guess she thinks we're unfit parents."

"We are."

"Yeah, I know."

"Are we going to be okay?"

"Well, yeah, I guess. We have the Social Security money, but that's hardly anything. If Mom and Carl had actually worked like normal people, we'd be getting a bigger check every month. My job is going to help a ton, but we're still going to come up short."

"I can help out a little."

Vallery nodded. "Yeah, okay. I mean, I hate to take your money. But if you want to buy groceries or something, that'd help."

"I can find something full-time."

"Don't be ridiculous."

"How's that ridiculous?"

"You're only eighteen. You should be out having fun. Not worrying about jobs and money and all that dumb stuff. Besides, I need you to help me at home. Maybe you can work more hours in the fall while Collin's in school."

"I might be in school too." I hadn't thought about school in a while. I didn't know what the plan was anymore.

"Crap, I forgot about that. Well, I don't want you to work any more than you have to. Especially if you're going to school."

"Why do you care?"

"I had to work my way through college, and I had to work in high school to help my dad with the bills. It's not fun."

"I don't think it'll be *fun*. But we have to do what we have to do."

Vallery sighed and leaned back in her chair. She looked up toward the ceiling. "Thanks a ton, Mom."

The doctor pulled the crayon out with a pair of pliers, then shone a flashlight in Collin's ear.

"How's it look?" Vallery asked. "Any waxy buildup?"

The doctor glared at her. I clamped my hand over my mouth to keep from laughing. No one in this place had a sense of humor.

"Everything looks fine," the doctor said. He handed the crayon to me. On the way out, I handed it to Vallery. "Here. Send it back to camp with him tomorrow."

"Why didn't they just pull it out with some pliers at school?" Vallery asked.

"His teacher didn't want to break it off in his ear and make it worse. Lawsuits and all that," I said.

As we crossed the parking lot, my cell phone rang. I looked at the caller ID. "It's Rodney," I said.

"Is he the guy?" Vallery asked.

"What guy?"

She grabbed my arm where the ugly bruise had been. "The *guy*."

I rolled my eyes. "No."

Vallery took Collin with her in the Mustang. I got into the Grand Am and answered the phone.

"Katie's going to squeal," Rodney said.

"Katie? I thought Yasmin worked on Wednesdays."

"Today's Tuesday."

"Oh. Really?"

"Yeah. She showed up half an hour early. I told her that you had stomach cramps and had to run to the bathroom. I made up this whole story about some bad Chinese you had last night. I told her I'd watch the kiosk until you got back, but she just stayed there and waited. When you never came back, she got really suspicious, and I'm pretty sure she's going to tell Bob."

"Oh great," I said. "This is very bad." Abandoning your kiosk was about the worst thing you could do.

"I know. I'm sorry. I probably should have just told her the truth, but I didn't want her to know you weren't even in the mall. I really thought she'd leave and come back when her shift started."

"That's okay. It would have looked bad anyway."

<hr>

As if the day couldn't get any worse, Kara was waiting on the porch when we got home. She had a wrapped present on her lap.

I sat in the Grand Am and watched as Vallery got out of the Mustang and unbuckled Collin.

Crap. Kara had called four days ago, and I hadn't even listened to her message. I pulled out my cell phone and called my voice mail.

Collin ran up to Kara.

Hey, Lainey, it's Kara. Christine and Wallace were just here, and they asked me what I'd gotten Collin for his birthday.

Kara handed the present to Collin. He smiled.

And I had to tell them that I hadn't gotten him anything, because my best friend Lainey didn't tell me about the party.

Kara hugged Collin.

Christine said, oh, she just sent out invitations. It probably got lost in the mail.

Vallery took Collin's hand. They walked inside the house.

So anyway, give me a call if my invitation got lost in the mail. Okay? Love you. Bye.

I hung up and got out of the car. Kara walked down the porch steps.

"Where are you going?" I asked.

Kara shrugged. "Home."

We stopped in the middle of the yard. Kara looked away from me.

"I just got your message. I'm sorry."

She shrugged. "Right. It's okay."

"It was really nice of you to get Collin a present anyway."

"Yeah. I would have brought it earlier, but it took me a while to convince myself that being mad at you wasn't a good reason to ignore the kid's birthday."

"I would have sent you an invitation, but I didn't think you'd want to go."

"You invited *Christine*."

"Come on, Kara, don't do this. I had one invitation left, and Christine's pregnant and into the whole kid thing, so I thought it'd matter more to her. You know? I really didn't think you'd care."

She rolled her eyes. "I have known the kid forever,

and I do care about his birthday."

"I know you do. And it's really not like that. I'm sorry."

"Okay."

"I'm glad you came over."

"Right," she said.

I sighed. "Can we go somewhere?"

She didn't answer, but I yelled into the house and told Vallery that Kara and I were going out for dinner. We ended up at the McDonald's because Kara wouldn't tell me where she wanted to go and it was the first place I came to.

Kara didn't talk to me while we waited in line, and I wasn't sure what to say. Finally, as we sat down with our chicken sandwiches, I apologized again. "Things have been crazy," I explained.

"What's going on with Riley?"

I shrugged. "Riley? Nothing."

"Christine said he seemed kind of mad at Collin's party, and then he left early."

"Well, yeah, he had to leave early. I don't know why Christine said he looked mad, though."

"Everything's fine with Riley?"

"Yeah," I said. "Just fine."

Kara put her sandwich down. "Lainey, I know you guys are still fighting. He called me and told me all about the party. He cried on the phone for like an hour."

"You know, we're not *fighting*. We broke up."

"He told me you're seeing some other guy, and that you had a hickey."

"It wasn't a hickey. It was a bruise. On my arm."

"A hickey is a bruise."

I rolled my eyes. "So what if I'm seeing someone new? How is that his business?"

Kara sighed. "It's not Riley's business, but I thought you might have told *me* about it."

"Oh."

"It's just weird that your boyfriend—your *ex*-boyfriend—is telling me all this stuff about you, and I had no idea it was going on."

"I'm sorry. I didn't think you'd want to hear about the new guy."

"Why wouldn't I want to know about the new guy?"

I shrugged. "You think I belong with Riley."

"You thought you belonged with Riley. That's what you always used to say."

"Well, I guess I was wrong."

"So who is he?"

"Nobody. Just a guy."

"Lainey."

"His name is Eric."

She threw a french fry at me and cracked a smile. "Very enlightening."

"Okay . . . he's in sales right now. But he's a ski instructor in PA during the winter. And he has his own place. He has a beard."

"And it's going okay?"

I shrugged. "Yeah, fine."

Kara nodded. "Okay." She dipped a french fry in my ketchup. "So are things crazy with your brother, too?"

"God, yes." And so I told her about Collin's birthday party, and about our trip to urgent care. By the time we left McDonald's, I'd gotten her laughing.

"Can I meet him?" she asked as we pulled up to my house.

"Eric? Yeah, we'll do something sometime."

"Okay. Call me."

We hugged on the sidewalk, and then Kara walked to her car and I went inside.

<hr />

The next morning Bob called and fired me. He said he'd send my last check in the mail.

I hung up on him before he was finished talking and threw the cell phone across the room. I cried. I'd never been fired before. And I hadn't even thought to defend myself. I'd had a perfectly good reason for leaving. It felt too late to call him back now, after I'd already hung up on him.

After I started to feel really stupid about crying, I wiped my eyes and picked my cell phone up off of the floor. I scrolled to K but realized that Kara was probably asleep, so I scrolled down to R and then shook my head and wondered what was wrong with me. I scrolled back up to E and dialed Eric.

"I got fired!" I whined into the phone.

"Oh, honey! I'm sorry. I know how much you loved that job."

"Shut up."

"Well, do you want to go to work with me today?" he asked. "Frank's on vacation."

"Um," I said. "All right."

"Cool. I'll pick you up in a few minutes."

I dressed in a red button-up shirt and black skirt and heels. I hadn't worn the shirt in a while, and it was relatively clean. The skirt? Well, it didn't have any visible stains, at least. My underwear, though, was brand-new. I'd finally run out of clean underwear, so I'd bought an economy variety pack of cotton briefs at Walmart. They would get me through the next few weeks.

"Now, this job works on commission," Eric explained in the car after he picked me up. "At the end of the day we'll split everything evenly, all right?"

"All right," I said.

"I figure you'll help me win over the male demographic. My biggest customers so far have been old ladies, because old ladies love me. Anyone younger than forty-five thinks my beard is creepy, but the old ladies dig it."

"I'm under forty-five," I said.

"And what do you think about my beard?"

I shrugged and smiled.

"Where are we going?" I asked.

"Annapolis."

"Annapolis?"

"Yeah. Frank and I already hit all the streets in Corben."

"Really. All of them?"

"Yeah."

"Then I guess it wasn't such a coincidence that we met again. It was just a matter of time."

"Nah, fate still had something to do with it. Would you have gotten out of bed to answer the door if Vallery hadn't stayed home from work?"

I shook my head. Absolutely not.

The houses in the Annapolis suburbs weren't that close together, so we did a lot of walking. Most people either weren't home or didn't answer the door. They were probably at work, which made sense. If you lived in a big brick house in a suburb of Annapolis, you probably needed a normal nine-to-five job to pay the bills, and that prevented you from being home in the middle of the day to answer the door for a couple of kids selling magazines.

After four hours of going door-to-door, I realized that selling was *hard*. Door-to-door salesmen aroused even more contempt than kiosk cashiers. But some people were receptive to our pitch (or to our charming good looks). We made a bit of money and decided to go out to lunch.

The burger place Eric picked out had peanut shells all over the floor. "This place is filthy," I said to Eric, kicking at the shells with my black heels.

"The food's good, though," he assured me.

"No, I like it," I said. "It makes me feel at home."

He rolled his eyes at me. "I can never tell when you're being facetious."

After we were seated and the waitress gave us a bowl of peanuts and went off to get our drinks, we stared at the menus and I thought about getting fired. I knew it was just a stupid mall job, but I couldn't stop thinking about it and wondering what I should have done differently.

"I should have just waited," I said to Eric. "He wasn't even in pain. And then we sat in the waiting room for half the night anyway."

"Your brother needed you," Eric said, cracking open a peanut. "Why don't you call Bob and explain?"

"I don't know. I think maybe I should find a full-time job. But I don't even know if I'm going to school in the fall." I looked at Eric. "What should I do? And what should I *order*?"

He reached his hand across the table and popped a peanut into my mouth. "You want the bacon and mushroom burger."

"Do I?" I chewed and swallowed the peanut as I looked down at the menu. No chicken. Just burgers. "Okay."

"To answer your other question, I believe everything

happens for a reason, and everything will turn out the way that it's supposed to turn out."

"Okay," I said. "That's nice and all, but it doesn't really help me out now."

"Why not? Don't you believe that everything will work out in the end?"

This was starting to sound like one of Mom's therapy sessions. "Well, yeah," I said. "I guess."

"If everything turns out right in the end, then everything that happened until then was leading up to that point in time. Therefore everything that happened had to happen."

"O-*kay*."

Eric grinned. "What I'm trying to say is don't stress out about making decisions. If everything is going to turn out right in the end, then it doesn't matter what you decide to do, because you can't make the wrong decision. You get what I'm saying? You can't do the wrong thing. If you believe that everything will turn out right in the end, then whatever you do, no matter what it is, it will be the right thing."

"But how do you know what the right thing is?" I asked.

"That's my point. You don't have to worry about it. You do what's in your heart and you don't second-guess yourself."

The waitress came back and dropped off our drinks. Eric ordered our burgers.

While we waited for our food, Eric made a big production out of building a tower of sugar packets. I stared out the window and thought about what he had said.

The problem with Eric's philosophy was that it was complete bullshit. Do what's in your *heart*? What did that even mean? The only thing in my heart was a lot of blood and arteries and ventricles. When people said that, they really meant do what you *feel*. But how was I supposed to know what I really felt about something, when my feelings changed every time I thought about it?

Right then, I kind of missed Riley and wouldn't have minded if I'd been sitting across from him instead of Eric. Riley would have given me a real answer—apologize to Bob, find a new job and help Vallery, whatever. He wouldn't have given me any do-what's-in-your-heart theoretical bullshit.

But I liked being with Eric most of the time. Earlier, when we were going door-to-door and selling magazines and then making fun of the people who'd been rude to us, I hadn't even thought about Riley for a second.

My feelings didn't change on a day-to-day basis. They changed hourly. They changed every minute.

Sometimes when Collin actually felt like cooperating and Vallery was in a good mood, we almost seemed like a real family, and I didn't feel like someone who just got in the way. But other times I couldn't stand Collin's temper and obstinacy and I didn't want to deal with being a family; I just wanted to deal with being myself, which was hard enough anyway.

How was I supposed to know what I should do? I had no idea, so I couldn't do anything. I couldn't leave Corben or get a new job or make any plans or register for college. I didn't feel qualified to make even the smallest decision by myself. Not even ordering my own food.

When the waitress came back with our burgers, I stared at mine and wondered why I'd let Eric order for me. I wasn't big on mushrooms, or bacon, so what would possess me to get a bacon and mushroom burger? Eric's burger, topped with chili and red onions, didn't look much better, so I couldn't even propose a trade.

I had no other option, so I lifted my burger and took a bite. I expected to hate it, but the mushrooms and bacon surprised me. "Oh my God," I said after swallowing. "This is the best burger I've ever had. Ever."

"Who takes care of you, baby?" Eric asked with a wink. He rubbed my knee under the table.

You just do what's in your heart.

Is this what was in my heart? Magazines, and this bearded man, and bacon mushroom burgers?

It could be. It felt good. It *tasted* good.

It wasn't so bad, leaving things for other people to decide. They seemed to know what they were doing.

14

BOOKS OF
CLICHÉS

As soon as Vallery got home, I handed her half of my magazine money and told her I'd been fired. The money wasn't much, but I knew it would help a little.

"You should call your dad," she said. She folded my money up and put it in her purse.

"What? Where did that come from?"

"Have you even seen him since Mom died?"

"Yes. He was at the funeral."

"He was? And you didn't tell me? Nice."

"You've met him before. You could have gone up and talked to him."

"I haven't seen him since I was a kid. I wouldn't have recognized him. Anyway, have you talked to him since then?"

"No."

"He hasn't called? You don't think that's a shitty

thing to do to your daughter, when you're her only living parent?"

"He called me on my birthday, but I didn't talk to him. We've never been close anyway. Hey, how often do you call *your* dad?"

"That's irrelevant to this conversation. Anyway, you need to call him and tell him you miss him and want to get together. Go have dinner or something. He'll ask how you've been, you tell him about Collin, about losing your job, he gives you some money."

"That's absolutely not going to happen."

"I'll call him and set up a dinner date for you."

"You're not going to pimp me out to my own father."

"Oh, Lainey, why is everything *dirty* to you? He's your dad. If he isn't going to support you emotionally, the least he can do is give us some money."

"I'll get a real job. With both of us working full-time, that should cover all the bills, right? Maybe I can work night shift at the diner with Kara. Then I'd be home during the day with Collin."

"I don't want you to do that."

"Of course you don't. Then you couldn't hold it over my head that you make all the money and I do nothing."

"Oh, stop it. I've never said anything like that, and you know it. We'll struggle through the summer and then you can get a job in the fall. It would help *now* if you could get some money from your dad, but if you don't want to, then whatever. We'll deal. We'll be fine, all right?"

I went to my room and pulled Mom's notebooks out from under my mattress. I piled them up and stared at them. How much would they be worth to Deborah? Enough to pay our bills for a month or two? Enough to make me feel better about losing my stupid job?

Pick them up. Take them to Vallery. Give her the phone number.

I couldn't do it. I didn't know why, but I couldn't.

I heard Vallery's footsteps coming up the stairs. I threw my blanket on top of the notebooks.

She knocked on my door. "Hey, I'm taking your money and going grocery shopping. Do you want anything?"

"No. Are you taking Collin?"

"Yeah, I can."

After I heard the Mustang drive away, I sat on my bed with Mom's notebooks. I opened the binder and flipped through the pages. It was full of things like notes on starting your own business. Tax forms and all that. Boring stuff. If Mom had been smart enough to gather all this information, why hadn't she been smart enough to invest her money? Stocks and bonds or whatever?

I closed the binder and opened to a random page in one of the notebooks.

The early bird catches the worm. So true. Set your sights on what you want and go out and get it. Don't take no for an answer. Don't let the wind knock you down.

Everything works out okay in the end! If it's not okay . . . it's not the end!

I closed the notebook and threw them all back under the mattress. I didn't know why Deborah would want to buy these books full of clichés. Couldn't she make up this crap on her own?

I sat on my bed. I looked at all the dirty laundry covering my floor and I got angry. Really angry.

I jumped up. I started shoving everything into my hamper. I dragged the hamper into the hallway, down the stairs, through the living room, to the kitchen, to the basement door.

And then I froze.

I opened the basement door. I flipped the light on.

I told myself to take one step, just drag the hamper down one step, but I couldn't move.

I pushed the hamper away. I'd try it without the hamper first.

I took one step down the basement stairs.

Then I jumped back into the kitchen and slammed the door shut.

Ridiculous.

———

Look at what you've done to me, Mom. I can't even walk down to my own basement. I can't even do my own fucking laundry. I'm buying panties in bulk from Walmart because you had to kill yourself and make me terrified of my own basement.

What the hell was wrong with you, Mom?

And not just in June, either. Not just when you decided to kill yourself. Earlier. Years ago. What was wrong with you then?

When something's over, you're supposed to remember the good times. You're not supposed to remember the sucky parts or the moments that you'd never in a million years want to live through again. You survived, and that's all that matters. At least that's how it's supposed to be. Obviously that's not how it's working out for me since you died. It's not that I *want* to keep remembering the bad times. It's not that I *want* to keep reliving every time you hurt me. I just can't forget. I want to, but I can't.

You were supposed to chaperone the field trip to the aquarium in first grade. You had a whole group of my classmates assigned to you and everything. I didn't remind you that morning because I was six—why would I remind you? And then you never showed up at school, and my group had to be divided up among the other groups, among the other parents who had remembered to show up. They asked me where my mother was, and I had no idea what to say, so I just cried instead.

You also missed: several parent-teacher conferences, fifth grade graduation, eighth grade graduation, and every American Education Week except the one in third grade. And it also took you three hours to come pick me up that time I had a really bad headache and the nurse was afraid

I might have meningitis. I didn't have meningitis, but how did you know that?

Why are these the things that I remember?

I know you loved Collin better because he needed a lot of love. And that was fine. Really, it was. You thought you didn't have to put any work into me. You thought I'd just coast through life and I'd make it okay no matter how much attention you paid to me. And I have.

After you got Collin, I thought you'd changed. I didn't understand why you loved Carl, and I know I mocked your group therapy stuff, but I knew that you were different—and believe me, I appreciated it. I thought, *Well, she doesn't love me any better and she hasn't apologized for any of the crap she put me through, but at least she loves Collin, at least she tries as hard as she can for him. She doesn't live for herself anymore. She lives for him.* But I was jealous—I was the kid you'd accidentally acquired, and he was the kid you'd tried so hard for.

But I had it wrong; you didn't live for Collin. You lived for Carl. And after Carl drove his stupid Kawasaki off the highway, you had nothing. It didn't matter that you'd finally made a nice life for yourself and your kids. It didn't matter that you still had Collin to raise. It didn't matter that you'd never see me and Riley get married or hold your grandkids. It didn't matter that you were helping those women in your groups.

Obviously you hadn't done it for yourself, or even for us. Everything you'd done was for him. Always him. A fat, uneducated, unemployed lazy man sitting in a La-Z-Boy. I don't understand, Mom. And I don't think I ever will.

I should take your blue binder and your composition books and call this Deborah woman. I should hand them over and take whatever I can get for them. Maybe Deborah's just in it for all the money she can make from the poor lonely women you used to counsel. But maybe she actually wants to help them like you used to. Maybe she actually cares. Maybe she'll stick around. Maybe she won't disappoint them.

15

HAMBURGERS AND SNOWBALLS

Saturday was moving day for Christine and Wallace. Christine couldn't lift much because of being very pregnant. Kara and I were both notoriously lacking in upper body strength. Joe was coming along, but he'd sprained his wrist at work, so he wouldn't be good for any heavy lifting. Everyone else was otherwise occupied. Jamie and her boyfriend were supposed to come but had to cancel at the last minute. Owen and a few others were working. No one told me anything about Riley's whereabouts, but I was sure they hadn't decided to invite me first over him. Christine had called and said to me, "Bring your new guy along if you want. We're going to have a little pizza party afterward." I knew they were only asking because they were desperate. And probably wanted to check out this new guy. I didn't know if Kara had told everyone about Eric, or if it had been a lucky guess. I mean, it *was* a valid assumption. If you were going to dump a great guy like Riley, you must have a new boyfriend already lined up. You didn't just walk away from something like that without a plan, not unless you were crazy.

— ••••• —

As soon as I stepped outside on Saturday morning, a woman shoved a paperback novel in my face and asked, "How much is this?

I took the book from her and looked at the price on the back. "Five ninety-nine," I said, and handed it back to her.

The woman rolled her eyes. "You can't charge the cover price."

I noticed the stack of paperbacks on the porch swing. Then I looked past the woman and noticed everything else. It wasn't just one crazy woman on our porch. It was a whole yard sale.

"All books are a quarter!" Vallery yelled from behind the woman.

"Thanks, hon," the woman called to Vallery. And then she handed me a quarter and walked off with the book.

Yard sales were a big deal in our neighborhood. Someone on our street had one just about every week in the summer, and now apparently it was our turn. Our neighbors traipsed around our tiny yard, digging through boxes of our stuff. They were even out on the sidewalk because Vallery had hung Mom's dresses and shirts on both sides of the fence. She'd even pulled out some of the extra chairs from the dining room.

I walked down the porch steps and pinched Vallery. "What the hell are you doing?"

She turned around and smiled. "Having a yard sale. Obviously."

"You shouldn't have done this without telling me!"

"Well, I need to make some extra money somehow."

"I gave you practically all of the money I made with Eric!" Eric had let me tag along for the rest of the week. Apparently Frank didn't have much of a work ethic. Eric had told me that he wasn't away on vacation—just at home playing Grand Theft Auto.

"If you want to get rid of some stuff too, bring it out. I'll give you your cut."

"What if there's stuff here that I don't want to give away?"

"It's just Mom's old clothes and a bunch of stuff that belonged to Carl. We don't need it. I've made over a hundred bucks already and I've only been out here an hour."

I recognized some of our neighbors. I spotted the woman with the long braid, Deborah, digging through boxes on the other side of the yard. I wondered if she'd already asked Vallery about Mom's notebooks, or if she was hoping to just come across them and buy them for a quarter.

I walked around and started looking down into boxes.

Then I came across a box that had LAINEY OLD CLOTHES written on the side.

I looked inside. Yes, definitely my old stuff. I held up the box to Vallery. "What does this say?"

"'Lainey old clothes.' Old! You clearly don't want them anymore. They've clearly been put aside for disposal."

I dug through the box. "Vallery!" I whispered. "There are *panties* in here." Panties! At a yard sale! Labeled with *my name* for all the neighbors to see!

"Oh for God's sake," Vallery said. "Just take them out."

I heard a car pull up, and I turned and saw Eric idling by the curb.

"I'll be home in a few hours," I said. I closed up the box and carried it to the car. I threw it in the backseat and got in beside Eric.

"What's in the box?" he asked.

I sighed. "Vallery was selling my underwear at her little yard sale."

Eric laughed and shook his head. "How much did she want for them?"

"Not funny."

"Did you have to buy them back from her?"

"Also not funny."

<hr>

I could tell right off that Eric was not making a great impression on the Old Crew. I should have gotten him to shave the beard off. Wallace and Joe shook his hand, and

Christine and Kara were friendly to him, but I knew they wanted to shake me and scream, "YOU LEFT RILEY FOR THIS GUY? WHAT IS WRONG WITH YOU?"

I mean, Eric wasn't bad. Obviously, *I* liked him. But Riley was a man's man. He fixed cars and played sports. Eric spouted off bizarre philosophies and had favorite movies that no one else had heard of. He just didn't fit in the way Riley did. Not that I fit in either. If it hadn't been for Kara, I wouldn't have talked to any of those people ever again.

But fortunately Eric had no trouble holding up his end of a sofa, and he was old enough to buy alcohol, so at least he wasn't a total outcast. Moving took way longer than I thought it would, and then Eric and I stopped by the liquor store on our last trip to the new apartment and bought a twelve-pack for those of us who weren't pregnant. Christine ordered pizza. Wallace put on a movie. It was like the old days, except we were in a strange place and Riley was missing.

Christine had drawn a diagram of where she wanted all the furniture to go, but now that everything was where she wanted it, she couldn't decide if she liked it. She kept asking me my opinion, and I kept telling her it looked fine. I kept trying to talk about other things, but then I'd catch her looking around the living room and I knew she was still thinking about the furniture.

I was on my third beer when I ended up alone in the kitchen with Kara, getting another slice of pizza. I grabbed her arm. "Do you like him?" I whispered.

"He's nice," Kara said. "Do *you* like him?"

"Of course I like him. Well, most of the time. I don't know. I miss Riley sometimes, you know? Why do I have to be such a crazy person?"

Kara opened her mouth to tell me, but I reached out and tried to cover her mouth with my hand. I grabbed her chin instead, but that shut her up. "Don't tell me I'm going through a difficult time," I warned her. I let go of her chin.

"I wasn't going to. I was just going to say, if you like Eric, be with Eric. If you like Riley, go be with Riley. They're both nice."

"And they're really different, you know?"

"Yeah, I know."

"So how am I supposed to know which one I really like? I mean, I don't know anything anymore, Kara. For real. Like I can't even decide what I want to eat. I sit around thinking and thinking and thinking and I can't make up my mind about anything."

She took my beer and handed me a can of Coke. "Maybe you should switch to soda."

"See, that's what I need. That was good. Make up my mind for me."

"Okay. Let's go back to the living room and drink our sodas."

"No, no, no, I mean about the boys. Which boy do I want?"

"You're with Eric. I thought you already made up your mind."

"But I miss Riley sometimes."

"Well, which one do you like better?"

"That's the problem, duh." I rolled my eyes. "I can't figure it out. Maybe it's Riley. But maybe I only think that because I had him for so long. It could be Eric because, you know, I liked him enough that he pulled me away from Riley. Right? So which one is it?"

"If you're confused, then maybe you don't need a boyfriend right now."

I laughed. "Who would help Wallace lift the sofa if I didn't have a boyfriend?"

Kara rolled her eyes. "I really don't understand you and Christine. Why you're like that."

"Like what?"

She shrugged. "I don't know. Never mind."

"It's not our fault we have boyfriends and you don't."

She didn't answer. She just stood there, staring at me.

"Kara?"

"What?"

"Are you mad at what I said?"

"No."

"Okay. Then please pick for me."

"Fine. Hold on. I'm thinking."

She stood there for at least an entire minute before she spoke again. "Okay, I'm not saying this is what *you* should do, I'm just saying this is what *I* would do. If *I* had to pick, I'd pick Riley. He worships you. Not that there's anything wrong with Eric. He seems really nice and interesting. But didn't you say he's moving to Pennsylvania or something? And besides, you have a history with Riley."

"It doesn't even matter what I want. Riley hates me now anyway."

"I guarantee he doesn't hate you."

"I messed everything up."

Kara shook her head. "You just have too many problems, Lainey St. James." She took my arm and guided me back into the living room.

On the drive home Eric's car sputtered to a stop.

I looked at Eric. "Are we out of gas?"

"Well, we drove around all damn day. I thought we'd have enough to make it home. I *hope* we're out of gas, actually. If not, it's something a lot worse."

I sighed.

"What?"

"It's my night to watch Collin."

"I'll call Frank, and he'll come take us to a gas station. Don't freak out."

"I'm not freaking out. I should just be home by now, that's all."

"Well I'm not the one who wanted to sit and drink beer with your friends for three hours."

"I knew it. You don't like my friends."

"I like your friends just fine."

"You think they're stupid." I kicked my feet around on the floor of Eric's car. There were CDs everywhere. Some of them weren't even in cases. "You should take better care of your CDs."

"Lainey, you had too much to drink, and I really don't want to talk to you right now."

Well, that was one thing Eric and Riley had in common: They both hated me when I was drunk.

"I didn't drink anything," I lied. I was a compulsive liar when I was drunk. That got me into trouble at parties too.

Eric rolled his eyes. "Just sit there and be quiet, and I'll call Frank."

"They just like my old boyfriend better, that's all. He would have known what was wrong with the car. He would have fixed it a long time ago before it broke down."

"I'm out of gas. It doesn't take a genius to figure that out."

"You're just guessing. He would know the difference. He would have fixed it."

"Oh yeah? Why didn't he fix your car? Why do you have to get under the hood every other time you try to start it?"

"Shut up."

He took out his cell phone and started dialing. I jumped out of the car. I pulled my box out of the backseat. I held it to my chest and stomped down the shoulder of the road.

Stupid Eric. Stupid Riley. Stupid Corona Light. Maybe

Kara was right. Maybe I didn't need a boyfriend. I'd be anti-Mom. I wouldn't need anyone.

Kara *had* been right, when I stopped to think about it. She wasn't jealous that Christine and I had boyfriends. Where had it gotten us, anyway? We'd been with the same guys since ninth grade, planned our lives around them, and now what? Now Christine was knocked up and living in a sad little apartment. I didn't even have a plan anymore, didn't even know if I was still going to community college in the fall. Kara knew what she was doing. She'd go to school. She would be a nurse. She'd never needed anyone, and she never would.

I'd probably walked about half a mile when Frank's car pulled up beside me. I saw Eric sitting in the passenger seat. *I'm sorry*, he mouthed to me. I stopped walking. I climbed in the backseat.

"What's with the box?" Frank asked.

"Her sister tried to sell her panties," Eric explained. "Now she has to take them with her everywhere and guard them with her life."

Frank turned and raised an eyebrow at me. "How much was she—"

"I don't want to talk about it," I snapped.

⊷⊶⊷

Vallery came in and sat on my bed that night. Collin had already fallen asleep, and I'd almost been out, too.

"Do you know a woman named Deborah?" she whispered.

247

"Deborah?" I asked.

"Yeah. She said she came by and talked to you a few weeks ago."

"Oh. That weird woman. With the hair."

"Yeah."

"She wanted to buy Mom's notebooks. I didn't know what she was talking about, though. I think Mom just made that stuff up off the top of her head."

"So you didn't find anything?"

I shook my head. I had at least ten composition and spiral-bound notebooks under my mattress, and that huge blue binder stuck between my mattress and the wall. And I lied to Vallery's face.

"Yeah, I looked through the whole house and I couldn't find anything either. God, that sucks. She wanted to give us a ton of money."

"How much is a ton?"

Vallery told me.

"Oh my God."

"Seriously."

"Maybe they'll turn up."

Vallery sighed. "Maybe. Okay, good night."

Vallery walked back across the hall to her bedroom.

Deborah seriously wanted to give us that much money?

That could pay the bills for a few months.

That could get me a new car. A cheap used one, at least.

I fantasized about taking the money and running off to Pennsylvania with Eric. He'd go out in the cold every day and teach people how to ski. I'd get a job working in the lodge, making hot chocolate or something.

I fell asleep and dreamed about snow.

——— ···✦··· ———

The Old Crew must have told Riley all about the new bearded, camouflage-coat-wearing guy I was dating, because he called and said he was coming over so we could talk.

We sat on the porch on the Walmart swing Mom had bought but never really used. She'd gotten it thinking that she and Carl could sit there on the porch during the summer while Collin played in the yard, but it didn't work out that way. Carl didn't like the porch because of the bugs flying around everywhere.

"I need to know if we still have a chance to make this work," Riley said. He didn't look at me. He looked at Collin. I watched Collin too, as he played in the grass with his toy soldiers and LEGOs.

"I guess everyone told you about the guy I was with last night."

"They didn't say much."

"Come on. I know they did. What did they tell you?"

"They said he was nice but a little strange, not your usual type. I didn't want details. I don't want to know who he is. I don't even want to know his name."

"Okay," I said.

"So you're with him now? Like really with him?"

"Well, yeah. I guess."

"I get that you're confused. Doubts are natural, you know? After my parents got engaged, a few months later my mom got cold feet and they took a break. But it all worked out. My mom wasn't dating another guy, though. Do you understand what I'm saying?"

I nodded. If I stayed with Eric, Riley wouldn't wait around for me to change my mind.

"You know what I think you should do. And Kara told you what she thinks you should do. Unfortunately your life isn't a democracy, so you get to do whatever you want. I mean, do you really like this guy?"

"Yeah. I like him okay."

Riley laughed like he didn't think anything was funny, and he grabbed my hand. I tried to pull it back, but he held on and stared at me. "You're going to throw away almost four years with me for a guy that you like 'okay.' Think about how that makes me feel. Just think for a second about that, Lainey."

I looked down at the ground. "I know how it sounds, but I'm really not trying to be a bitch about it."

"I know you're not. But I just need to know what we're doing here."

"Why? Are you going to start dating someone else?"

Riley didn't answer right away, and I jumped up and pointed my finger at him. "Oh my God, you *are*!"

"I'm not *dating* anyone. A girl asked me out. That's all. We're supposed to go out on Wednesday after work. I don't even really want to go. But if you're telling me we're over, if you're dating this other guy, then why shouldn't I go and have a good time and meet new people?"

I sat back down. "Well, I don't care what you do."

"Really."

"I don't. Date a girl. What do I care? We should both move on."

"Road!" Riley screamed. He jumped up and pushed past me. I spun around and saw that Collin had climbed the fence. I ran toward Collin, but Riley had enough sense to run for the gate. While I helplessly reached over the fence toward Collin, Riley intercepted him at the sidewalk.

"No road!" I screamed at Collin as Riley carried him back into the yard. He set him down in front of me, and I grabbed Collin's hand and smacked it. "What's wrong with you? You could get hurt!" I looked at Riley. "We're going to have a time-out. I'll see you later."

"No!" Collin screamed. If Riley said bye, I didn't hear it. I dragged Collin into the house kicking and screaming.

"My LEGOs!" he yelled, and tried to yank away from me.

"You're punished from LEGOs." I threw Collin down on the couch. "Time-out for five minutes."

"No time-out!"

"Yes, time-out." I sat down beside him and threw my leg over his lap so he couldn't move. "If you fight, it will be five more minutes."

I stared at Collin and wondered what would possess him to climb the fence and run for the road. There was nothing there. No ball rolling away. No cute puppy. No ice cream truck. Nothing that would entice a normal kid to run into the street. But of course I wasn't dealing with a normal kid.

And of course I hadn't been the one to protect him. That had been Riley yet again. And probably for the last time. What would have happened if we'd been out in the yard, just the two of us, without Riley? I might not have even noticed.

When I started crying, Collin stopped struggling to get free. He turned and looked up at me. I pulled my leg off him. He climbed onto my lap. "What's wrong?" he asked.

"Don't run in the road," I said. "It's very bad."

He held my chin and stared into my eyes. The tears made him look blurry, and I could hardly make out his face. "Don't cry," he whispered. "Feel happy." He kissed me on the cheek.

"I'm happy," I said. I wiped my eyes and forced a smile. "Go play. Time-out's over."

He jumped up and ran off. I went outside and brought in his LEGOs.

Feel happy. If only it could be that easy.

While Collin played in the bathroom with his toy soldiers, I got the phone to call Kara. "Do not flush them," I said one more time before I dialed.

I didn't bother with hello. "Who is Riley dating?" I asked when she answered.

"I don't think he's *dating* anyone," Kara said carefully.

"He told me a girl asked him out. And since *I'm* your best friend, not Riley, I want you to tell me who the girl is."

"Christine really knows more about it than I do."

"Fine, I'm calling Christine."

I hung up on Kara and dialed Christine's number as I paced in the hallway.

"Who is Riley dating?" I asked when she answered.

"I don't think—"

"Come on, I just had this exact same conversation with Kara."

"As far as I know, he's just going out on a date with this girl Gina."

"Did you set him up with her?"

"Lainey, please."

"Well, where'd he meet her?"

"We were having lunch at José Yummy's—"

"I knew this was going to have something to do with you."

"Do you want to hear the story or not?"

"Yes."

"So we went there for lunch, me and Riley and Wallace, and Gina was working there, and she was kind of flirty with Riley, so afterward Wallace told him to go get her number and he didn't want to, obviously because he's still in love with you. But then Wallace said, 'Maybe it will make Lainey jealous.' So Riley went up and got her number. And I assure you he was only doing it to make you jealous. And you're obviously jealous, so it worked. Are you guys back together?"

"Why would I call you and ask you who Riley's dating if Riley and I were back together?"

"Is that one of your sarcastic questions that I'm not really supposed to have an answer for?"

"He's going out with her."

"Well it's your own fault. You should have told him not to."

I heard a crash in the bathroom. "I have to go." I hung up on Christine and then ran to the bathroom to see what Collin had broken now.

Riley wanted to date? Whatever. I had Eric. Eric was cute. Nice. Funny. Cooler than Gina. On the day of Riley's date, I invited myself over to Eric's. We had an absolutely thrilling afternoon, wrapped up in blankets on the couch bed watching TV. He kept the air conditioner blasting all day long and it was always freezing cold in his room. Or apartment. Or basement. Whatever you wanted to call it.

"I'm hungry," I said, running my hands through the hair on his chest. Riley had been relatively hairless. Yet another reason my new boyfriend was far superior to my old one. Older, wiser, hairier.

"What do you want?" Eric asked.

"I don't know."

"We can make grilled cheese."

"Grilled cheese?"

"Yeah. We'll put the sandwiches between our hot bodies and melt the cheese."

I rolled my eyes, but Eric couldn't see. Despite the fact that I wouldn't let him do much more than kiss me, he thought his naughty jokes were hilarious.

"Didn't you like my joke?" he asked.

"I think it's the cheesiest thing anyone has ever said."

"Cheesiest?" Eric asked. "Was that a pun?"

"Yes," I said.

Eric cracked up, so I gave in and laughed too. "I don't even have cheese," he finally said. "Let's try again."

"How about burgers?"

"Burgers?"

"Mmm, yummy burgers."

"What kind of yummy burgers?"

"From the place we went the first time I worked with you."

"Oh, that place in Annapolis? I'm not going to take you back there if you're planning on getting the same thing."

"Why not?"

"Because you said it was the best burger you'd ever had. And if I take you back, you'll just be disappointed."

"Okay, that's dumb."

"No, it's not. Every time you eat something that blows your mind, and then go back and have it again, it's not as good. And that depresses the hell out of me."

"Well, maybe it will be just as good."

"In my experience, that's never true."

"But it could be."

"I'm going to tell you a story."

"All right. I like stories." I laid my head on his chest. Eric kissed my forehead.

"Once upon a time I worked at a supermarket, and in the same shopping center as this supermarket, there was a snowball stand. So every day after work I stopped at the snowball stand and got a raspberry-flavored snowball. But on one particular day, I was feeling rather decadent, so I opted instead for something called chocolate-covered cherry. It was mind-blowingly delicious. It stopped the world. I could have died happy right then and there eating that snowball. You know what I did the next day?"

I rolled my eyes. "You got another chocolate-covered cherry snowball, and it sucked."

"No. Because I was *smart*, I went back to raspberry. I knew that the conditions of that particular day could never be replicated again, and that the chocolate-covered cherry snowball wasn't going to be the same to me as it had been the day before. And I wanted to remember that perfect moment forever. I didn't want to remember it as the flavor that disappointed me. I want to remember it as the flavor that stopped the world on that hot August afternoon. Instead of spoiling it, I'm never going to get that flavor ever again."

"That's an awful story. You're needlessly depriving yourself."

"You never take anything I say seriously."

"You just keep talking and I'm way too hungry to listen."

"Fine, you want burgers?"

I nodded.

Eric sat up. "All right, we'll get burgers. But you're going to be sorry."

"The chef could be different today," he said as we sat at the table eating peanuts and waiting for our burgers. "Maybe the chef who makes the amazing burgers is off on Wednesdays."

"You're insane."

"Maybe you were really hungry the first time and that's why it tasted so good."

"I'm really hungry now."

"Maybe your body thought it really needed red meat that day."

"My body really wants red meat today too."

"There's a difference between what you need and what you want."

"I'm beginning to think you're too philosophical for a guy who sells magazine subscriptions door-to-door."

"I'm beginning to think you're a little too cocky for a girl who got fired from her job at the mall."

I rolled my eyes.

When our burgers came, Eric didn't touch his; he sat and watched me. I'd already made up my mind that no matter how it tasted, I was going to pretend that it was the best burger ever. So I bit into it and mmmmm'ed and smiled as I chewed.

"It's good?" Eric asked.

"It's perfection," I said.

"Well, I'm glad."

"You're not glad," I said. "You're upset that I proved you wrong."

"I'm paying nine bucks for that burger. Trust me, I'm glad you're enjoying it."

"You know, I have a philosophy too."

"Yeah, what's that?"

"You don't know until you try."

"That's a fine philosophy."

"Thank you very much."

I finished my burger and then picked at my fries until the cashier brought the check. After we'd paid and walked out to the parking lot, I asked Eric, "Can we check out that snowball stand now?"

The snowball stand was outside of Weil's, the grocery store that Mom and I used to shop at when we lived in the old house. It had been the closest one and we could walk there. There hadn't been a snowball stand in the parking lot back then. I wondered if Eric had ever gone shopping there with his mom before the existence of the snowball stand, if maybe we'd passed by each other in the aisles.

A pretty girl with long dark hair greeted us at the snowball stand and stood there patiently while I looked at the menu. It had been ages since I'd had a snowball.

"What do you recommend?" I asked the girl.

She shrugged. "I don't eat them. I don't like sweets."

"I've heard good things about the raspberry," Eric said, running his fingers through my hair.

"Okay," I told the girl. "One raspberry and one chocolate-covered cherry." While the girl made our snowballs, I poked Eric in the ribs. "My philosophy is about to kick your philosophy's butt."

"We'll see," he said. "You know, you can't even find snowballs outside of Baltimore."

"I don't believe that," I said.

"It's true. You might be able to get a snow cone, but it's not the same. Not as good."

We took our snowballs and carried them to the car. He put his snowball in the cup holder and we drove back to his place.

"Please take a bite," I said.

He shook his head. "Can't eat and drive."

"You're just wasting time."

"I'll take a bite when we get home."

The longer he waited, the more nervous I got. He was going to hate it.

When we got back to Eric's place, he mixed the snowball together and then took a bite.

"Well?" I asked. But his face told me it was not going to stop the world. At least not in a good way.

"Way too sweet," he said. "Way too rich."

"Take another bite."

He did and then pushed the cup away.

"No, I can't even eat this. I must have been ready to go into a diabetic coma that day if I thought something this sweet tasted that good."

I sat down on the bed. "I'm sorry."

Eric smiled and rubbed my shoulder. "It's just a snowball."

"But I ruined your memory."

"No, you didn't," he said.

I held out my raspberry. "Trade?"

He kissed me on the cheek and we traded snowballs.

"You just can't go back and expect your mind to be blown by the same thing every time," he said. "Life doesn't work that way."

"Then why didn't you try a new flavor every day?" I asked. "You said you always got raspberry."

He thought about it for a moment. "Well, there's

something to be said for consistency. Monogamy, if you will."

"But consistency doesn't blow your mind."

"No, it doesn't."

"It's boring to do the same thing over and over."

"Yeah, but it's safe."

"It's more fun to be different."

"It is." Eric grinned at me. "You don't know until you try, right?"

—————

My cell phone rang that night just as I was trying to put Collin to bed. I reached for it, and Collin bolted for his room.

"Hello?" I said.

"Hi, is this Lainey?" A girl's voice.

"Yeah, who's this?"

"I just wanted to say thank you," she said. "I had a great time with Riley tonight." I heard giggling in the background. Then she hung up.

16

REVENGE

Vallery and I sat on the couch at six o'clock on Saturday looking down at our legs. Mabel had begged us to let her keep Collin overnight. It was sweet how she did us a favor but made it seem like we were doing her one. It made me feel bad for all the times I'd silently mocked her Basket Bingo nights. As a result of Mabel keeping Collin, Vallery and I had no idea what to do with ourselves.

"Margaritas?" Vallery suggested.

"Absolutely not."

"What do you want to do, then?"

I shrugged. "We could go out to dinner."

"Yeah," she said. "That would be nice. What did you have in mind?"

"We could go to José Yummy's."

"What the hell is José Yummy's?"

"It's this Mexican place. I've been wanting to try it out."

"I didn't think you liked Mexican food."

"It's supposed to be really good. I'll pay."

"How do you have any money?"

"I don't give you *everything*. I keep gas money."

"And taco money."

"Do you want to go, or not?"

"Fine."

Vallery grabbed my arm as we walked in. "Oh my God. They're freaking me out," she said.

I stopped walking. Three girls stood behind the counter. I didn't want to get too close, just in case. "Who?"

"The peppers."

"What?" I asked. I tried to read the name tags of the girls behind the counter, but we were too far away.

She pointed at the wall. "The peppers have faces. And they're wearing sombreros."

"Get over it," I said. "They won't hurt you."

And then I saw her there behind the counter in her green T-shirt and white apron. It was the handbag kiosk girl. Awful remedial math class girl! It was her. She was Gina. I didn't even have to see her name tag to know it.

"What is wrong with you tonight?" Vallery asked. "You're being weird."

I handed her my wallet. "Just get me whatever you're getting. I'll get a table."

I walked away before she could argue. I sat down in the corner and stared at Gina. I watched as she doled out cheese, tomatoes, lettuce, sour cream. She looked strong and tan and had her hair up in one of those side pony-tails like the girls on the field hockey team used to wear. I couldn't remember if she'd been on the field hockey team. I wondered if she could see me in the corner star-ing at her.

What was she doing working here, anyway? Had she quit the kiosk job, or did she work both? Maybe she was saving up for college like Kara.

Vallery walked over with a tray and sat down across from me.

"Do you think that girl's pretty?" I asked. "The one who puts the cheese and lettuce and stuff on the tacos."

"Uh, are you interested in her?" Vallery asked.

"No. She's dating Riley."

"He's dating already? What a bastard."

"Yeah, well, I'm dating someone else too."

"That's different. You dumped him. He's supposed to pine after you."

"Well, he's not."

"How'd you find out?"

"He told me. He asked if it was okay."

Vallery rolled her eyes and shook her head. "And you told him it was okay."

"Well, what else was I supposed to tell him?"

She tilted her head to the side and twirled her hair. "'I

love you, Riley; please don't ever love anyone but me.'"

"If you're trying to mimic me, you're doing a really bad job. Anyway, she called me."

"Who?"

"That girl. Gina."

"She called you? And said what?"

"She thanked me. For dumping him. I guess they had a really great time."

"You're kidding me."

I shook my head.

"What a bitch. I can't believe we let her touch our tacos." She pushed her food away.

I pushed it back toward her. "It's my own fault, anyway."

"Why would he think it's okay to date that skank? He knows you're just being wishy-washy and that you're going to come back to him. And he's only trying to make you jealous. And then letting her call you? That's so wrong."

"Okay, first, I'm dating Eric. I don't want Riley back."

"Liar. If you're so serious about Eric, why haven't I ever met him?"

"You met him. He came over with his friend Frank."

"No, I never met him. You're getting me confused with your other sister."

I sighed. "*Glamour, Cosmo.* Does this ring a bell?"

Vallery looked at me. "The magazine guy? You're dating the magazine guy?"

I nodded.

Vallery laughed. I sat there and rolled my eyes until she got it out of her system.

"Finished?" I asked.

"No. So wait, you're selling magazines too?"

"Yes. What did you think I was doing?"

"I don't know."

"I thought you knew. You never asked."

"I thought you were doing something shady that you didn't want to tell me about."

"Like what?"

"I don't know. We can get back to that later. Right now, let's talk about this Gina girl. I wish you were telling the truth about not wanting Riley back, because any guy who's going to let his new girlfriend call up his old girlfriend is no kind of guy you want to be dating."

"I doubt he was with her when she called. She probably got my number from Christine."

Vallery raised her eyebrows. "Nice friend."

I shrugged.

"Gina sounds like a huge bitch. I bet she's been plotting to steal Riley away from you."

"Vallery." I sighed.

But she was right. Gina *was* kind of a bitch. The way she'd rubbed my ninety-seven percent in my face every week. The way she never said hi to me like the other kiosk employees did, just tried to sell me her stupid handbags.

"I wonder if it was her," I muttered. I hadn't even meant to say it out loud.

"What?" Vallery asked. "What was her?"

I shook my head. "Nothing."

"Come on, you already started to tell me. You have to finish."

"Remember when you made me leave work early to take Collin to the hospital?"

"Don't start on that again."

"I'm not. Anyway, she was working that day. At the handbag kiosk. She watched me leave. I wonder if she ratted me out."

"Huh. I bet she did. Do you want me to take care of her?"

I shook my head. "No, it was definitely Katie. Rodney said she showed up early that day. She knew I left. And what do you mean, take care of her?"

"I'll take care of her."

"What, like hire a hitman?"

Vallery shushed me. "Lainey! First, don't ever talk like that in public. You never know who's listening. Second, no, I'm not going to hurt her. I'll just make her life a little miserable for a while."

"She didn't get me fired. And it's not her fault I dumped Riley."

"Well, she still sounds like a bitch. I'll take care of her. I know you want me to. I'll just ignore any protesting."

"Please don't do anything."

"Sure thing, Lainey." She winked.

When I called Eric later that night, hoping he'd want to do something that didn't involve lying in bed at his apartment, he told me he had to go to the Laundromat. Any normal girl would have yawned and called someone else, but I sat straight up and asked, "Oh my God, are you serious?"

Laundromat. So obvious, yet it had never occurred to me.

"Unfortunately," Eric said. "The dryer here has been broken for a while now. My stepmom just hangs their clothes on the line. But that's not my style."

"Can I go with you?"

"You want to go to the Laundromat with me?"

"I have so much laundry to do. You have no idea."

"I have some idea. I've seen your room. Is your dryer broken too?"

"No. I just think it'll be fun."

He laughed. "You're weird."

"Give me ten minutes. I'll meet you at your place."

I'd driven past the twenty-four-hour Laundromat before and wondered why there was a need for a twenty-four-hour Laundromat. Who did their laundry at such odd hours that they needed to use a twenty-four-hour Laundromat?

The answer was me and Eric.

We were the only people in the whole Laundromat except for the woman who worked there. She sat inside a big glass room watching a mini TV on her desk. She didn't even look up at us when we came in.

Eric only had one load to do, and he looked really amused as I pulled my dirty clothes out of the hamper and shoved them into three separate washing machines.

"When's the last time you did laundry?" he asked.

I shrugged. "June."

"You don't strike me as that kind of girl."

"What kind of girl?"

"The kind of girl who doesn't stay on top of things. I mean, I've seen your room, so I know you can be a little messy. But otherwise, you seem like you've got it together. What's your deal with laundry?"

"I just don't like doing laundry."

Lie. I'd always loved doing laundry. I loved the smell of the detergent and the dryer sheets and the clothes after they came out of the dryer.

"Is it the washing or the drying that bothers you?" Eric asked.

"Can we talk about something else?"

"Ouch," Eric said. "I'm hitting a nerve. Interesting. Childhood trauma?"

"What kind of childhood trauma could result in me not liking to wash my clothes?"

He shrugged. "Maybe Vallery shoved you in the dryer

when you were a kid."

I realized then how little Eric actually knew about me. Well, he knew who I was that summer—mostly unemployed, a little irritated all the time, jointly responsible for my brother's well-being. But he didn't know Old Lainey at all. He thought Vallery and I had grown up together like normal sisters. No one who knew me would have suggested that Vallery had shoved me in a dryer. Anyone else would have known she'd never had the opportunity.

Eric poked me. "Well?"

"No one ever shoved me in a dryer."

"Well, you clearly have issues with laundry."

"I clearly don't want to talk about laundry anymore."

"Do you keep a journal?"

I slammed the quarters into the last machine and turned to him. "What?"

"A journal. Where you write down your feelings. It seems like you have a lot of stuff bottled up inside."

I thought about Mom's groups, all the women who brought their journals to our living room every week. How many times had Mom said those words to me? *Write down your feelings, don't keep everything bottled up.*

"I don't have anything bottled up. And you're starting to sound like my mother."

Eric laughed. "I'm starting to sound like my own mother."

I sat down next to Eric in one of the bright yellow

plastic chairs. "Your mother told you to keep a journal?"

"Oh, yeah. A few years back, she went to some kind of class, and she'd come home and tell me about all the stuff she'd learned. Like the journaling, writing down your feelings, trusting that everything will turn out all right. All that kind of stuff."

"You got all that from your mom?"

He nodded. "Are you disappointed that I didn't actually come up with all that on my own?"

I shook my head. "So your mom took a class?"

"Yeah. It was a feel-good workshop kind of thing. But my mom really loved it. It changed her life. Anyway, you might want to think about that journaling thing. Maybe it will help you work through your laundry issues."

My mother? He couldn't be talking about my mother.

Well, he could. It was possible.

No, it wasn't. His mom lived in Indiana.

"Where'd your mom take the class?" I asked.

"I'm not sure, but I think it was at this woman's house."

"In Indiana?"

"No, it was before we moved there."

"Where did you live before you moved there?"

"Here. We all lived here before the divorce, then Mom and I went to Indiana, then I came back." Eric grinned. "Are you interested? I can call my mom and find out the details."

"No," I said. "I'm not interested."

My mother. It had to be. All of Eric's theories and advice—straight from my mother. Oh my God. I couldn't get away from her. *Think about that journaling thing.* Even now, even dead, Mom still could nag me.

For two weeks I wore clean clothes. I picked Collin up from camp every afternoon and watched him until Vallery got home from work. Every other night he slept in my bed. I looked at job advertisements in the newspaper, but I didn't call about anything. I went to work with Eric every other day and tried not to engage him in any philosophical discussions out of fear that he'd spout off more of my mother's teachings. I wondered why I didn't just tell him, *Hey, my mom taught those workshops your mom took!* and it could be another neat coincidence to add to the list of neat coincidences that it seemed our relationship had been built on.

Things fell into a routine. Things felt almost normal. And then Christine called one afternoon while I sat on the couch watching TV with Collin.

"You're so selfish!" she screamed after I said hello.

"Okay," I said. "What's your problem?" It had been months since I'd heard Christine this angry. I'd thought impending motherhood had somehow mellowed her.

"You can't just let him be happy, can you? You have to ruin everything."

"I don't know what you're talking about."

"Gina!"

I thought about that night at José Yummy's, when I'd pointed Gina out to Vallery.

She'd done something. Vallery had done something to get even with Gina for doing absolutely nothing to me.

"Okay, Christine, whatever happened, I can guarantee you it wasn't me."

"Oh yeah, right."

My call waiting beeped. It was Kara. Good. Maybe she could let me know what was going on.

"Kara's calling, gotta go," I said to Christine, and then clicked over to Kara.

"Please tell me what Christine has up her ass," I said.

"She just called and asked me to pick sides."

"Sides for what?"

"Apparently whatever you did to this Gina girl has created some huge rift in Christine's world. Gina is Jamie's boyfriend's cousin or something, and now the boyfriend is upset that his cousin is upset, and Jamie's upset that her boyfriend is upset, and they know you had something to do with it, and they know Christine and I are good friends with you, so they think we might have something to do with it. It's all very complicated and ridiculous."

"I didn't have anything to do with this," I said. "It was all Vallery. She threatened to get back at Gina for me, but I told her not to do anything. God, she's nuts. What happened to Gina?"

"She lost her job. And broke out in some kind of rash.

273

There may be more to it than that, but that's all I could get out of Christine."

"You know I didn't have anything to do with this. You're on my side, right?"

Kara laughed. "I'm not getting in the middle of this."

"Oh my God. Okay. I have to talk to Vallery. I'll call you back."

<hr/>

I started to dial Vallery's work number, but then I hung up. Ruining my life probably didn't count as an emergency to Vallery, so I waited patiently until she got home.

"What did you do to Gina?" I asked as she walked in the door. "Christine called me today, flipping out about whatever you did to her."

I expected her to deny it, but she just smiled and put her purse on the counter. "Sit down and I'll tell you all about it."

I sat down on the couch. Vallery came in and sat across from me in Carl's recliner.

"Well, first I had to get Gina's work schedule. I went back to José Yummy's that night. I waited for Gina to leave, then I called the restaurant pretending to be her and I asked for her schedule."

"Oh my God, you are such a stalker."

"Anyway. I started to go in during Gina's shift. I'd order something weird every time, you know, make it real complicated and yell if she got it wrong, and make her redo everything two or three times."

"I cannot believe you."

Vallery smiled. "I complained and told her the bathrooms were dirty. I told her the fountain Coke tasted funny. I let Collin run around and make a mess. It was pretty damn hilarious, but of course it drove her nuts. Finally I got her to blow up at me. You would not believe the things that came out of this girl's mouth. Before I even had to chance to say I wanted to talk to her manager, she threw her apron down and walked out."

She winked at me—winked at me!—and then went into the kitchen and opened the refrigerator.

I walked up behind her. "Why would you do that?" I asked. "Now that she's unemployed, she just has more time to spend with Riley."

Vallery took a pickle out of the jar and sat down at the table. "No. Trust me. This doesn't reflect well on her. Would you want to date a girl who couldn't handle working at a taco restaurant?"

"God, Vallery, what if Riley realized it was you? He's going to think we're completely crazy."

"He has no idea."

"She probably called him every night and told him about the bitchy blond girl and the crazy Puerto Rican boy who terrorized her. Vallery! God!"

"Later you're going to think about this and appreciate everything I did for you."

"What's up with the rash? How'd you give her a rash?"

Vallery laughed. "Christine said I gave her a *rash*? How would I even do that? Voodoo?"

"I don't know. You tell me."

"I didn't give her a rash."

"I don't believe you."

"You and your friends are paranoid."

"You're ruining my life, do you realize that?"

She shook her head. "You'll think about it later and you'll thank me."

17

AN UNEXPECTED ARRIVAL

Vallery had started making little to-do lists for me every morning. The fact that she was quickly ruining my life had no impact whatsoever on whether or not I still had to spend part of my day running her errands. The next morning she left this list for me:

1. Go to grocery store and get: bread (whole wheat, not that white crap), dozen eggs (large, check them), snacks for Collin's lunch, 2-liter Diet Coke, 1 lb ground beef, whatever else you think we need.
2. Put ground beef in fridge. Sloppy joes tonight?
3. Wash dishes. Rewash big pan—it looks cruddy.
4. Buy stamps and put bills in mail.

I rinsed off the pan and put it in the dish rack, then crossed it off the list. I wasn't washing that stupid pan again. I'd done a perfectly good job the first time. If she didn't like it, she could wash it herself. I grabbed the list and the bills and headed for the door.

When I opened the door, I saw a man with slicked-back hair walking up to the house. He wore jeans and a denim shirt with the sleeves rolled up to his elbows. His arms, at least from what I could see, were covered in tattoos. He had a goatee, and a hoop earring in each ear. I looked past him and saw a motorcycle parked in front of our house. Judging by the tattoos and the bike, he could have been one of Carl's old friends. But considering the denim outfit and stupid earrings, he was probably one of Mom's ex-boyfriends. A little younger, but sometimes she went for the younger ones.

"Are you looking for Carl or Lisa?" I asked. "'Cause they're both dead."

He stopped at the bottom of the porch steps and gave me a funny look. "Uh, I'm actually looking for Vallery Lancaster."

"Oh. Who are you?"

He smiled and shook his head. "Pardon me, I forgot my manners." He held out his hand. I took a few steps toward him and he took a few steps up to the porch. "I'm Lenard Fry Jr."

"Nice to meet you," I said.

"So is Vallery around?"

Since I was about five, I'd been trained on how to handle men who come to the door: Get rid of them for Mommy. If Vallery was anything like Mom, she wouldn't want me to tell Mr. Lenard Fry Jr. where she was. And who *was* this guy? As far as I knew, the only people Vallery had met in Baltimore I didn't already know were from work. If she knew this guy from work, he'd know she wouldn't be home in the middle of the day. I shouldn't do her any favors, but this guy seemed shady.

I shook my head. "She doesn't live here. Haven't heard from her lately either. Are you a bill collector? Is she giving people this address again?"

He shook his head. "I knew her back in Dallas. She came home from work one day and told me her mom was dead. Then she just disappeared. I can't get ahold of her. I just wanted to know if things were all right. Are you her sister?"

I nodded.

"She told me about you. I pictured you younger."

"How did you know where we live?"

He gave me a half smile. "It's kind of embarrassing."

I shrugged.

"Well, I looked up all the obituaries in Baltimore and found her mother. Your mother, I mean. Then I looked your mother up in the phone book and found the address."

Stalker. Vallery and this guy had probably been perfect for each other. "What do you want Vallery for?" I asked.

"Well . . . I just wanted to see what happened to her. I got worried, you know."

"You couldn't call?"

"I tried."

"Well, she was here for the funeral. But she left, I don't know, maybe two months ago."

"No kidding?"

I nodded.

He shook his head and looked away from me.

"I'm real sorry," I said.

He ran his hands through his hair. "I just really needed to see her. Listen, I don't know where I'm staying yet, but maybe I can stop by tomorrow and give you the number? In case you hear from her?"

I nodded. "Okay. I don't expect to hear from her soon, though."

I watched Lenard Fry Jr. walk back to his motorcycle and ride off. Then I ran through the house, made sure all the doors and windows were locked, and went out to run Vallery's errands.

Collin's teacher called my cell phone just as I left the post office.

"Hello, Miss Pike. This is Mrs. Young. How are you?"

I squeezed my eyes shut and forced some cheerfulness

into my voice. "I'm fine, Mrs. Young. What can I do for you?"

"I'd like to have a meeting with you this afternoon when you come to pick up Collin. I just spoke to Ms. Lancaster, and she said you'd be available."

"Absolutely!" I said. "See you then!"

<hr/>

It was weird being in an elementary school again after so long. I felt ten years old again, like I shouldn't be walking around without a hall pass.

When I walked into the office and sat down beside Collin, I felt nauseous, like I was the one in trouble.

"What did you do?" I whispered to Collin.

He didn't answer. He stared straight ahead and kicked his chair.

After the rest of the kids had gotten on the bus or been picked up by their parents, Mrs. Young walked in and had us follow her back to her classroom. She sat at her desk. She took off her glasses and let them hang from a chain around her neck.

"Collin had a bad day," she said.

I nodded. "That happens." I held my hand out to Collin in case he wanted to hold it, but he didn't move.

"I'm afraid he got out of hand during art time today and hit our friend Zachary Milligan."

I raised my eyebrows. "Our friend?"

Mrs. Young tried to smile, but her lips didn't quite make it. "That's how we refer to everyone here at camp."

I looked down at Collin. "Isn't Zachary the same boy who made you shove a crayon in your ear?"

He nodded but wouldn't look at me.

Mrs. Young shook her head. "That's not what happened, Miss Pike."

"Did you see it happen?"

Mrs. Young shook her head. "Several students told me what happened."

"Well, I don't believe everyone else. I believe my brother, and this Zachary kid sounds like he's a bully. If Collin hit him, he probably deserved it."

"We do not condone violence in the classroom under any circumstances. Mrs. Milligan is understandably quite upset about the incident, and we'd like to have a meeting on Monday afternoon to discuss it."

"That's fine. My sister Vallery will be attending that meeting."

"Okay. I'll call your sister and we'll discuss it further."

"All right."

I took Collin's hand and we walked out to the Grand Am.

He didn't say anything, but I knew what he was thinking. He had that deer-in-the-headlights, I'm-going-to-get-it-now expression on his face. Like when I caught him eating a whole box of Twinkies, or when I found him crouched on my dresser after he broke my snow globe.

"I'm not mad," I said to him. He only had one more

week of camp left anyway, so who cares if he couldn't get along with Zach Milligan. "I know you probably didn't even do anything wrong. But listen, we're going to visit Vallery at work now, so I need you to be very good for me. Okay?"

He nodded.

I knew Collin's being injured hadn't been that urgent to her, and I wasn't sure if Lenard Fry Jr.'s sudden appearance constituted an emergency either, but I thought it was better to be safe. I had no idea what kind of trouble she might have gotten herself into back in Dallas before she left.

Vallery's office was about a ten-minute drive up the beltway. It wasn't anything fancy—just a plain brown building. The elevator didn't come fast enough, so we took the stairs. The second door down the hallway had a little sign on it that said PARKER ASSOCIATES. I rang the buzzer. When we walked in, Vallery was on the phone. She pointed to a couple of chairs by the door and we sat down. I gave Collin a fishing magazine to look at. He flipped through the pages and swung his legs.

Vallery hung up the phone and walked over. "I already heard. That was Mrs. Young."

"Does the name Lenard Fry Jr. mean anything to you?"

Vallery stared at me without blinking. "Where did you hear that name?" she whispered. "Did he call?"

I wondered if Lenard Fry Jr. was a bounty hunter. They'd done a story line like that on *Heartstrings* a few years ago. One of the new characters in town had murdered a guy in another state, and the bounty hunter caught up with him.

"I met him today, actually."

"You're *kidding* me!" Vallery whispered. "He came to the *house*?"

"You know him?"

"Jesus. Yes, I know him."

"Is he a bounty hunter?"

"What?"

"Please tell me he's not your boyfriend."

"Lainey, I don't need this."

"Oh God, he is!"

"He *was* my boyfriend. Back in Dallas."

"I can't believe you just left and didn't tell him you weren't coming back!"

"I can't believe *him*. How did he *get* here?"

"He was on a motorcycle. I can't believe you didn't tell me about him."

"He was an idiot. He must have stolen the bike from his brother. He only tracked me down because of the car. He doesn't care that I left—he just wants the goddamned Mustang."

"You stole his car?"

Vallery glared at me. "Of course not. It's my car. It's in my name. I pay for it. But he might have had the impression that I bought it for him."

"Oh God."

"Lainey, shut up."

"You're Mom!"

"Shut up!"

"Lenard Fry Jr. is your Carl Snodgrass."

"I know you think that saying I'm like Mom is the meanest thing you can say to me, so I'm choosing to ignore it. Anyway, what did you tell Len?"

"I told him you came for the funeral and then left, and that I didn't know when I'd hear from you."

Vallery cracked a smile. "You seriously told him that?"

"Yeah. I've been trained to lie to men who knock on the door."

"That was sweet."

"Yeah, well, he's not leaving. He said he's going to find somewhere to stay and then he's coming back tomorrow to give me the number."

"He's probably doing surveillance on the house right now. I'll ask Bunny if I can stay with her tonight."

"You know a girl named Bunny?"

"Don't make fun. You were named after a whore on a soap opera."

"I was not. What am I supposed to do?"

"Well, you and Collin need to go home or he'll get suspicious."

It wasn't my night to keep Collin but I decided to let

it slide. "Wait, what if he tries to break in?"

"Oh for God's sake, Lainey, he just wants the stupid car. He knows you're not hiding it in the house. I know he looks simple, but he's not that dumb. And he's not violent. Don't worry."

"Fine," I said. I didn't believe her, but I couldn't stand in her office all afternoon arguing with her.

"Okay," Vallery said. "Just go home, be cool, and I'll call you tomorrow."

The Grand Am died half a block from the supermarket after we got off the beltway. I managed to guide it onto the shoulder before it sputtered to a stop. I sighed and pulled out my cell phone. I dialed Eric.

"Have a few minutes to come pick up a cute girl and her delinquent brother?"

"You broke down?" he asked.

"Of course."

He sighed. "It was only a matter of time."

I told him where we were, and he talked to me as he drove. He told me how many magazines he and Frank had sold. I told him about the errands Vallery had me run. I considered telling him about Lenard Fry Jr., but then I realized I'd have to explain entirely too much for the story to make sense, so I didn't bother.

When he got there, Eric piled the groceries in the trunk while I strapped Collin and his booster seat into Eric's car.

"Long day," I said to Eric, and shook my head.

When we got to my house, I didn't see Lenard Fry Jr. hiding in the bushes. Collin ran to his room.

"Want to stay with me tonight?" I asked Eric. "Collin has to sleep with us, though."

Eric shrugged. "All right."

He went into the living room and turned on the television. I pulled out my cell phone and called Vallery at work.

"It's your night to keep Collin," I said.

"Lainey!"

"Do me a favor and I'll let it slide."

"Fine, what do you need?"

"The Grand Am is broken down on Franklin Boulevard."

"Okay, I'll call a tow truck or something. I'll talk to you tomorrow."

"Bye, Val."

⊷ ⋯⋙✦⋘⋯ ⊶

Eric and I hadn't spent the night together before. With a six-year-old boy between us, it got even more awkward. Eric rolled over about fifteen times before I jabbed him in the side and said, "Just go sleep on the couch." He kissed me on the cheek and then climbed over me and Collin and left the room. I would have just sent him home, but I wanted him there in case I needed him. I'd found a baseball bat in the garage and left it by my door, thinking that Collin and I could hide under my bed and I would call the police while Eric fought off Vallery's boyfriend.

"Time to play?" Collin asked.

"No," I whispered. I wrapped my arm around him. "Bedtime. Sleep."

I wanted to feel safe knowing that Eric was in the living room and could take Vallery's wimpy Texas boyfriend if it came down to it. Well, he probably could. Eric had skinny arms and he seemed like kind of a pacifist, but he'd do what he had to do.

I wouldn't have worried at all if Riley had been there. He wasn't a violent guy, but I knew he could throw a punch.

And he knew how to keep Collin in check.

And he seemed to fit perfectly in my bed. He'd never bail on me and sleep on the couch.

But he was probably, at that very moment, falling more and more in love with Gina and her stupid side ponytail.

As Collin snored beside me, I made a mental list of all the clichés Mom might have used in this situation.

A good man is hard to find.

The grass is always greener.

If you love something, set it free.

You always want what you can't have.

18

AN UNEXPECTED
DEPARTURE

After Collin woke up the next morning and ran for the television, Eric came back to my room and fell asleep beside me. We got out of bed a few hours later, and I went to the kitchen. I looked out the window and didn't see anything suspicious.

"What are we looking for?" Eric asked. I turned and saw him at the window in the living room.

"Nothing. What do you want to eat?"

"Who's that guy in your yard?"

I ran to the window, expecting to see Lenard Fry. Instead I saw Riley bent under the hood of the Grand Am.

"Oh, that's Riley."

"The old boyfriend?"

"The mechanic."

"The old boyfriend."

I nodded. "The old boyfriend."

"When did you call him?"

"I didn't. Anyway, breakfast?"

"Actually, I was going to head home." He gestured to his clothes. "I've been wearing the same thing for like three days."

I shrugged. "All right. I'll walk you out."

I stood on the front steps and hugged Eric. "Give me a call?" he asked. I nodded. He kissed me and then walked to his car.

As Eric drove off, I walked over to the Grand Am.

"Riley?" I said.

He stood up and pushed his hair off his forehead. "Hey."

"What are you doing here?"

He waved his wrench around. "Trying to fix your car."

"But—?" I stood there looking stupid and confused.

"Vallery called me."

"Jesus. I swear I didn't tell her to. I just asked her to take care of it. I thought she'd—"

"Look, I'm just fixing your car, all right? That's what I do. That's my job. It's business. Don't freak out or anything."

"Why aren't you fixing it at the shop?"

"This is a charity case. We can't take charity cases to the shop."

"I'll *pay* you. I'm not a charity case."

Riley shrugged.

"Well, do you at least want something to eat?" I asked. "I'm getting ready to make Collin breakfast."

He looked at his watch. "You haven't fed him yet?"

I rolled my eyes. "Never mind. Invitation revoked."

"That's fine. I have plans later, so I want to get a good start on this now."

Plans. Gina.

Bastard.

My phone rang. I pulled it out of my pocket and held it up. "Sorry, I have to take this," I said to Riley, and walked back into the house. It was only Vallery, but I wanted him to wonder.

"Vallery, what the hell did you think—"

"No, no, no," she interrupted me. "We'll have plenty of time for that later. You have to listen to me now. All right? I need you to pack some things for us. Get a couple days' worth of clothes for you and Collin. And get about ten different outfits for me, because I don't trust your judgment. Casual stuff, though, because I'm skipping work for a few days. And don't touch my underwear—I'll buy more. All right? And grab my Keds. And you and Collin wear comfortable shoes."

"What's going on? Are we entering the witness protection program or something?"

"Just pack. Then meet me on the corner in twenty minutes."

"Are you serious? What's going on?"

Vallery hung up.

I went to the front window and looked for Vallery's ex-boyfriend. If we had to leave the house for a few days, he must be more dangerous than Vallery had been willing to admit.

I went to Vallery's room, grabbed her suitcase, and piled in as many T-shirts, shorts, and socks as would fit. I threw in a handful of underwear too, just because she'd told me not to. I went to Collin's room and packed some clothes in his backpack. Then I went to my room and packed. Before I zipped my bag, I picked up my mother's copy of *Another Day* off the floor and threw it into my bag. I didn't know where we were going or how boring it might be, so it was best to be prepared.

I went into the living room. "Come here, Collin," I said. He ignored me, of course, and stood in front of the television, hopping on one foot. I slid his backpack onto his shoulders, which wasn't easy to do when he decided to hop and not cooperate.

"School today?" he asked.

"No school. We're going for a drive in the car."

I went around the house again and made sure all the doors were locked. Then I put my backpack on and picked up Vallery's suitcase. I turned off the TV and grabbed Collin's hand and went outside. Riley must have gone into the garage, because I didn't see him when we walked outside. "Be quiet and hurry up," I whispered to Collin as I pulled him across the yard. I didn't know which corner

Vallery had meant, so I just walked to the left.

We didn't have to wait long before Vallery pulled up in the convertible.

"Get in the car, Collin," I said. I threw our bags in the back. I buckled Collin in and then climbed into the front seat.

"Where are we going?" I asked. "Are we staying with Bunny?"

Vallery looked at me. "No."

"Are we going to a hotel?"

"Yes."

"Lenard Fry really is dangerous? Shouldn't we call the cops?"

"No, Lainey, he's harmless. I just don't want to deal with him."

"So . . . we're just going to hide?"

Vallery nodded.

She turned onto the interstate. The top of the convertible was down, like always, and the wind whipped my hair around. We drove for about fifteen minutes, and then I started wondering where we were going. After thirty minutes, I asked. "Um, where exactly is this hotel?"

"Lainey, can't we just have a quiet drive?"

"I'd just like to know where we're going."

"I want it to be a surprise."

"Fine, but give me a hint."

"Okay. Your hint is: It's a long drive."

"How long is a long drive?"

"Um, a few hours."

"*Hours*? How many hours?"

"I don't know exactly. Maybe fifteen."

"Vallery! You're taking us back to Dallas?"

"No. Dallas? No way."

"Do you realize that we're running away?"

"It's a trip. Not running away."

"So where are we going?"

Vallery sighed. "Florida," she whispered.

"Florida?" I screamed.

"God, Lainey!"

"Disney World?" Collin yelled from the backseat.

"Yes," Vallery said, glancing back at him. "That's exactly where we're going."

"Oh my God," I muttered. And after that we had a quiet drive for a while because I was too shocked to form a coherent thought.

⋆⋅☆⋅⋆

After we crossed into Virginia, my cell-phone battery died. Had I packed the charger? Of course not. I convinced Vallery to stop at the next rest area so I could use the bathroom. While she was at the vending machines outside buying snacks, I went inside and looked around. Lottery tickets? Check. Virginia mugs? Check. Beef jerky? Check. Cell-phone chargers? Of course not. Well, it wasn't like anyone wanted to talk to me anyway.

When I came back out, Collin and Vallery were both eating chocolate bars. Vallery handed one to me.

"Thanks," I said. We got back in the Mustang, and Vallery drove back onto the highway.

"We're really actually going to Orlando?" I asked. "All the way to Orlando?"

"Yes."

"Just because you don't want to face your ex-boyfriend."

"Oh, it's more than that. I don't want to deal with Len. And I don't want to go to work on Monday and answer the stupid telephone. I don't want to go to this conference and talk to this woman whose kid Collin beat up. I don't want to look at all of Mom's stuff still lying around my room. I don't want to think about the bills. Don't you ever just lose it? All the little stuff adds up and then you snap?"

"Mom called it being on the verge," I said. "But she never drove us all the way to Orlando when it happened. She usually just cried."

"Well, your mother and I are very different."

"First, she's your mother too. And second, no, you're not."

"Whatever, Lainey. I guess you'd know better than I would. It's not like I ever got to know her. I barely existed."

"I know what you mean."

"You do not."

"Yes, I do. After she got Collin, I was practically invisible."

"You were what, twelve?"

"Fourteen."

"Yeah, well, Mom divorced my dad when I was three. She let him have custody and she picked me up on the weekends. Some weekends. And sometimes only for just an hour. And then you were born when I was seven, and she couldn't deal with two kids at the same time, so guess which one she forgot all about?"

I didn't know what to say. I'd never really thought of it that way before, that Mom had let Vallery go. I'd always assumed that Vallery's dad decided to take her away and there wasn't much Mom could do about it. "I'm sorry, Val."

"The funny thing is, I was excited when she got pregnant. You have no idea how much I wanted a sister. Did you ever wonder why I didn't come around, or did she just pretend like I didn't exist?"

Okay, honestly? I'd kind of liked it that she was far away. I'd never wanted a brother or sister. I'd never wanted to share anything.

"I don't know," I said. "I always thought you were lucky, because you got to leave."

"Are you on *crack*?" Vallery asked. "I have maybe three good memories of Mom. Collin's hardly going to remember her at all. You have almost eighteen years of memories of her. Eighteen years!"

"They're not good memories. I hated living with her. I always wished she'd let me move in with my grandmother."

"Well that's really sad. She's your *mother*."

"But she wasn't a *good* mother."

"Yeah, well at least she kept you. And at least she didn't kill herself before you even started first grade."

"Oh God, let's not do this. Let's not argue over who Mom screwed over more."

"It's Collin," Vallery said. "There's no argument."

I nodded. "You're right. Can we put the top up now?"

"No."

"Well, can I drive for a while?"

"Not yet. You can drive when I'm tired."

"So how long are we staying? How will we know when Lenard Fry's gone?"

"I don't know."

"Maybe he's really just upset that you left him," I suggested. "Maybe he came to Baltimore to win you back."

Vallery snorted. "You met him. Does he look like the sentimental type? He just wants the stupid car. He thinks I'll be dumb enough to give it to him like I was dumb enough to do everything for him before. And why do you want to go home, anyway? You have no job. You're caught up in this ridiculous love triangle. All your friends are mad at you."

"I sell magazines." Sometimes. When Frank didn't feel like it.

"That's not a real job."

"Have I been giving you real money?"

"Sorry. Point taken."

"Are you sure we can't put the top up?"

"Just deal with it."

I reached into the backseat and grabbed my backpack, hoping I'd find a ponytail holder to wrangle my hair under control. As I dug around in the pocket, my hand closed around something sticky and melted and disgusting.

"Oh no," I muttered. I pulled my hand out, and it was covered in chocolate.

Vallery looked over. "Oh, nasty. Don't touch anything!"

"Well, get me some napkins!"

Vallery steered with one hand and dug around in the glove compartment with the other. "Why are you so *messy*?"

"It wasn't *me*!" I turned to look at Collin. "Did you stick your chocolate bar in my backpack?"

Collin looked away.

I shook my head. "Why do you care if I get chocolate on the seats anyway? You're going to have to give it back to Lenard Fry soon."

"I'm leaving you at the next rest area," Vallery said. She found a handful of napkins under her seat and flung them at me. One blew away in the wind, and I grabbed the rest and wiped off my hands and then did the best I could to clean the chocolate out of my bag.

"How many more hours?" I asked.

"I don't know. But no more food in the car. I knew that was a bad idea."

——◆——

As we drove through North Carolina, the signs for South of the Border accosted us at every mile. I wasn't even sure what it was—some sort of bizarre amusement park rest stop? But we'd been driving for so long. Come on, how could you read a billboard that said "You never sausage a place" and *not* stop?

"Please, Vallery," I said as we passed another billboard.

She knew exactly what I was talking about. "It's just a stupid tourist trap." She sighed.

"I think Collin needs to learn about his Mexican heritage."

"I'm not falling for that. You already told me he's not Mexican."

For the next twenty miles I started the argument every time we passed a new billboard. I'd given up on actually going to South of the Border. Now the fun was just in seeing how much I could annoy Vallery. But as we crossed the state line into South Carolina, Vallery took the first exit.

"You're the best sister ever!" I screamed when I realized we were headed for the Border. I'd been cooped up in the car for hours. I was getting kind of giddy.

After Vallery parked, I led the way to a gift shop, which I figured would be air-conditioned. Vallery wandered off, so I took Collin's hand, and we walked up and down the aisles. He picked up every other thing and asked if I'd buy it for him. Finally I bought him a sombrero because he looked adorable in it, and I got "Amigo of Pedro" buttons for each of us. I pinned mine on and then stuck one to Collin's shirt.

"We should get some dinner," Vallery said, catching up with us as we walked away from the register.

I looked at my watch. "Yeah, I guess so. Hey, I got you something."

Vallery stepped back when I came at her with the button. "No way am I wearing that. You are not punching holes in this shirt."

"Vallery, come on. Are you seriously going to be uptight on *vacation?*"

"Yes."

Collin pointed to his button. "I got one," he said. "Lainey's got one."

Collin and I both stared at her until she finally took the button from me and pinned it to the belt loop on her jean shorts.

When we got outside, Collin ran straight for a cactus statue, so Vallery and I sat in the grass and watched him climb on it. After a while a family with about ten kids came up. The mom had her camera ready. The kids stared at Collin. The family turned and gave us dirty looks, but Collin didn't get down, and we didn't make him. Finally the mom hustled the kids over to another statue. After they were gone, Collin hopped down and ran over to us, waving his sombrero.

"I'm hungry," he said. So we walked to the closest restaurant, where they shockingly didn't even sell tacos, which was good because now tacos made me think of stupid Gina. We ate hot dogs and Collin wanted seconds, so Vallery got back in line to get him another hot dog and an ice cream cone for herself. Then we went back outside and walked around. The night was still hot but had gotten bearable since the sun went down. Collin ran ahead of us, cramming his hot dog into his mouth with one hand and holding on to his sombrero with the other. I smiled. Maybe running away hadn't been such a bad idea. For the first time ever, I seemed to be having a nice evening with my sister and my brother simultaneously.

And then Vallery grabbed my arm. "Back to the car," she whispered in my ear.

"What's wrong?" She spun around and changed directions and headed back for the parking lot. I ran and grabbed Collin's hand. His sombrero fell off. I picked it up and we hurried after Vallery.

She looked over her shoulder. "You drive so I can eat my ice cream." She tossed me the keys.

"No food in the car," I reminded her.

"Oh, shut up."

I buckled Collin in and then started the car. I turned back onto the highway. I kept glancing over at Vallery so she'd know I was waiting for her to explain herself, but she sat there with her ice cream and didn't look at me.

"What was the big deal back there?" I finally asked.

"I thought I saw someone I used to know."

"Do you always run from people you know?"

I didn't look over at her, but I could feel her glaring at me. "Only when I don't want to talk to them."

"Who'd you see?"

"This girl I went to college with. I guess it probably wasn't even her, though. I mean, what are the odds? This friggin' ice cream is melting so fast. Why is it still so hot?"

"We're in the south. Do you realize you are *crazy* paranoid?"

I glanced over at Vallery. The ice cream had melted onto her hands. She couldn't lick it because the wind whipped her hair into her face, and she couldn't touch her hair with her sticky hands.

"Lainey, I think we need to pull over."

"All right."

"This is running down my arm. Gross."

Collin started humming.

The dish detergent commercial. I groaned.

"Enjoy your feast—then cut the grease! CUT THE GREASE!"

"Please, Collin. Not now," I said.

I put the blinker on and checked the mirror. Then I

thought about the chocolate-bar incident. This was karma in action. I shouldn't make it easy for Vallery. I flew past the next exit.

"CUT THE GREASE!" Collin yelled.

"Collin, please."

Vallery smacked my arm. "What are you doing?"

"I'm going to the next rest stop. I don't want to pull off just anywhere. We don't know what kind of neighborhoods are around here."

"Fine. Good point."

Vallery was quiet until we passed a sign that said the next rest area was seventeen miles away.

"This ice cream is going to be all over the car by the time we get there!" she screamed. "Pull over!"

I got off at the next exit and turned into the first McDonald's. "If you'd let me put the roof up, you would have been able to eat your ice cream instead of wearing it," I said. "And if you weren't so friggin' paranoid, we could have walked around South of the Border like a bunch of normal people."

Vallery turned and glared at me. Her hair stuck to her face in a very unattractive way. Mine probably didn't look much better, but at least I wasn't covered in ice cream. "Come open the door for me," she said.

I laughed at how helpless she'd become.

"Come on!" she yelled.

I got out of the car and went around to the passenger's side. Vallery held the ice cream up and away from the car.

I opened her door. As she stepped out, she reached out and smeared ice cream on my cheek.

My mouth dropped open. Vallery grinned her stupid wicked grin.

I'd had about enough of Vallery. I grabbed the ice cream out of her hand and smashed it into her forehead. The cone fell to the ground, and ice cream rolled down her face. She wiped it out of her eyes. I laughed. And then before I knew what had happened, she'd knocked me over into the grass.

Vallery pinned me to the ground and wiped the ice cream off of her face and into my hair. Sticks and leaves poked into my back and legs. I reached up and stuck my finger in her ear. She grabbed my arm and bit me—bit me!—and pinned my other arm to the ground with her knee. I hit her in the shoulder with my free hand and then stuck my finger up her nose.

"Gross!" she screamed. "You are *gross*!"

I pushed her off me and rolled on top of her. "Truce?" I yelled.

"Fine, fine, truce!"

I rolled off her and quickly realized that we had an audience. One of the workers from the McDonald's stood by the entrance, fanning herself with her visor. A man and woman in a pickup had stopped just past the drive-thru to stare at us. A man climbed out of his tractor-trailer and walked across the parking lot toward us. He had a big grin on his face.

"Oh Jesus," I muttered as I helped Vallery up. "Look what you did."

Vallery brushed twigs off her legs. "We can't get into the car like this," she said. "No friggin' way."

"We have to," I said. "These people are freaking me out." The pickup drove off, but the McDonald's worker and the tractor-trailer guy were still staring at us from across the parking lot. "Let's at least act like we're leaving, and maybe they'll go away."

"Fine."

Vallery walked toward the driver's side of the Mustang, and I walked to the passenger side. We noticed the empty backseat at the same time.

Vallery turned toward the trees. "Collin!"

I bent down and looked on the floor to make sure he wasn't just hiding from us. I thought about the pickup and wondered if they'd snatched him. I couldn't remember what kind of truck it had been, or even the color. I didn't know what the people had looked like.

And then Vallery ran across the parking lot toward the McDonald's. I looked over and saw Collin walking up to her with his arms full of paper towels. Vallery picked him up and carried him back to the car, holding him to her chest.

"What is wrong with you?" I yelled at Collin. "Don't ever get out of the car unless we tell you to!"

He stared at me as Vallery let him down. He held out the paper towels. "You were sticky," he said.

I sighed.

"At least he's being sweet," Vallery hissed at me. "Say thank you."

"I'm not thanking him for almost getting kidnapped."

Vallery rolled her eyes at me and took the paper towels. We wiped the ice cream and dirt off of us as best we could and then laid the rest of the paper towels on the seats.

"I can't wait to take a shower," I said. "We're stopping at the very next motel we see. I don't care how shady it looks."

"We're not stopping now," Vallery said. "Orlando or bust."

"Orlando or *bust*? Are you kidding me? We're covered in ice cream."

"We only have two states to go."

"We have like eight hours to go!"

"Come on, it's not that late. We'll get to Orlando before morning, take a shower, sleep for a while, then go see Mickey Mouse."

I rolled my eyes. "At least stop at the next rest area so we can change our clothes."

"Fine."

We changed our clothes at the next rest stop. I tried to stay awake while Vallery drove, but eventually I leaned the seat back and fell asleep. Vallery woke me up a few hours later.

"Are we there?" I asked. Then I looked around and realized we were at another rest stop. I looked in the backseat and saw Collin slumped over, asleep.

"We've got a few more hours," Vallery said. "Can you let me take a nap?"

"Fine," I mumbled. We got out of the car and switched places. Vallery fell asleep before we were even out of the parking lot.

I listened to the radio, but every time I found a good station, I drove out of its signal area. After a while I decided I would play the alphabet game, except I'd find words instead of thinking them up. That would keep me alert and paying attention to the road instead of falling asleep and driving into a tree.

So *A*. That was easy. The van in front of me with Georgia plates had an Alpharetta High School bumper sticker.

B was easy too. The word *business* on a billboard for cell phones.

C took a while, but finally I spotted a Checkers restaurant advertised on one of those blue signs that tell you what's coming up at the next exit.

Then I saw *Days Inn* on the next blue sign.

Ten minutes went by and I couldn't find an *E*. I flipped through the stations on the radio. I spent ten more minutes looking for an *E*. Then my eyes started to shut.

"Orlando or bust," I muttered to myself. I slapped my cheek. I opened my eyes wide. I pinched my leg.

I tried to find an *E*, but I could barely hold my eyes open.

Finally I crossed the border into Florida.

"Close enough," I said. I pulled off at the Florida welcome center and shook Vallery awake. "I'm tired," I said. "Tag."

Vallery got out and rubbed her eyes as she walked around the car. I climbed over into the passenger seat.

"I don't know if I can stay awake," she said.

"You better," I snapped.

"What's your problem?"

"I'm tired."

"Like I'm not."

"You wanted to keep driving."

"Lainey."

"Vallery."

She adjusted the rearview mirror. "Will you talk to me?"

"You didn't talk to me. Just play the alphabet game like I did. I got stuck on *E*."

Vallery yawned. "Okay."

I leaned my head back against the seat and shut my eyes. Vallery started the car and pulled back onto the highway. She slapped my leg. "Exit, Lainey. Duh."

"Mmmm," I mumbled.

"Let's see," she said. "*F*—"

"No," I said. "You play in your head."

19

A FUN FAMILY VACATION

The next time I woke up, we were parked in front of a motel.

Vallery checked in and came back to the car with our keys. Collin was sleeping, so I carried him inside and laid him on one of the double beds. Vallery went into the bathroom to take a shower. I sat down on the bed with Collin.

Then I realized: *We're in Orlando!*

I walked across the room and opened the dresser drawers until I found the white pages. I sat on the bed and looked up Elaine Pike. Still there. I tore the page out and then looked up Aunt Liz. I tore out that page too. I folded them and slipped them into my pocket. I put the phone book away and lay down on the bed beside Collin.

Vallery came out twenty minutes later in her pajamas with her hair wrapped up in a towel. We watched TV while I waited for the hot water to heat up. Neither of us bothered to change the channel, which played some cheesy advertisement for Disney World. When the ad started playing again from the beginning, I went and took a shower.

"My hair smells like sour milk," I said to Vallery as I came out of the bathroom. She was sprawled out on the bed with her eyes barely open.

"Should have used shampoo."

"I did." I leaned down and sniffed her hair. "You smell too."

"I guess that's what happens when you let ice cream sit in your hair for hours."

"Yeah, that was my idea."

"Good night, Lainey."

"Yeah. Good night." I turned off the light and got into bed with Collin.

——◆——

We slept until the afternoon, and then Vallery went down to the lobby and brought up a bunch of brochures. She spread them out on the bed and told Collin we could do whatever he wanted. He spent about half an hour looking at all the brochures before he finally decided that we should go to the go-cart track next door, which we could see out of our motel window.

"Look at those prices," Vallery whispered to me as we stood in front of the go-cart track.

"Didn't you know everything down here was going to

be expensive?" I asked.

Vallery didn't answer because Collin was pulling on her shirt. "What is it, Collin?" she asked.

He turned around and pointed. "Feed the gators."

We both looked behind us, and Vallery read the sign aloud. "'Feed our gators. Two dollars.' Collin, if we feed the gators, we can't ride go-carts."

"Okay," Collin said.

"Which would you rather do?"

"Gators."

Vallery winked at me. She took Collin's hand, and they walked up to the counter to buy gator food. I walked over and looked into the pit at the alligators swimming around. Did it not occur to her that maybe I'd rather ride go-carts, or did she just not care? I hadn't been on a go-cart since my ninth birthday. I wouldn't do it alone, though. I didn't have the money for it, and that wouldn't be much fun anyway.

Money. How the hell were we paying for this, anyway? We'd already spent a ton on gas, and the motel didn't look all that cheap, either.

Vallery and Collin came back with the food, which turned out to be sandwich bags full of hot-dog pieces. Vallery reached for a fishing pole. "Want to feed the gators, Lainey?"

"Um, no thanks."

"It'll be fun."

I rolled my eyes.

Collin ran over to the side of the pit and grabbed a fishing pole. Vallery slid a piece of hot dog onto the plastic prong at the end of the string. Collin swung the string into the water. We leaned over and watched as the alligators swam up and jumped for the hot dog. Water splashed as the alligators jostled around in the water and fought over the hot dog. Collin and Vallery laughed. I wondered if the slower alligators eventually starved to death. Survival of the fittest and all that.

"God, we need a camera," Vallery said. "Lainey, go look in the store and see if they have a disposable one or something."

I waited a second to see if she'd hand me any money, but she didn't even look at me. I had exactly fourteen dollars in my pocket, and not much more than that in my bank account. I walked over to the gift shop. I saw the disposable cameras right away, but I walked around looking at sunglasses and gum and then stood at the front of the store and watched Collin and Vallery through the window.

I couldn't believe that we'd spent sixteen hours in the car to get to Orlando to feed hot dogs on fishing poles to alligators. And that Vallery and Collin were actually enjoying it.

I bought a disposable camera. On my way out, I passed by a pay phone and thought about the white pages in my pocket. It occurred to me that I really *could* run away. I could stay here with Aunt Liz. I didn't have my clothes or my car or any of my other stuff, but so what? I'd get a job. I'd replace it all. Fresh start. Clean slate.

"Lainey!" Vallery yelled. "Come take pictures!"

"Are you ready to go to Disney World today and meet Mickey Mouse?" Vallery asked as she got Collin dressed the next morning.

"No," Collin said.

Vallery looked at me. Obviously, the entire point of running away to Orlando had been taking Collin to Disney World. And now he was going to be a brat about it and tell us no?

"Why not?" I asked.

He ran back to his bed and picked up one of the brochures. He handed it to Vallery. "'Holy Land Experience,'" Vallery read. "This is where you want to go?"

Collin nodded.

"For real?" she asked. "Instead of Disney World?"

He nodded again.

Vallery went down to the lobby and brought back our complimentary breakfast of bagels and orange juice. We sat out on the balcony while Collin ate on his bed.

"Were you guys, like, *religious*?" Vallery asked. "Did Mom take him to Sunday school or something?"

"No," I said.

"Well, maybe it will be fun. Who knows."

"You don't have to really go there just because he says he wants to."

313

"I'm not going to tell the kid he has to meet Mickey Mouse if he really just wants to meet Jesus."

"He probably doesn't even know who Jesus is."

"Do you think they have a Jesus impersonator there? Like, do you think you can have your picture taken with Jesus?"

I shrugged.

I realized this was my chance to see Aunt Liz. I couldn't have justified missing Disney World, but Vallery couldn't guilt me into seeing the Holy Land. "I guess you'll find out," I said.

Vallery shook her head and took another bite of her bagel. Then she turned to me. "Wait, what do you mean, *I'll* find out?"

I touched my head. "You know, I really don't feel well."

Vallery glared. "Are you freaking kidding me?"

"No," I said. "I haven't felt well since yesterday."

"I can't believe you're faking sick to get out of seeing the Holy Land."

"I seriously don't feel well. I don't care if you don't believe me."

"You're really sick?" She reached out and touched my forehead. "You do feel a little warm. And you've been looking kind of spacey. What exactly is wrong? Tell me your symptoms. I need to call in sick to work in a few minutes."

She actually believed me?

Mom had never believed me when I faked sick.

"It's just my head. Like, a really bad headache."

"That's not going to be enough. I think I'll tell them I have the stomach flu."

"All right. So I guess I'll spend the day resting."

"I can't believe you're doing this to me. I hope you feel better tomorrow."

I sighed. "I'll make it up to you tomorrow. You can stay home and I'll take him wherever he wants."

"No," Vallery said. "Tomorrow I'll have him convinced he wants to see Mickey."

After Vallery and Collin left, I walked to the pay phone outside the motel and dialed Aunt Liz's phone number.

"Hey, Aunt Liz. It's Lainey."

"Lainey! How are you, sweetheart?"

"I'm fine. Guess what?"

"What?"

"I'm in Orlando."

"Oh, how nice! What are you doing in town?"

There was no way I was telling her the truth. Then she'd want to see Vallery and Collin. I wasn't sure why that was such a bad thing, but it was.

"I'm here with a few girls looking at colleges. They're, uh, off doing some stuff today, so I was wondering if maybe I could stop by."

"Oh, of course! I'm glad you caught me on my day off. Where are you staying, honey? I'll come get you."

I told Aunt Liz where I was staying and then waited outside the lobby. While I waited, I imagined what it would be like to drive away with Aunt Liz and never come back. To start over in Florida with nothing but five outfits. Never arguing with Vallery again. Never fighting with Collin to get him to go to sleep at night. Not having to decide how I really felt about Riley or Eric. No more dealing with Old Crew nonsense.

When Aunt Liz pulled up to the curb, I caught my reflection in her passenger window. I was smiling.

"Oh my," she said as I climbed into the car. She moved her purse off the seat. "Look at you! You're all grown up."

We hugged awkwardly with the center console between us. I tried to remember the last time I'd seen Aunt Liz. Probably when I was ten.

"Don't tell me I look just like my mother," I warned her.

She laughed. "Well, I never thought you did to begin with. I always thought you favored our side of the family. How's your dad doing?"

I shrugged. "He's fine."

"Well, that's good to hear. I'm glad he has you up there with him, at least. He was really broken up when he called to tell us about your poor mother. I mean, it was so tragic."

As we drove out of the tourist zone, the motels and gift shops and miniature golf courses gave way to dentists' offices and supermarkets. We turned down a residential street, and Aunt Liz parked in front of a beige rancher. All the houses on the street looked just like hers. I knew that Grandma Elaine had lived two doors down, but I didn't know which direction. The house on the left had boarded-up windows. The house on the right had a playpen in the front yard full of broken-down cardboard boxes.

"Which house was Grandma Elaine's?" I asked as we sat in the car.

She pointed in the direction of the house with the playpen. "That one right there. We sold it to a nice young couple after your grandma died, and they lived in it for about a month and then rented it out to some of their redneck relatives. We're not happy about that at all, let me tell you. Should've just rented it out ourselves and handpicked our neighbors, you know?"

I nodded.

"Of course, it didn't look anything like that when your grandma lived there. She had such lovely flowers. The rednecks let them all die. And the grass, too. They can't even keep the grass alive."

"I wish I could have seen it," I said.

"I've got pictures. Plenty of pictures. We'll look at them, all right?"

"Okay," I said.

We sat in the car and stared at Grandma Elaine's old house. "Do you have any pictures of her headstone?" I asked. "I never got to see what it looked like."

"Oh, honey," Aunt Liz said. "We don't need pictures. We'll go visit."

She started the car back up and backed out of the driveway. "How are you and your brother holding up?" Aunt Liz asked.

"Fine," I said.

"And your sister, too—how's she doing? Your dad said she moved back to Maryland to look after your brother. I bet that's a big help to you."

"Yeah. She's actually Collin's guardian; I just help her out."

"You kids," Aunt Liz said, shaking her head. "You all turned out so well. It's just terrible about Lisa. I wish she could be here to see how responsible you are and how well you're all doing."

"She could have been here if she wanted to," I said. "She *killed* herself."

Aunt Liz looked ahead and drove. "She had a lot of problems that caused her to do that. I'm sure she would have much rather stayed with you kids."

I shrugged and looked out the window. "Everyone makes excuses for her."

We turned into a cemetery. "You know, your grandmother drank a bit in her day," Aunt Liz said.

"I know."

"She smoked for forty-five years."

"That long?"

Aunt Liz nodded. "She let her cholesterol get too

high, plus she had the diabetes. She wasn't one for exercise. She never even would have gone in for her checkups if I hadn't made her."

I turned to Aunt Liz and gave her a look as if to say, *What's your point?*

"I'm just saying if she'd taken better care of herself, we could have had another ten or fifteen good years with her. She could have gone to your wedding and held her great-grandbabies. But she made her choices, just like your mom did, and we have to live with them."

I shook my head. "I don't know how you can even compare them."

"Some people slowly kill themselves, Lainey. They don't all do it with a bullet or a noose or some pills, but they sure enough do it."

"Grandma Elaine was *sick*. How could you even say something like that?"

Aunt Liz touched my arm. "I'm not trying to upset you, honey. I'm just trying to get you to look at it from a different point of view. Maybe you shouldn't judge your mother so harshly. I'm just saying maybe she was sick too. In a different way."

"Let's not talk about my mother. Okay?"

Aunt Liz looked at me closely. "You're really angry, huh?"

I laughed. "Of course I'm angry."

"Is it doing you any good?"

I didn't answer her, because I thought that was a

stupid question. I knew it wasn't doing me any good. But how was I supposed to stop? What else was I supposed to be?

"I know she put you in this awful situation, but you can't change it, and she's not coming back. You need to just hold on to your happy memories, don't think about the bad stuff."

"It's not that easy."

"Have you tried?"

Aunt Liz parked and got out of the car. I got out and followed her to Grandma Elaine's grave.

I'd never understood the appeal of visiting cemeteries, but I thought I would feel something, some kind of connection, when I stood there where Grandma Elaine was buried. At one time it had been so important for me to go there and see it for myself, but now I didn't feel much of anything. I didn't feel closer to my grandmother. She was dead, in the ground, and I was probably getting sunburned.

It should have been Riley standing there beside me with his arm around me, instead of Aunt Liz standing behind me with her arms crossed. That had been our plan, after she'd died. We couldn't make it for the funeral, but he'd promised he'd get me there eventually. Except I'd screwed that all up. Riley wouldn't take me anywhere ever again. Now Christine hated me too, and eventually Kara would decide it was easier to stop being friends with me, and then Eric would move to Pennsylvania and I'd have no one, nothing. Not even a job.

I didn't like being here with Aunt Liz standing behind me. It didn't matter if what she said was true. I didn't want to hear it.

I looked at Grandma Elaine's headstone and realized there was nothing for me in Orlando either. It had been fun to daydream about, but I wouldn't start over in Florida. What would be the point of that? Nothing would be better here than it was at home.

There was nowhere to go but back, whether I liked it or not.

—— ·—✦—· ——

When I got back to the motel, Vallery and Collin were already there. Collin lay on one bed with a huge Band-Aid on his chin, watching TV, and Vallery lay on the other bed, reading a Disney brochure.

"Good news and bad news," Vallery announced.

"What happened to his chin?" I asked. I bent down and looked at Collin's face. He turned his head away from me.

"That's the bad news, but it's not all that bad. He fell and busted his chin open on our way into the Holy Land. No stitches, but it was pretty bloody."

She'd been alone with him for not even an hour before he hurt himself. Nice.

"Are you okay?" I asked Collin. He nodded and waved me away. I was blocking the television.

"So," I said to Vallery. "Good news?"

"We're going to Disney tomorrow. If you're feeling better."

"I am."

"Good."

I took *Another Day* off the nightstand and went out to the balcony.

Vallery came out a minute later and sat down in the chair beside me. "Where'd you go today?"

"I rested and then took a walk."

"Long walk, huh?"

I shrugged.

"We've been back for hours, so I know you've been gone all day. Do you have a guy in Orlando or something?"

I glared at her and then looked back down at my book.

"What? You have two in Baltimore. I thought you might have a few spread out across the country. Or maybe a traveling salesman or something."

"Shut up, Vallery."

"Then what were you doing today?"

"It's none of your business."

"By acting evasive, you're only increasing my interest."

I sighed. "Fine. I saw my aunt."

"That's the big secret? That's seriously what you did?"

"Yeah. We went to the cemetery and I saw my grand-mother's grave; then we went to the mall and had lunch, and then I hung out at her house for a few hours with her and my uncle and my cousin."

"Why couldn't you just tell me that?"

"I just did."

"But you acted like you didn't want me to know. Like you don't want me to have anything to do with your other family."

"It's not that I don't want you to have anything to do with them. You can't make a generalization like that based on one incident."

"You wouldn't let me talk to your dad, either."

"Whatever, Vallery."

"Okay, listen. I'm not sure why you're in a pissy mood, but I want you to know that we missed you today. If you'd been there, Collin wouldn't have fallen. I wasn't holding his hand like I should have. You always remember to hold his hand."

"So you only missed me because you can't keep the kid from falling down?"

Vallery sighed. "You know, it's getting really hard to have a fun family vacation with you around."

I took my book and went down to the pool. Vallery didn't try to stop me.

<hr/>

Vallery and Collin both had big smiles the next morning as we sat in the lobby and ate our complimentary breakfast.

Vallery poked my arm and grinned.

I glared at her. "Why are you so happy?" I asked.

"Because we're in Orlando on our fun family vacation."

"Okay."

"Look, you're going to have a good time whether you like it or not. I've decided that you will."

That seemed to be the new theme for my life: doing things whether I liked them or not.

"I'm doing this for all of us, you know," Vallery said. "And it's upsetting me that you're trying to ruin it."

"I'm sorry. I'm not trying to ruin anything."

"So what's your problem? Do you miss your boyfriends?"

Boyfriends. I probably should have called Eric by now. I didn't even know his number by heart. I had it programmed into my cell phone with the dead battery.

"No."

"Then what?"

I shrugged and spun my empty juice glass around on the table. Everything sucked. How many reasons did she want?

"Can you try?" she asked.

"Try what?"

"To be happy. At least while we're in Disney World. The happiest place on Earth."

"How do you try to be happy?"

"Like this," Vallery said. "Like what I'm doing."

I looked at her. She smiled.

"Just smile?" I asked. "You want me to fake it?"

"Well, you'll only have to fake it at first. Smiling releases endorphins that make you happy. It's a scientific fact."

"All right," I said. I flashed Vallery a fake smile.

"Not bad," she said. "Keep working on it."

※

As we entered Disney's Magic Kingdom, Collin stopped walking and stared straight ahead at Cinderella's Castle. Vallery whipped out the disposable camera and took his picture.

"We have to keep walking," I whispered to Collin as the people behind us glared, then shoved around us. So much for being the happiest place on Earth.

"Let's look at the map," Vallery said. She pushed through the crowd and led us over to a bench.

I unfolded the park map and spread it across Collin's lap. Vallery pulled a pen out of her purse and handed it to him. "Here. Circle what you want to do."

I sat beside him and helped him read the descriptions. And then I heard Vallery say, "Smile!"

I looked up and saw her aiming the disposable camera at us. I put my arm around Collin.

"Look happy," I said to him.

"I am happy," he said. And we both smiled for Vallery.

※

We stayed until the park closed, but we'd made it through only half the things Collin wanted to do. "We'll come back tomorrow," Vallery promised. Collin fell asleep in the car on the way back to the motel. I carried him inside and then sat on the bed beside him and opened *Another Day*.

"I think you had fun today," Vallery said. She squeezed onto the bed beside me even though there wasn't all that much room for her.

I nodded. "I did."

"Good. You know, I'd been planning this. I mean, not *this*, not a spur-of-the-moment trip. But ever since Collin's awful birthday party, I've been trying to put away money so we could go on vacation. But then there were just too many bills, and I had to start using my savings to make sure stuff got paid on time. Then last week just *sucked*, and I figured we all needed to get away."

"How are we paying for this?"

Vallery shrugged. "Credit cards. I'll sort it out when we get back." She looked down at Collin. "Didn't you desperately want to go to Disney World when you were his age?"

"Sure," I said. "Every kid does."

"And you knew Mom was never going to take you," Vallery said. "Just like I knew my dad was never going to take me. So I thought it would be nice to do this for Collin, and for us."

"Mom would have taken *him*," I said. "Eventually."

"You're probably right. She really changed, didn't she?"

I thought about Mom, how she'd always been there

for Collin, how she'd been around for me sometimes, how she'd hardly been there for Vallery at all. It seemed like she got better with each kid. Until she decided to leave all of us.

"She was always changing," I said.

"You know, if things hadn't happened like they happened, we wouldn't be here."

"No kidding," I said.

"I mean, we never would have known each other. You would have just been the bratty little sister I was jealous of, and I would have been the drunk older sister you only knew for one summer. Neither of us would have spent this much time with Collin. I probably never would have met him at all. I'm not saying it's a *good* thing that she did what she did, I'm just saying . . ."

"No, I get it. Mom would have said that things always work out for the best in the end."

"So this is the best?" Vallery asked. "This is the best thing that could have happened?"

I thought about it. The three of us together, in a motel room in Florida, going further into debt to spend a few days faking happy at the happiest place on Earth.

I shrugged. "If it hasn't worked out, then it's not the end."

⋯⋯✦⋯⋯

Back at the motel after our second day at the Magic Kingdom, Vallery explained to Collin that we had to go back to Baltimore soon so he could start first grade.

Really, her credit cards were almost maxed out.

"No!" Collin screamed.

"Yes," Vallery said patiently. We sat on the balcony and let him cry it out for a while, and then I went back inside the room.

"If you stop crying, we have a special treat for you tomorrow."

"What?" he asked. He narrowed his eyes at me like he didn't really believe me, and then he wiped some snot off his lip.

We'd anticipated a tantrum, so we had a plan. "There's a store here in Florida that sells nothing but LEGOs," I said.

"LEGOs?" he asked.

I nodded. "And if you're good, we'll go there tomorrow and let you pick out one thing that you want. All right?"

Collin nodded. "All right."

<hr>

After Collin fell asleep, we sat on the balcony and read. Vallery had taken an old newspaper from the lobby. I finished *Another Day*. It wasn't my kind of novel, but I could see why Mom had liked it. Michaela Davis was married to a cop but had fallen in love with some kind of mobster. I'd thought maybe the book would help me with the Riley-Eric dilemma, but I couldn't figure out which of them was the cop and which was the mobster. At first I thought Riley would be the cop since he'd been my boyfriend and

Eric had been the other man. But the cop's personality was more like Eric's and the mobster was more like Riley. And then I remembered it didn't matter anyway, because Riley had moved on. And Eric was probably going to be mad at me, too. We didn't have a daily-phone-call kind of relationship, but I hadn't talked to him at all since we'd left for Florida, and I figured that probably wasn't a good thing.

Maybe by the time I got home, they would both hate me, and it'd be too late to date either of them. I knew I wouldn't have an infinite number of chances to change my mind.

⸺ ✦ ⸺

The next day at the LEGO store, Vallery watched Collin stare at boxes and boxes of LEGO sets while I stood behind her looking at the rack of personalized mugs.

"You know what we all have in common?" I asked.

"What?"

I held up a mug that said "Lisa." "We can never find anything with our name on it."

"Huh," Vallery said. "That's true."

"Is he getting close to deciding?" I asked.

"Not at all."

I kneeled down beside Collin. "So what are you thinking?"

He shrugged.

"Trains?" I checked the price tag. "No, not trains. Um. Oh, look, Batman."

I checked the prices on three of the Batman sets and laid them on the floor in front of Collin. "Okay, here, I narrowed it down. Pick your favorite."

I stood back up and looked around for Vallery, but she'd disappeared. Collin stared at the LEGOs.

"Are you thinking about it or just staring?" I asked.

"Thinking."

"Okay."

Several years passed before Collin decided on the Batmobile. When we turned, I saw Vallery running over to us.

"Look what I got," she said with a smile. "I had them personalized." She held up a plastic bag. I took a step closer and looked inside.

Three LEGO blocks, each one engraved with one of our names.

20

THE LAINEY PIKE WHIRLWIND RECONCILIATION TOUR

Before we left Orlando, we stopped at a drugstore. They had a one-hour photo lab. So while I shopped for snacks and a new cell-phone charger, Vallery handed over our twenty disposable cameras.

We sat in the Mustang and looked at the pictures. Pictures of Collin with Disney characters. Pictures of either me or Vallery on rides with Collin, waving and smiling. Pictures that Collin had taken himself, usually crooked and off-center.

We'd gotten only one picture of all three of us together. After standing in line for an hour to meet Mickey Mouse, Vallery'd gotten impatient and insisted that all three of us get in the same picture. She handed our camera to the people in line behind us. It wasn't such a bad picture. Collin hadn't looked at the camera, but at least we'd all smiled.

"Let's look again," he said when we'd looked at the last stack of pictures.

"We have to go home." I passed them back to him. "Here. You can look, but don't let them blow away." I opened up my new cell-phone charger and plugged it in.

"Want to drive?" Vallery asked.

"Sure," I said. "Why?"

"You think I have ulterior motives just because I'm letting you drive?"

"Yes." She got out and walked around to the passenger's side. I climbed over to the driver's seat.

Vallery grinned. "Okay, I wanted to read that book you've been carrying around. I read the back and it sounds pretty good."

I shrugged. "All right. It's in my bag."

"I'm a fast reader. We can talk about it when I'm done. Like a book club."

I'd like to say that we had a quiet drive while Vallery read and Collin looked at the pictures, but that wasn't how it happened.

Vallery turned a page in the book. "Oh my God, I can't believe he just did that."

Collin flipped through the pictures. "Goofy!" he screamed.

"What chapter?" I asked Vallery.

"Twelve. When they go to the ball."

"Oh yeah, that sucked."

"Lainey eats a pretzel!" Collin laughed.

Vallery kept me constantly updated on her progress. Collin looked at pictures and narrated our entire trip. But it was better than being covered in ice cream and arguing. It was better than CUT THE GREASE.

––•❈•––

Before we even stopped for lunch, Vallery had finished the book.

She set it down on her lap. "This isn't the kind of book I imagined you'd read. I thought you'd read Dickens just to prove how smart you are."

"It was Mom's. Her favorite book."

"Well, that makes sense. I thought for sure that Michaela was going to stay with her husband."

"Me too. But the mobster was actually better for her in the end, wasn't he?"

"It seemed like he was. But she had to give up everything to be with him."

As we drove on I-95 north toward Baltimore, toward home, we talked about the book. And it was nice. I'd never read a book and talked about it with someone else before, outside of English class, and that really wasn't the same at all. Vallery and I talked about the characters like they were people, not like we were looking for symbolism or a moral or anything. And then it occurred to me that if I'd actually finished the book the first time I'd started it, when Mom had given it to me, I could have had this conversation with her. It could have gone on my short list of happy memories. But I'd screwed that all up, hadn't I?

That night, while Vallery and Collin slept, Mom's song came on the radio. It was a cheesy love song that she'd liked for as long as I could remember. It had been her and Carl's song. And her and Daddy Steve's song. Every time she got really serious about a man, it had been their song. I hadn't heard it since Mom died. I didn't usually play the easy-listening stations, but we'd been driving so long, I'd stopped caring what was on the radio, as long as it wasn't static.

As I drove down the highway, I remembered Mom singing in the car as she drove me to school. If her song came on while she made dinner, she'd stop in the kitchen and dance. With Daddy Whoever, or with me, or just by herself. Even in her Dark Days, the song had been enough to cheer her up, at least for a few minutes.

I remembered what Aunt Liz had said about digging deep for those happy memories of Mom. I pictured Mom dancing. I pictured her smiling. I tried to remember.

I'd hated dancing with her. I'd complain and pull away. Sometimes I'd give in and sway with her, but most of the time, especially the older I got, I'd just roll my eyes and walk away.

Would it have really killed me to dance with her and not act like I hated every second of it?

I'd never made much of an effort, now that I thought about it.

I could have tried. I could have gone along with it when she tried to include me in her and Carl and Collin's goofy family activities. I could have taken that step-aerobics class with her. I could have sat in on her groups once in a while. I could have listened to her when she talked. I could have talked to her about Riley. Maybe she could have talked to me about Carl and I could have understood why she loved him. She probably knew things about him that I didn't know, things that might have helped me like him. I could have let her keep treating me like a queen on my birthdays. There had been so many times I'd spent so much energy pushing her away when it would have been easier to have given in and danced.

As Mom's song played, my chest felt tight and for a second I was afraid I might be having a heart attack. Then I started to cry.

I cried for Mom, because she'd never get to sing again. I cried for Collin because he'd never remember her singing at all. And I cried for myself.

Mom hadn't been the only problem lately. *I'd* been the problem, too.

I didn't have an infinite number of chances.

And it was too late now.

I drove all night and let Vallery sleep. As we approached the Maryland state line, I finally unplugged my phone charger and turned the phone on. I had seventeen new messages.

Lainey, it's Riley. Please come to the door and let me in. I just want to talk about your car. Okay? I'm waiting.

Okay, maybe you're not home? Or maybe you don't have your phone on you? I don't know. Anyway, your car is running fine now. I'll leave the key under the mat. Call me.

It's Rodney. Please call me as soon as you get this. You're never going to believe who just showed up at my kiosk.

Hey, it's Eric. Just wanted to see if you want to grab some burgers or something. Call me.

Hi, sweetheart, it's Mabel. I haven't seen you kids around in a few days and I just wanted to check in. Please call me. I'll try the house phone again.

Lainey, I don't like what you're doing. I can't get ahold of Vallery or you. You're not home. I'm starting to worry. Please call me. (Riley for the third time.)

Hey, Laine. It's Kara. Riley asked me to check in. He hopes you're ignoring him, but he's kind of worried that something's wrong. Please give him a call and let him know you're all right. Okay? And then call me back. Love you. Bye.

Okay, Lainey. I sat outside of Collin's school, and you didn't come to get him, and neither did Vallery. I saw a weird guy hanging around your house the other day when I was fixing your car—that was the last day I saw you, actually, and I'm really worried. Call me.

Hey, Laine. It's Kara again. Riley's freaked. I tried to explain that when you're upset you just want to be alone. But he said, "It's not just Lainey, they're all gone." So I said maybe your whole family's just like you and maybe you're all upset and want to be alone. I told him that your phone is off so you probably haven't gotten any of his messages. He said he's going to break into your house if he doesn't hear from you by tonight. So please just call him.

Hey, it's Eric. Could you please just give me a call and tell me what's going on? I know we never made anything official, but I kind of felt like we were heading in a certain direction, and if that's not the direction you want to head in, that's fine, but I think

I deserve a little better than just being ignored. So call me, all right? See ya.

I just busted out your back window and looked through the house to see if I could find . . . I don't even know what the hell I was looking for. But I don't know where you are, and this is really not cool, Lainey. For real. I'm going to fix your window, and then if I don't hear from you soon, I'm going to the police.

Hi, Lainey, it's your father. I had two interesting phone calls this morning. First Liz called to say you'd been by to visit her. So you're in Florida? I wish you'd told me. It would have been nice to see you before you left. But I guess you're busy with your girl friends. (Loud sigh.) *Oh, so then your friend Kara called me. She didn't seem to know where you were and she was pretty worried. I didn't know if your trip with your other friends was a secret or whatnot, so I just told her that I'd talked to you this morning and you were fine. So you might want to give Kara a call. And me, too, if you want. I miss you, kid. It's been so long since I heard from you. I love you. Drive safe.*

Oh God. Dad. I found it so easy to push him out of my mind and forget that he even existed. And there he was, worried about me, sounding like a normal father.

He'd even lied to Kara for me.

I still had five messages.

Hey, it's Eric. You know what? I wish you'd talk to me, but I guess I'll take a hint. I'm sorry if I did something wrong.

Kara just called and said she talked to your dad. I didn't even think of calling him. Anyway, he said he heard from you, so that makes me feel a million times better. But what the hell is wrong with you that you'd let us worry for so long? I'm going to beat you when I see you. No kidding. You might want to lay low for a few more days. I love you, Lainey, even if you are a huge pain in the ass.

Riley still loved me?

Well, that didn't mean anything. Kara loved me too, but she didn't pine after me.

Okay, I talked to your dad and he said he heard from you and you're fine. Now I'm more worried than ever. What the hell are you doing calling your dad but not us? Is he lying? Did he really kill you and bury you in his backyard? Jesus Christ, call me.

Oh my God, it's Kara again. Christine is in labor. Like, right now. I'll call you when I know more.

Oh my God, it's Kara again. Christine had the baby. It's a girl! I wish you were here. Call me.

As we got closer to Baltimore, I waited for everything to look familiar again. But nothing did. We were ten miles from home, and then five miles, and everything still looked strange. Every highway looked the same.

But then I exited the highway and recognized Corben, the supermarkets and the gas stations and the stores and the trash and graffiti. And then our street, finally.

I shook Vallery. "We're home."

<hr />

Vallery listened to the messages on our answering machine. They were pretty much the same as the ones on my voice mail, except for one from Deborah, the woman who wanted to buy Mom's notebooks.

"I guess I should call that woman back and tell her I couldn't find anything," Vallery said.

"Yeah," I said. "Are you going to work?"

She nodded. "What are you doing? Can you stay with Collin?"

"You're not taking him to camp?"

"It's the last day. Why bother? I'll ask if Mabel wants to watch him."

After Vallery had changed into her work clothes and taken Collin next door, I thought about what to do next. There were so many people to call back. I started to make a list in my head, in no particular order, of people I really should make up with before the day ended:

Eric—even though he'd written me off and wasn't even worried that I might be dead. He deserved an explanation.

Riley—even though he was probably completely in love with Stupid Gina by now and only loved me as a friend.

Christine—under the circumstances I could probably just stop talking to her completely. High school was over and I didn't have to see her every day anymore. But she *had* always tried to be a good friend to me. And I kind of wanted to go to the hospital and see the baby and apologize to her for Vallery being a lunatic, so things could be normal again.

Kara—apologize and thank her for dealing with Riley for me.

Deborah—well, not really make up with her, but decide what I was going to do about her.

Dad—apologize for being a jerk. Maybe even explain why. Maybe even thank him for lying to Kara for me.

I hesitated for a second and then I added Mom to my list. I wasn't sure how I was going to make up with her, but I knew I had to. Since it hadn't all been her fault.

I was about to call Kara (to start with an easy one), but then I remembered Rodney's message about his mystery visitor. I decided that would make a good lighthearted warm-up phone call. I could practice my explanation on someone who hadn't been all that bothered by my absence. Perfect.

"Hello?" Rodney said.

"Hey, it's Lainey. I just got your message. I'm so sorry. There was this guy . . . from Texas . . . and then I told Vallery, and she flipped out, and we drove to Orlando, and . . . then we came home. . . ." Okay, so maybe my explanation needed a lot more practice. "Anyway, who was your mystery visitor?"

Rodney laughed. "Your boyfriend."

"Boyfriend?"

"Yeah. Well, I guess you guys broke up or whatever. I forget his name. Soccer boy."

Oh. So he'd just seen Riley at the mall. No big deal. "Yeah?" I asked.

"Well, he wanted to talk to me."

"About what?"

"You." Rodney started to laugh. "He told me that he respects you as a person and he respects your decisions, but he's really in love with you and he thinks he might still have a shot. He'd appreciate it if I'd step aside and let him have one more try to win you over."

I didn't even know what to say. "He thinks I'm dating you?"

Rodney laughed. "Apparently. Anyway, he wasn't a dick about it at all. He came and said what he had to say, and I tried to convince him that there's nothing going on between us—and that I hadn't even known you two had broken up, actually, thanks for telling me—but he just kept saying, 'It's cool, man.' Then he rambled on some more about how much he loves you. I didn't know what to do. So finally I agreed to step aside. Anyway, what happened? How'd he try to win you back?"

"He hasn't. I haven't talked to him yet."

"Well, you gotta let me know what happens. I've never seen someone so heartsick in my life. It was sad and hilarious all at the same time."

After I got off the phone with Rodney, I called Kara. I didn't even want to take a moment to think about what Rodney had just told me. If I let myself get sidetracked, I'd never get through my list.

"I'm sorry," I said to Kara.

"It's all right. Where have you been hiding out? Did you elope with Eric?"

"We went to Orlando for a few days," I said. "Not me and Eric. Me and Vallery and Collin." An inadequate explanation, but at least it was coherent.

"Jesus. You could have let someone know."

"You're right, I should have. But it was kind of a surprise. Vallery's ex-boyfriend showed up, and she freaked out, and we left and then just kind of had a vacation for Collin, to make up for his birthday party sucking so bad."

"That's sweet. But you still should have called."

"I know. I'm an awful person. Anyway, are you still at the hospital?"

"No, I'm at home. I have to work tonight, so I need to get some sleep."

"Oh. I didn't mean to keep you up. I'm sorry."

"You're not bothering me. It's good to hear your voice."

After I got off the phone with Kara, I emptied my book bag on the floor. I pulled Mom's notebooks out from under my mattress and shoved them inside. I slung the bag over my shoulder and went out to the car. I wasn't sure what I was going to do with them, but I wanted to have them with me.

There was a note taped to the steering wheel.

No, not a note. My list of everything wrong with the Grand Am.

Everything was crossed off in red marker except the part about the volume control. Riley had written a note: "It doesn't do this for me. You must be crazy."

So this was how he was going to win me back. He'd fixed everything. He'd replaced the windshield. The windows rolled up and down again. The lights worked. I didn't even want to think about all the money I owed him.

The next step on the Lainey Pike Whirlwind Reconciliation Tour was Eric's house. I didn't know what I was going to say to him, but whatever it was, I knew I had to say it in person. I went around to the basement door and knocked.

"I'm sorry," I said when he opened the door. That was going to be my mantra for the day: I'm sorry, I know I should have called, I'm so sorry.

He stood there wearing just his pajama bottoms. He

didn't say anything, so I guessed I was supposed to keep apologizing. "My sister's ex-boyfriend showed up and she freaked out and we left. We drove to Orlando. We took my brother to Disney World. My cell phone died. I couldn't call anyone."

He shrugged and smiled. "That's cool. I hope you had a nice time."

"Um, okay. I just wanted to say I was sorry for not telling you I left. We didn't tell anyone. Everybody was really worried about us. I know it was a stupid thing to do."

"I didn't know what was going on. I stopped by a few times. That other guy was at your house all week, fixing your car."

I nodded. "Yeah, my sister asked him to fix it after it broke down."

"I would have taken care of it for you, if you'd asked."

"You said you don't know anything about cars."

"I could have taken it to a mechanic."

"But he is a mechanic."

"Oh. Are you getting back together with him? I'm kind of getting that vibe."

I shrugged.

He reached out and touched my arm. "Hey, if that's what you want to do, don't feel bad," Eric said. "I'm a big boy."

"You're moving," I said.

He nodded. "Not far, though."

"It seems far. You remember what you told me before, about doing what's in my heart?"

He shook his head. "You don't have to apologize. I've already gotten used to the idea. I just . . . I don't want to think I wasted your time. Or screwed anything up for you."

"No," I said. "No way. He's just . . . do you remember when we got snowballs? He's like my raspberry, you know? And I don't know if that's good or bad, but . . . it is what it is."

Eric kind of laughed. "I can appreciate that. But that makes me your chocolate-covered cherry, yeah?"

I nodded.

He grinned. "So did I stop the world? Even for a little while?"

"Oh my God, you are so cheesy." I turned away from Eric because I didn't want him to see that I'd started to cry just a little. I'd never cried so much in my life as I'd cried already that year.

"Oh, honey," Eric said. He held out his arms and I let him hug me. He kissed my forehead. "You tried something new," he whispered. "That was brave. And we had fun, right? We had fun. Don't be upset."

I didn't think I'd been brave. I'd been silly and reckless and selfish. I'd hurt Riley. I'd gotten Gina and her stupid side ponytail involved. Now I was hurting Eric, even though he'd been nothing but awesome, even though we'd had fun, even though it felt so good to let him hold me. I didn't want to turn and walk away from him knowing I'd never be able to run my fingers through his chest hair again.

But love wasn't a buffet. I couldn't have everything that looked good.

"Maybe I'll see you around?" he said. "On those late-night Slurpee runs?"

I grinned and pulled away from him. "Yeah. Maybe."

I was glad we didn't say anything about staying friends, because that was always a lie. Real people didn't do that. I'd seen the Old Crew girls try, and it never worked out. We wouldn't be friends. He'd fade away. I'd forget the way he smelled, the way it felt to snuggle up next to him in the cool basement. He'd go off to Pennsylvania for the winter. He'd meet new people, maybe a new girl, maybe a few new girls. I'd be a girl he had once dated, for what? A month? In the grand scheme of a person's life, that wasn't a long time at all. Insignificant, really. I told myself that over and over as I walked to my car and resisted the urge to run back in and tell him, no, we'd make it work. Somehow.

I turned the car on, but I didn't want to drive away. I felt like there was so much I still had to say to him. I wanted to ask him about his mother. If he told me more about his mother, it'd be like he was telling me more about my own mother. And now I finally cared, now that it was too late to ask him anything. Why had it bothered me so much before, the thought that his mother and my mother had known each other? Why was it a bad thing?

I'd wanted to forget she even existed. I didn't want Eric to know about her. The best thing about Eric had probably been that he had no idea who I really was.

But I didn't need Eric to tell me about my mother.

I had that book bag full of notebooks.

As I drove to Riley's house, I thought about how crappy it was that I'd broken up with him, ignored him for days after he fixed my car, and then hadn't even bought him a key chain or anything from Disney World. I mean, even the worst (ex-)girlfriend in the world could have been *that* thoughtful.

To be honest, I didn't know if going back to Riley was the right thing to do. I didn't know if I was doing it because I was jealous and didn't want a stupid jock girl with a stupid hairdo to have him. I didn't know if I was doing it because I was scared to be without him and things were just easier when he was around. I didn't know if I was doing it because he'd been sweet and fixed my car and was obviously so in love with me. I didn't know if I was doing it because I thought I needed him around to help me with Collin. I just knew that it was what I felt like doing, so it was what I was going to do. Kara approved. Eric understood. I knew I shouldn't have to back up my own feelings with anyone else's approval, but it felt good to have it.

Riley was coming down the front walk before I'd even gotten out of the car. He grabbed me and lifted me off my feet.

"Riley, I—"

"Shhh," he said. And he just stood there on the sidewalk holding me up like I was a little kid. I wrapped my arms around him.

"You don't have to win me back," I said. "The car and everything, that was great, but—"

"Doesn't even matter," he said. "I'm just glad you're okay."

"What happened to beating me?"

He smiled and shrugged. "Changed my mind. Listen, I made something while you were gone," he said. He put me back down on my feet.

"What is it?" I asked.

"Come on," he said. He took my hand and we walked toward the house. I followed him to his room. He picked up a photo album and handed it to me. I opened it up. And then I realized it wasn't a photo album. It was a scrapbook. For Collin.

I flipped the pages. It started with pictures of Carl and Mom. Then pictures of Collin. Pictures of all of us. Christmas and birthdays. The pictures from Collin's graduation—the last pictures we'd ever have of Mom. The second half of the book was empty.

"We have to take more pictures," Riley said. "So we can fill the second half."

I flipped back to a page at the beginning. "What's up with these little squares?" I asked. Almost every page had a different colored square.

"That's the journaling block," Riley said. "You're supposed to write about what's happening in the picture. Or whatever. Whatever you want to write. I figured you should do that yourself. I mean, I know I've known him as long as you have. But it still seemed like, you know, the words should come from you."

"He'll love it. We got our Disney World pictures printed at this one-hour place before we left Orlando. He looked at them over and over again on the drive home. I mean, over and over."

Riley grinned. "I told you."

"Hey, have you been to the hospital?" I asked. "To see the baby?"

He hadn't, so we got in the pickup and drove to the hospital. On the way, I told him all about the trip, what Collin liked and didn't like, what we'd have to do again if we ever went back. He never asked if I'd take him back, and I never asked if he'd take *me* back, but things felt right again.

When we got to the hospital, Christine was asleep and Wallace was sitting in her room, looking at the baby.

"Where've you been?" Wallace asked with a grin. I saw him look down. Riley and I were holding hands.

"Disney World," I said.

He laughed. He probably couldn't tell if I was serious

or just giving him a flip answer.

"Want to hold her?" he asked.

I nodded. He picked the baby up out of her crib and handed her to me. I sat in the chair by the window. It was amazing how tiny and shriveled up they were when they were just born. It was hard to believe that they grew up to be real people. I thought about Collin and how little he'd seemed when we'd first gotten him, but he would have been huge compared to Christine's baby. I'd never seen Collin this small, not even in pictures.

Riley stood beside me with his hand on my shoulder. He looked down at me and Christine's baby and smiled.

"Don't even think about it," I whispered.

"It's okay to just *think* about it," he said. "One day."

"Not any day soon."

He shrugged. "When Collin's older."

"Much older."

Riley had to go to work, so I went to work with him for the first two hours of his shift and sat in the waiting room, drinking gross coffee out of a Styrofoam cup. I caught glimpses of him in the garage, through the big glass window, and when he came into the waiting room and announced, "2002 Jeep Cherokee?" and waited to see which customer stood up.

While I sat there, I started reading Mom's notes. I started with one of the composition books. There were no dates, so I didn't know what came first. Her handwriting wasn't that great. I read slowly, but I didn't give up; and I knew I'd eventually make it through all the books plus the binder. I didn't know if it would be enough, but I figured it was the least I could do.

And then, scribbled in one of the margins, I read this:

everyone deserves the benefit of the doubt and a second chance.

When I got back to the house, Lenard Fry Jr. was sitting on the front step. I thought about staying in the car and driving away, but I didn't. I parked and walked up to him.

"Hey, Lenard," I said.

He stood up. "I knocked. She won't let me in. I know she's in there. That's her car."

Her car. Lenard didn't want the car. Vallery's paranoia was out of control.

"Why are you here?" I asked. "Really?"

"I miss her," he said. "She just took off."

I walked past Lenard Fry Jr. and stuck my key into the lock. "Come on in," I said.

Lenard followed me into the house. Collin was jumping on the couch and watching TV. "No jumping," I said to Collin. I swatted at him. He crashed down on the couch and sat still for about three seconds before I heard him stand up and start jumping again.

I led Lenard into the kitchen and got him a glass of

water. "I'll go get Vallery," I said.

"I appreciate it," he said, and sipped his water.

I found Vallery in her room, digging through boxes in the closet. Probably looking for Mom's notebooks one more time before she called Deborah.

"Vallery, I have to tell you something. You're probably going to be mad."

She sighed. "You let Len into the house, didn't you?"

I dropped my book bag on the floor.

"I'm not doing your laundry," she said.

I unzipped it. She leaned over and looked inside.

"Is that what I think it is?" she asked.

"All of Mom's notebooks."

"Let's not talk about where you found them. Or how long you've had them."

"No, let's not. Anyway, you can sell them to Deborah, but I want to read them first. I know it's probably just a bunch of clichéd nonsense, but still."

Vallery shrugged. "Sounds like a plan. This will pay off all the credit cards. It'll pay for Florida. And then some." Vallery laughed. "So I guess Mom kind of did take us to Disney World after all."

"Hey, Vallery," I said. "There's something else."

She sighed. "You *did* let Lenard in, didn't you?"

"He's in the kitchen. Listen, you need to set things right with him. I've been apologizing to people all day. It's fun. He may be a loser, but he deserves an explanation, you know? And he doesn't want your stupid car.

He's just hurt. Give him the benefit of the doubt."

Vallery sighed. "Fine." She shoved a handful of papers back into the box.

As Vallery walked away, I realized that for the first time in years, I was intentionally following and repeating my mother's advice.

⊷ ⊷⊱⊰⊷ ⊶

Riley came over after work. "That weird guy I told you about is sitting in your kitchen," he said as he walked into my room.

"That's Vallery's ex-boyfriend. The reason why we ran off to Orlando."

"I see." He pulled something out of his back pocket and handed it to me. "I got you some pens. For the journaling. They're acid free."

"Acid free?"

"Yeah. That means they won't damage the pictures. You know. Over time. If the ink had acid, it would eat away at the pictures."

"You got really hard-core about this scrapbooking stuff, didn't you?"

Riley sat down on the bed beside me. "You haven't registered for fall classes yet, have you?" he asked.

I shook my head. "Things were so crazy. I didn't know what the plan was anymore."

"The plan is whatever you want the plan to be."

"Well, I'm sure everything is full, so I'll be left with whatever no one else wanted to take. That's my plan."

He grinned. "At least you have a plan. Did you guys eat yet, or has Vallery just been sitting in the kitchen talking?"

"Talking."

"Mind if I go start something?"

"Of course not. I'll be down in a few minutes. I have to make a call."

Riley raised an eyebrow. "Checking in with your other boyfriend?"

I couldn't tell if he was being serious. "No. I broke up with him this morning."

"Good."

"Did you break up with your other girlfriend?"

"You mean that girl who talked on her cell phone all night whenever we hung out?"

"Yeah. Her."

"Yeah, I dumped her."

"Good. Anyway, I actually have to call my dad."

"Didn't you talk to him yesterday?"

"I didn't. It's a long story."

Riley shrugged. "All right. See you in a few." He kissed me and then walked out into the hallway.

The only reason I had my dad's number programmed into my cell phone was so I'd know not to answer the phone when he called. How mature, right? So when I hit "send" on the phone, it was probably the first time I'd called him in years.

Just lunch, I told myself. *We'll just have lunch. And if he breaks any promises, then oh well, at least I tried.*

And you never know until you try, right?

"Hello?" my father answered.

I heard Collin shrieking and laughing. I pictured Riley tickling him mercilessly. I pictured Vallery in the kitchen, still talking to poor Lenard Fry Jr. hours after I'd let him into the house.

"Hey, Dad? It's Lainey."

I could keep holding a grudge for all the things he'd done wrong. Or I could let him make it right. He didn't deserve an infinite number of chances, but it couldn't hurt to give him one more.

ACKNOWLEDGMENTS

I wouldn't be anything without the love, encouragement, and support of my wonderful family.

It's hard to imagine how my life would have turned out if I hadn't spent those three years at Carver, under the guidance of Bonny Boto, writing, learning, and being validated. I'm also grateful to all my writing professors and classmates at UMD who read my stories and taught me how to take criticism. Thanks especially to Patrick McKenna and Tom Whitmire, who went out of their way to befriend the quiet girl, and Kristen Sabrina Shahmir for giving me the last push I needed. Dara Granoff, Joanna Mechlinski, Lauren Hopkins Karcz, and Tom Nichols offered keen observations and suggestions on the earliest draft of this novel. Eternal gratitude to Karl Langkam for making me laugh and driving me crazy. Thanks to Sara Crowe, Jill Santopolo, and everyone else at HarperCollins who helped along the way.

Finally, thanks to Brian Bauer for being there when I wrote this, for feeding me, picking me up when I fell down, taking me to Florida, and generally putting up with me.

HOLLY NICOLE HOXTER was born and raised in Baltimore, Maryland. Like her character Lainey, she was named after a soap opera heroine. After receiving her BA in English from the University of Maryland, she went on to work as a bookseller, relay operator for the deaf, housecleaner, legal word processor, and dog walker. She currently masquerades as a medical transcriber and begrudgingly still resides in Baltimore with her three adorable cats. THE SNOWBALL EFFECT is her debut novel. You can visit her online at www.hollynicolehoxter.com.